THE LITTLE BLONDE NIGHTMARE

The Complete

THE BLACK MASK

Cases of Reverend Daunt

Volume 1: 1924–25

J. PAUL SUTER

BLACK MASK

2024

Table of Contents

The Problem of the Man
Who Sowed the Wind

With this story, Black Mask *readers are introduced to one of the strangest and most fascinating characters in fiction—The Reverend McGregor Daunt, clergyman by profession and detective by choice. The character, says Mr. Suter, is taken from life; and if readers will turn to the end of this story, they will find something unique in magazine publishing—a letter from the character himself!*

THE HUNTING LODGE of the Reverend McGregor Daunt lay twenty miles due south of his city church, this distance being calculated not as the crow flies, but according to the reckoning of Stubbs, the manservant, who left the city each morning at five with an oddly-shaped box in his care. This box was an especially built vacuum device. It had three compartments. They contained, respectively, the breakfast, the lunch, and the dinner of the Reverend McGregor Daunt.

Seventeen miles of the twenty Stubbs covered speedily in a roadster. Two of the miles, still in the roadster, he crawled more or less slowly, according to the condition of the dirt road into which he was obliged to turn. An unprogressive farmhouse sprawled at a bend in this road. There, by special arrangement, the roadster was left, and Stubbs finished the remaining mile through the woods on a grey mare. Thus, too, journeyed the Reverend McGregor Daunt, on his comings and goings—except that, on a fine day, he sometimes walked that woodland mile.

Every clergyman would do well to consider the advantages of being a millionaire. It is possible then to support a French chef, whose duties when one is occupying one's hunting lodge embrace the preparation of absentee meals. It is feasible to own such a hunting lodge, in which one lives alone for days on end, but does not hunt. Even the captious demands of one's congregation, too often the humiliation of him who discourses from a pulpit, can be stilled. The Reverend McGregor controlled every such demand by seldom preaching from his pulpit. He was able to hire that done. To insure variety and lift his course above all possible criticism, he retained only the brightest ornaments among ecclesiastics, and never the same individual for more than two Sabbaths in succession. His large congregation was expensively supplied.

A certain reputation for profundity which the Reverend McGregor enjoyed was not belied by his appearance. He wore a seven-and-seven-eighths hat with a wide brim—not the customary head gear among clergymen of his denomination; but he fancied it. His forehead was both high and broad; his were feature's rather coldly chiseled; his face, though rotund, at the same time was subtly ascetic in expression. Sitting, he had the appearance of a very large man; his shoulders were wide, his torso was imposing. When he rose, however, his lower members were seen to be disproportionately short, and he preferred to walk with a cane.

Natural bent had directed him toward the studious professions. He had seized first upon the law; had passed the bar examination; had even pleaded a few cases. Some medical point in one of the latter intriguing him, he had put law to one side and taken up medicine. The course had proved well within his very broad limitations. He had graduated in a little more than half the usual time, and had spent part of the customary year in a hospital. But the combination of an exceptionally keen man, who was dying one night in the ward, and an attending clergyman rather shaky in theology, had turned his thoughts toward the intellectual side of religion. He had dropped medicine; had graduated with signal honors from a seminary; had entered the clergy. At length, in a moment of clear inspiration, he had evolved the conception of his palatial hunting lodge, where he could be alone and think.

Thither he went when solitude called to him. But men discovered him and came the twenty miles from the city to have him think for them. Most of them came in summer, in the daytime, for it was easier then to make the somewhat rugged trip through the woods. Some chose winter, if it so chanced that their thinking was of a kind which could not await his return to town. The Reverend McGregor welcomed them impartially. They were as likely—or as unlikely—to find him at one season as at another. One of the advantages of a hunting lodge in which the owner thinks but does not hunt, is its complaisance toward any sort of weather.

MR. FREDERICK BRAINE came at night, very late, and on the wings of a blizzard. The winter of that year was making its last desperate stand before spring.

For half-an-hour or so, the Reverend McGregor Daunt, lying abed in his comfortable darkness, had been luxuriously permitting the knocker on his door to edge him toward sleep, as it was lifted and then released with drowsy monotony by the wind. Its tattoo was, of course, but one of the antics of the storm. The owner of the lodge accorded general recognition to the others. Buffeting gusts against the adequate sides of his house; shrieking calls around its corners; the tempest-song through high branches; an occasional breaking limb far or near—these were harmony instruments in the symphony, but his mind continued to single out the insistent solo of his knocker. Had not the shout of a human voice raised itself desperately at last above an opportune lull in the storm, he

by
J. PAUL
SUTER

The Problems of the Reverend McGregor Daunt

would, until sleep came, have credited that solo to the wind; in which case he might have found Mr. Frederick Braine stiff upon his doorstep in the morning.

The late visitor was stiff enough and cold enough, at that. Daunt let him in through the system of double storm doors and entries, guaranteed to keep storms on the outside of the lodge where they belonged; and the stiffness of his guest aroused the clergyman's interest more than the cold did his compassion. The latter could be remedied, in fact was now on its way to be; but it seemed evident that the former never would, since it must have been born and bred with the man. Mr. Frederick Braine introduced himself; in careful words, with due attention to the quantity of each vowel sound, apologized for his late intrusion, explaining that he had been wandering in the blizzard for some hours seeking the lodge; and then tumbled over in a faint.

The Reverend McGregor took proper measures—not with any great concern, for his medical knowledge told him that the man was merely done up with exposure, and in no danger. He laid Mr. Braine in bed in the guest room—which Stubbs, the servant who brought his meals, put into order each day before leaving for town—and prepared to resume his own flirtation with sleep.

After a very brief waking period, his guest's swoon seemed to have passed into healthy slumber. But, as Daunt was stumping out of the room, Frederick Braine sat up in bed.

"If you will pardon me, sir, I have a tremendous disclosure to make," he said, in a well-bred, rather high-pitched voice.

He himself looked the reverse of tremendous. He was a very slight, small-jointed man, on whom the pajamas with which his host had invested him hung like the skin of a pink-and-white striped elephant. He wore a trifling moustache, cut to the latest angle. As he importuned, his arching brown eyebrows, fastidiously trimmed, almost exactly joined rather marked crow's-feet, so that nature appeared to have equipped him with the rims of a pair of goggles, minus their lenses. His hair, it seemed, was superior to the blizzard and to the enormous collared ulster which he had worn for protection; it had not been ruffled. The Reverend McGregor Daunt surveyed him with humorous appreciation, but not without annoyance.

"Can't your matter wait until morning?" he demanded, rather shortly.

The long pajama sleeves fell down, and revealed the hands which Mr. Frederick Braine lifted in appeal.

"I am a sinful and desperate man, sir. I have thrown myself on your compassion, because I must confide in someone, and you are the only man of judgment whom I dare trust. Should I delay until morning, I may not be able to speak. The weight of my guilt and apprehension may have killed me."

Very deliberately, his host drew up a cushioned rocker for himself beside the bed.

"I prefer to have you alive when you leave," he said, with resignation.

"I was certain you would be indulgent, sir." Mr. Braine assumed an air of rather smug satisfaction. "What I have to tell will repay your loss of sleep, even on this wild night. You are a thinker, Mr. Daunt. I venture you have never before bent your thoughts on a problem as unusual as the one I shall present to you. I, sir, am the private secretary of Dr. Laidlaw Lanthorne."

Daunt started.

"The Egyptologist?"

"The greatest Egyptologist in the world," his guest returned, gravely.

"I agree with you." The Reverend McGregor picked his words carefully, to avoid any seeming lack of modesty in what he meant to say. "I have often thought of going into Egyptology, chiefly with the object of making Dr. Lanthorne's acquaintance. You have been kind enough to call me a thinker. It seems a pity that I should have a church in the city near which the Doctor makes his home, yet should never have had the privilege of his friendship."

The little man inclined his head.

"A great pity. Dr. Lanthorne is one of the wisest of men. Admitting that, and my profound admiration for him, you will appreciate how much it pains me to confess that, through a number of the years in which I have been a member of the household. Mrs. Lanthorne has been my mistress."

The Reverend McGregor Daunt nearly catapulted from his rocking-chair; but he remembered that the word, "mistress," may be susceptible of two meanings. With an effort, he remained silent. Mr. Braine appeared to divine his confusion.

"I have been her paramour," he elucidated.

The little man hurried on, occasionally flicking back his pajama sleeves with a tiny air of annoyance, but otherwise betraying only tenuous emotion.

"Dr. Lanthorne, of course, has not known of our relations— at least, we have always felt that he did not. He is typically the scientist, Mr. Daunt—much older than Bertha. She was very young when she married him, and she feels that his eminence dazzled her. He has been uniformly kind and indulgent, but I think he does not know the meaning of love."

An echoing crash, nearby, told of a decayed tree which had yielded to wind and weight of snow. Mr. Braine shivered.

"I noticed a number of large trees very close to the lodge," he remarked, diffidently. "If one of them should fall, it might crush in the roof."

"That is entirely possible," agreed Daunt, dryly.

"Then we are actually in danger?" the little man demanded, with what, for him, was unusually spontaneous emphasis.

The clergyman's even, slightly disgusted expression did not change.

"I fancy, sir," he said, "that you are safer in this place than at the scene of your daily labors; probably safer now than may be the case at some time in the future."

Mr. Frederick Braine gave him a questioning and distinctly terrified look, as if inclined to read something sinister into the words; but since his host favored him with no further thoughts along that line, and continued to sit with hands patiently folded across his plump stomach, the narrator plunged again into his story.

"I shall be frank. Bertha and I have been situated very conveniently for our amours. Though I am Dr. Lanthorne's secretary, my work consists principally of his correspondence, his business affairs, and the details of his lecture dates. His scientific work is solitary. He locks himself into the suite of rooms which comprise his study and laboratory, and frequently is not seen for days at a time. We leave his meals at the outside of the study door. I say 'we,' for, up to six months ago, Bertha and I arranged all the household details. We relieved the doctor's mind of everything but his scientific work."

"And since the date you mention?" Daunt suggested, as the little man paused, with some show of emotion.

"Since that date, Mr. Daunt, I have arranged them. Bertha has not been with me."

He hid his neatly tailored face in the flowing sleeves of the pajamas, and continued to wrestle with his feelings for so long that his host felt brutality to be, perhaps, the best tonic.

"You mean she is dead?"

Mr. Braine looked up. He had been in tears.

"Worse than dead, Mr. Daunt. Be patient with me. I shall not give way again. I will tell you what I have seen, and it may be your mind will be able to probe to the bottom of it."

He paused to wipe his eyes. When he resumed, his voice had regained its high-pitched, impersonal quality.

"Six months ago, I came down one morning from my room in the third story, intending to go to my desk, which is in a little office on the ground floor, to open the morning mail. I found the doctor at my desk before me. The mail was unopened. He was sitting in my office chair, unshaven, his big head sunk on his breast. Dr. Lanthorne is an exceptionally large and strong man, as perhaps you are aware, sir."

"I have heard so," Daunt assented.

"At my entrance, he rose, but sank immediately into another chair, and motioned me to my own. 'Braine,' he said, 'a terrible thing occurred in this house last night.'

"I was very much alarmed, Mr. Daunt. You can imagine what I feared—that we had been found out. But Dr. Lanthorne put those apprehensions to rest at once, and immediately sank me into an agony of grief. He told me that Bertha had been taken desperately ill, with a malady which he recognized. It was a disease of ancient Egypt. The house is filled to overflowing with Egyptian antiques. New ones are forever coming in. The doctor surmised that the germ of this disease, hidden in a mummy case which he had lately received, had lain dormant through the centuries only to strike at last.

"I offered to telephone for a physician; but that was where I received my second shock. He told me positively that no physician would be of the slightest use. He himself is a doctor, Mr. Daunt. What little is known about these Egyptian diseases, he knows. He reminded me of that, and said that he had moved Bertha, with her bed, into his laboratory, so as to treat her himself."

"One moment," interjected Daunt. "Did you see the lady at this time?"

"Neither then, nor for months afterward. That was one of the disquieting conditions, Mr. Daunt. According to Dr.

Lanthorne, her malady was of a nervous nature. She was to be kept strictly incommunicado. You will note that it came suddenly. She was apparently well the evening before, and in good spirits, as I myself can testify. At some time in the night, she was taken ill, and, before morning, the doctor had moved her and all her belongings to his laboratory—this without arousing me or the servants."

Daunt nodded.

"Have you seen her at all since this sudden seizure?"

The little man hesitated. His hands, from which the loose sleeves had fallen back, worked convulsively.

"For more than four months I did not," he answered. "When I inquired as to her condition—which I did daily—Dr. Lanthorne merely replied that she was improving slowly. He never vouchsafed any details, and I hardly thought myself in a position to request them. One afternoon, however, he came into my office, and then, for the first time, I learned that her illness had made her deaf and dumb—whether permanently or only for the time he could not say. Her strength had returned to some extent, however—so much so that he invited me to dine with the two of them that evening. I usually dined by myself, you understand, since the doctor's habits as to his meals are irregular."

"In inviting me to this dinner, he made a further, very curious explanation. He was almost apologetic about it. 'Bertha's illness is of a nervous nature,' he said. 'I have told you that, but have not told you of its effect upon her facial muscles. Should you see her now, you might not recognize her. She is very sensitive on the subject. For that reason, she will be heavily veiled, to-night. You will understand, Braine, and make allowances for her?'"

"Of course, I agreed. But I cannot describe to you the horror, Mr. Daunt, with which I regarded that silent, veiled figure at our meal. The doctor brought her in, in a wheel-chair. She nodded to me. It was her only sign of recognition. She made no attempt to dine. Dr. Lanthorne stated that she preferred to do so only in private—why, he did not say. She was at our table chiefly as a favor to me, in recognition of our old friendship, and in token of her convalescence. When the meal was concluded, she was wheeled out again."

The Reverend McGregor Daunt, chin on hand, seemed at last profoundly interested.

"Have you seen her since?" he inquired.

"Three times," said his guest. "Each time under the same circumstances."

"Though she did not speak, she nodded—she actually moved?"

"Yes."

"There's another angle to the matter," said the Reverend McGregor. "You are asking me to think—at least, I take it that you are. I've hardly enough fuel for intelligent thinking. I don't really know your chief character. Dr. Lanthorne is a great scientist. He lives in a large house filled with Egyptian antiques. He is an outstanding man. So much is definite. Has he any interests, any hobbies or accomplishments, outside of pure science?"

Braine nodded.

"He has. He is a marvelous conversationalist, when he wishes to be. He can throw a spell over any company. His knowledge along the lines of electricity and mechanics is profound. Have you ever heard of Nefertiti, Mr. Daunt?"

His host's reply was prompt and precise.

"She was queen to the Pharaoh Ahknaton, of the eighteenth dynasty."

"Exactly. Your knowledge of Egyptology is beyond the average, sir. You may be aware, also, that the head of Nefertiti, in the Museum at Berlin, is considered the supreme example of Egyptian sculpture. Dr. Lanthorne has one of the two known copies of it. Now, sir—to illustrate his strange versatility—I will tell you this: I have been present at dinners in which he has made the sculptured eyes of this image actually glow with fire; he has caused the statue to move; he has even wrung speech from its lips."

"Ventriloquism?" Daunt suggested.

"And electrical effects—but wonderfully done, I have seen ladies faint when they looked at that head of Nefertiti. I have even been affected myself, sir, and I was 'behind the scenes,' so to speak."

They were both silent. The storm, quieter, interrupted their reverie with only an occasional hoot and scream around the corners of the lodge. Presently, the Reverend McGregor rose and looked meaningly at a marble clock on the mantel of his guest-room.

"It is half-past four," he stated. "You have hardly roamed the woods and fought a blizzard merely to tell me of something which has been going on for months."

The little man nodded, solemnly.

"You are correct, sir. Much though I appreciate your condescension, in listening to me at the expense of your sleep, it is as you suggest. I should not have come through the storm just for this. All I have told you is merely a prelude, so that you may help me to a decision, if you will. It will be the great decision of my life. Will you oblige me with my coat?"

His host silently did so. Mr. Frederick Braine shook back the obtrusive pajama sleeves, and removed a letter from the inside pocket of the coat. The envelope and the paper inside it were a delicate pink. There clung to them a faint odor suggesting musk.

"May I request you to read this aloud, sir?" He handed the letter to the Reverend McGregor. "I should like another opportunity to fasten the words in my mind. After nightfall, my eyes are not what they should be."

Daunt accepted the epistle, and slowly read it aloud.

My dearest: Come to me at eleven on Thursday night. He is to be out of the city—an engagement I am sure he will not break. You know where to find me. The door will not be locked.

Your Bertha.

The little man's narrow shoulders trembled with controlled emotion.

"It is her writing, sir."

"I have made some little study of handwriting," said Daunt, studying the pink missive. "I should say this was written by a woman in the best of health. There is not the slightest indication of illness. How did it reach you?"

"I returned to my desk this morning, after a short absence. The letter was under some of my papers."

The clergyman was still pondering.

"Tell me this—" he suggested; "would you say the lady could have been induced by force—even by torture—to write such a note as the one we have here?"

"No, Mr. Daunt."

"Torture is a powerful argument."

"Not so powerful, I think, with a woman as with a man. They have more courage and endurance. No matter what the circumstances, I am certain Bertha would not have written that letter to trap me."

For the first time, the Reverend McGregor Daunt's glance at his companion revealed a degree of grudging admiration. He nodded.

"You are right. I am a bachelor, and known as something of a woman hater; but I grant them that. They have stronger stuff than we. Now, I am come to the bottom of your visit. You wish my advice: shall you go, on next Thursday evening—which is the day after tomorrow—or shall you not?"

"You have divined my request, sir."

"My advice will not be binding on you, of course," continued the clergyman. "After I have spoken, you will still be a free agent. With that understanding, and in the light of what you have told me, I say—Go!"

The little man sprang from his bed—a ludicrously draped figure—and, shaking back the insistent sleeve, held out his hand.

"I thank you, sir. You confirm my own decision. I am aware of no one else whose word would have given me so much confidence. I shall go."

"Suppose, then, we use such of the night as is left for sleep?" suggested the Reverend McGregor Daunt.

ONE OF THE pleasant features attending the last storm of the winter is that spring comes tip-toeing in upon its departure, and, finding no opposition, takes off her things and stays. On Thursday evening, the Reverend McGregor Daunt found himself in town, at the manse, which adjoined the rear of his church; and it was spring. He was not unexpected, since the servant who carried his meals to the hunting lodge already had executed a commission for him, in preparation for what was to be done that night. This servant was short and heavily built, like his master, though somewhat more evenly proportioned. His eyes were small and his nose long. There was that about the droop of his mouth, particularly when he lifted his upper lip and showed two long teeth in a smile, which had been known to make nervous householders grateful that Stubbs was a clergyman's servant—therefore, of course, incapable of what he seemed adapted for. The Reverend McGregor, whose tastes were peculiar, also felt grateful. In his case, it was gratitude that the power of wealth had enabled him to reclaim a noted burglar, who now found it to his financial advantage to remain a reputable member of society. Burglary is a talent, like any other. Any talent comes in appropriately, once in a while.

"What information have you, Stubbs?" inquired the clergyman, behind the locked doors of his town study. Stubbs answered in the low and rather hoarse tones which were characteristic of him, but very explicitly.

"The place is wide open, sir. They go to bed just after the birds. I could take the Prince of Wales through with a band, sir, any time from half-past-nine on, and if anyone saw us, he'd roll over on the other side and go to sleep, for fear he'd miss the rest of the dream."

"You think you can smuggle me into the laboratory about ten o'clock?"

"There or anywhere else, sir. I could put you in Dr. Lanthorne's private safe if you wanted me to."

"I'll be satisfied with the laboratory. Hold yourself in readiness to leave here about nine-thirty."

"Yes, sir. And I found a place for you to hide, sir. It's a sort of a closet, with a glass window about five feet up. I'll bring along a stool for you to stand on, sir."

"This closet is in the laboratory?"

"Over on one side of it, sir. It'll give you as good a view of the laboratory, sir, as the bride has of the parson. There's other things there, too, sir."

"There would be, in a laboratory," said the clergyman, rather shortly. "That will be all until nine-thirty, Stubbs."

Not being a completely trained millionaire's man, as yet, Stubbs continued to speak, as he opened the door.

"Quite so, sir. And, begging your pardon and in particular, sir, there's something covered up that I took a peek at. Just as I lifted the cover, it moved, sir; and I remembered then you told me to come straight home. Yes, sir."

He was gone. His master was of a mind to call him and demand an amplification of his last remarks, but decided not to. After all, that along with a number of other matters, was due to be settled definitely within the next few hours.

ON THE WAY to the Lanthorne residence, Daunt was troubled by another consideration—a rather obvious one, too—which had escaped him: suppose someone else should reach the laboratory first? How, then, was he to enter the closet which Stubbs had spotted? His man, however, had not overlooked that point.

"You'll leave it to me, sir; or you'll leave it to whoever it was that put up the closet. It might have been built for spying, sir. The little glass window is on the laboratory side—looking for all the world like a window in coffin, only longer; but the closet door opens into the hall, sir. Very convenient, sir."

"Almost too convenient," his master returned, thoughtfully, stumping along beside the valet.

They had left the automobile some blocks away from Dr. Lanthorne's. The two of them, both well muffled against the damp night air, looked curiously alike: squat, solid, rather slow; though the Reverend McGregor walked stiffly and tapped on the sidewalk with his heavy cane.

"This way into the backyard, sir."

Daunt followed, down a narrow, stone-flagged passage, between the house and a high board fence. The big brick mansion was dark.

"I'll give you a boost, sir. When you're high enough, just raise that back window and climb in. You'll be in the rear hall. I'll guarantee everyone's in bed dreaming dreams. The hall to the laboratory is up a little flight of four stairs, sir."

Any misgivings which the Reverend McGregor Daunt may have had were not bred of his clergyman's conscience. *That* was sufficiently broad, erected, as it was on legal and medical foundations. He was rather doubtful, however, of his ability to master the window sill. But he did so. He had waited only a moment in the dark hallway, when Stubbs, grunting rather heavily, joined him, via the same route.

"Right along this way, sir," instructed his guide in a hoarse whisper. "If you feel you're getting lost, grab my coat-tails. Better leave the talking to me, sir, when we've climbed the stairs."

Stubbs' hand, thrust backward at the critical instant, sustained his master in the act of falling over the bottom stair. After that, their upward progress was relatively quiet. Daunt followed blindly through the second hall. It seemed to him absolutely dark. Why did not people keep subdued hall light, for the convenience of—well, of visitors? He grinned at the goal to which his logic had led him, though, when he was frank with himself, he felt too serious to grin. This little visit had altruistic motives. He had justified it to himself, over and over. He was there to probe a mystery, and mysteries were the breath of life to him. But justifying it to an unsympathetic and legally minded third party—a judge, for instance—might be difficult. Even millionaires have been known to go to jail. Daunt had to be content with the hope that, if an officer of the law should intrude into this affair, it might be one he knew personally. His acquaintance among the force was extensive, so the hope was not unreasonable.

"This is the door to the closet, sir. And here's the little stool. I'll set the stool inside, by the window, and you can climb on it when you're ready. I guess they'll light up the laboratory, if anything's going to happen."

"Where will you be, Stubbs?" demanded the Reverend McGregor.

"Right out here in the hall, sir. I'll get you away, like a fish off of a hook, when you're ready to call it a night." Daunt entered the dark closet, and, by careful feeling, managed to climb upon the stool without overturning it. He heard the closet door shut quietly behind him.

The window was perceptible, just before him, as he straightened up. Through it he could see dimly the objects in the laboratory. He could identify a large table, a long, low bench, a number of chairs and stools. Something rather vague and formless, like a draped figure, in a chair, was by itself at the side farthest from the table. He strained his eyes to make out its nature. It might be a draped figure or merely a dark cloth thrown over some object on the chair. Whatever it was, it made him shiver, though he could not have explained why.

His eyes, searching the opposite wall for the place the man he awaited probably would enter, found a door, obliquely to the left. A window near it afforded what light there was. The rays of a street lamp, ricocheted from some building or wall on the outside, relieved the gloom of the laboratory.

He turned his attention to nearer objects. The window in the closet appeared to be of the sliding kind. When he touched it, it moved, laterally. It had already been opened a little at the farther end. Daunt observed this fact, but for the moment attached no significance to it, as his ears caught a sound from the front of the house.

The sound resolved itself into cautious footsteps, timorous and hesitating. They reached the door in the opposite wall. There they stopped.

A soft light flooded the laboratory. Daunt's gaze darted from one end of the long room to the other, to learn who had turned it on. He found no one, but his eyes rested, with apprehension, on the mysterious object in the chair. It appeared to be only a mass of drapery.

With a little gasp of relief, he allowed his eyes to wander again; and immediately he ceased breathing.

Within the closet, not two feet from him, stood a very large and distinguished-looking man. The man was looking at him with curious interest. A slight smile curled the corners of the firm, rather humorous mouth.

Before the Reverend McGregor Daunt had resumed his arrested breathing, the man extended a big hand. There was now enough light in the closet to make his action perfectly clear.

"I am Laidlaw Lanthorne. Whom have I the honor of entertaining?"

The tone of the words, uttered in a deep whisper, was courteous in the extreme. Daunt responded in the proper form, also whispering, though he found difficulty in speech of any kind.

"May I request you to remain exactly where you are; also, to be silent?"

Again, his manner was courteous; there seemed no hint of menace in it: but the clergyman was sensible of the fact that implicit obedience would be his best course. He nodded without speaking.

A little shuffle at the other side of the laboratory was followed by a flicker of movement. The door had begun to open.

Daunt's companion at once turned his attention to the scene before him. The Reverend McGregor, in whose mind a number of conflicting emotions were hopelessly entangled, did likewise.

The door opened inward. It swung almost imperceptibly, a half inch at a time. There was a noticeable interval before enough space was made to admit the apprehensive, extremely diffident countenance of Mr. Frederick Braine.

Even after it was all within the room, Mr. Braine's head gave no evidence of rash precipitancy. It oscillated inquiringly from side to side, like the forward part of a measuring worm. The small, plum-like eyes, within their large circles popped suspicion at every object in turn.

Braine pushed the door a little wider; and someone breathed the one word:

"Frederick!"

With a cry, Braine staggered toward the mass of drapery in the chair. The mass seemed to be putting out, with horrible, unnatural stiffness, two bandaged arms.

Braine mumbled her name, over and over. He sank with his arms around her knees.

"Speak to me again, Bertha!" he sobbed.

It was an unmanly exhibition; but Daunt pulled away with aversion when he sensed that the spectator beside him was quietly laughing to himself.

"If you can't speak, at least show your face!" entreated the little man.

The mass of drapery remained still. Braine rose unsteadily, and made one or two upward movements, but let his arms sink again. At last, with hands that trembled in a wide arc, he plucked hold of the drapery. He made a false motion, even then, and nearly lost his grasp, before he reverently drew the sheet aside.

It fell, exposing the face.

Daunt craned his neck for a view, but Braine was in his way. The secretary acted strangely. He reached forward, with a motion as if to stroke the face. He paused, with the action unperformed. The rapid, rough sob of his breathing was audible. He reached again. His right hand, in advance of the other, achieved its object.

He staggered back to his knees, with a scream. Daunt saw the face. Dr. Lanthorne chuckled.

The bandaged arms of the figure in the chair lifted slowly, vibrating from side to side as they came up, with an invitation to Mr. Frederick Braine.

He jumped back. His hands tore at his face and his hair. His screams crowded one another, tumultuously.

Daunt was still trying to understand the face in the chair. His efforts were interrupted by Braine, whose screams had quavered into silence.

The little man began to laugh. He turned for a moment, by chance, toward the closet, and disclosed blood dripping from his upper lip, where he had seized the foppish little moustache with fingers of steel and uprooted it. Then he directed his attention once more to the figure in the chair. He laughed uncontrollably at sight of it, and grasped the outstretched hands. The next instant, he was capering around the laboratory, with both arms around the dead, stiff waist of a mummy.

Daunt felt an iron hand on his shoulder.

"Will you step into the hall with me, sir?" requested Dr. Laidlaw Lanthorne.

As they left the closet, the doctor switched on a light. It disclosed the astounded figure of Stubbs, crouching in a corner. When Stubbs perceived who accompanied his master, he appeared to consider the end of all things at hand. But Dr. Lanthorne bowed pleasantly.

"I am honored with visitors, it seems, for what I thought was to be a private exhibition," he remarked. "If both of you will enter this room, I can promise you comfortable chairs."

Daunt found himself in what appeared to be a private office. Possibly it was the one which had belonged to Mr. Frederick Braine. Dr. Lanthorne, seating himself heavily in an arm chair after his guests had been disposed, held up one large hand with an air of urgency.

"I am due for an appointment very soon," he said. "May I request that you permit me to speak without interruption? I am fortunate in having two voluntary witnesses, to whom this situation can be explained."

"I must be brief. The man whom you saw and my wife were lovers. I made sure of this one day, six months ago, chancing to intercept a note she had written him. I had trusted them both, implicitly. A man of science must be able to trust those about him. Without trust—confidence—the mind wears itself out, and can accomplish nothing."

He paused, with clenched hands. His dark eyes stared intensely at his two listeners. Beads of sweat appeared on his forehead.

"I disposed of her according to the ancient Egyptian custom. While she still lived, I made her into a mummy. It is a horrible death, but I felt that possibly the horror of it might even then save her soul. She died quickly—within perhaps the space of an hour."

"The rest is a matter of detail. I am skilled in many curious playgrounds of science—mechanics, electricity, ventriloquism. I used them to toy with Braine. He has sat at the same table as the mummy of my wife, and thought her alive. I postponed the final reckoning with him until some work I was doing should be finished. Tonight, I was ready for the ultimate scene. I lured him here by the very note which I intercepted, six months ago—it mentioned Thursday evening, but omitted the date. It was my plan to lead him to the mummy through ventriloquism and electrical effects; to let him learn what he actually embraced; then to kill him. It seems the penalty has been taken from my hands. He has become a madman. I am entirely satisfied."

The doctor rose, with extended hand.

"Gentlemen, I have an appointment. I must bid you good evening. I...."

Daunt sprang forward, in time to ease the giant figure of Dr. Lanthorne to the floor.

"Poison?" inquired Stubbs, nonchalantly.

His master nodded.

"We cannot help him. The servants are in the laboratory now. Suppose we go?"

As they rounded the corner of the hall, a door from it into the laboratory opened, and Daunt glanced back. He saw the slobbering, laughter-distorted face of Mr. Frederick Braine.

"THE SCIENTIFIC TYPE of mind has curious limitations, Stubbs," the Reverend McGregor Daunt observed, later, on the occasion of a night in town. "That man, who now grins and gibbers in the asylum, came to me for advice. He had heard of some reputation I may have as a thinker. With all of his facts in its possession, my mind persisted in treating the matter as an intellectual problem only. I told him to obey the summons in the note. I thought that the quickest way to solve the problem—and I sent him to his doom."

"The old boy would have got him anyhow, one way or another," Stubbs consoled.

"It may be." Daunt sighed. "Perhaps, by telling him to go, I actually saved his life. But of what use is it to him now?"

There seemed no answer to this. The Reverend McGregor

Daunt pondered sadly, but at length shrugged his shoulders and looked up with a brisker expression.

"I shall leave in the morning for the lodge, Stubbs. There is a text in one of the Apocryphal books which I wish to think over for a future sermon. It is, 'By whatsoever things a man sins, by these he is punished.' Did you ever know that to work out in life, Stubbs?"

"I can't say I ever did, sir," replied Stubbs, scratching his head.

A Letter from the Rev. MacGregor Daunt

Editors of BLACK MASK,

Dear Sirs:

"It is a somewhat unusual experience to find one's self walking, talking, eating, acting in a story by one's bosom friend of many years. As I read with interest Suter's translation of my character to the pages of his series of "Macgregor Daunt" stories, I enjoy an experience surely novel enough. I am afraid I am delineated rather correctly in some of my idiosyncrasies, but I must beg to plead not guilty to the possession of so acute a mind as seems to be at the command of Daunt. And as for means, I am in the class with the average clergyman in that regard. Although, were I like Daunt, independently rich, I can imagine myself leading just such a life as he chooses for himself. At any rate under any and all circumstances, I would be a clergyman. I cannot imagine myself out of that calling.

"Of course, the friendship of many, many years standing may make me partial. But I cannot but feel that these stories are well conceived, cleverly constructed, and of genuine and novel interest. You do credit to your perspicuity as an editor in giving place in your excellent periodical to a writer of the promise I believe Suter to be.

Sincerely yours,

Rev. A.W. MacN.

("Macgregor Daunt.")

The Problem of the Little Blond Nightmare

The Reverend McGregor Daunt, clergyman by profession and detective by choice, has come to take his place in Black Mask *along with Race Williams, the Continental Detective, Prentice, and a host of other* Black Mask *characters. Though the problems of ministers in general are of but little interest to most readers, the intellectual Daunt is an exception to the rule—his problems being those which usually concern the police.*

1

AT TIMES, THE Reverend McGregor Daunt, clergy-man by profession and detective because he chose to be, was compelled by circumstances to spend several consecutive weeks in town. He would have preferred remaining at his hunting lodge in the woods; but even clergymen of wealth must some-times act counter to their desires. If a man's bank balance be large enough, he can forestall most of life's annoyances. But not all.

Though Daunt grumbled, he faced the music. And because he was bored, one such stay in the city (a rather longer stay than usual) had this curious result: that he tired of the priceless concoctions of his French chef, Gaston. He craved a change, even to restaurant cooking. So the versatile clergyman, whose means were sufficient to buy him anything in reason that could be bought, fell into the commonplace habit of stumping about town, looking up new places to eat.

He found them; a few good, but all rather sad producers in comparison with Gaston's handiwork. He stalked the elusive chop houses assiduously. Cunning restaurant keepers cocked their eyes for him—and might have spared themselves the trouble. For his appearance on a street, walking stiffly with the heavy cane he affected, his great head riding majestically on his squat body, revealed nothing of his intentions. He could pass the most enticing odors. He could nod cynically to Monsieur le Proprietaire, and walk on around the corner to another eating-house. He could—he did—sometimes leave the restaurant district altogether, and, in the hope of finding the unfindable, plunge into some street which he should have known perfectly well boasted no place to dine in all its length.

Thus he meandered one noon-day into Starling Street—the warehouse thoroughfare, where furniture is stored while the owners are settling the custody of the children and like points. It is a street of blind walls and cobblestone pavements, over which moving vans rumble from seven to five. Occasional hardware trucks dispute right-of-way with them, coming from a firm at the north end of the street. Not far down Starling from the hardware storehouse is an alley—wide enough for the vans—which crosses two railroads within three squares and comes out on the river front. The alley serves as a convenient short cut for vans plying to the boats. Its cobblestones were laid in pre-sidewalk days, and they touch the brick walls of the warehouses.

On the day that he chanced into Starling Street, Daunt was feeling contrary. Had he been able to find a more unlikely street for restaurants he might have taken it. When he perceived the alley (McGuire Court it is called) he recognized at once that this, with its blind walls, *was* less likely than the street. So he turned into it. And halfway to the first railroad crossing, he met an irresponsible hardware truck, the driver of which took pleasure in making the reverend gentleman leap for his life into a nearby overhung doorway.

Blind chance? Absolutely! Over that doorway was a swinging sign, hung parallel to the door to prevent its projecting into the street and being wrenched loose by passing trucks; and on the sign was the most atrocious picture the Reverend McGregor had seen outside of the Metropolitan Art Museum.

The picture, painted in garish hues, was that of a horrid but pretty little lady with straw-colored hair through which horns projected. She was smiling hideously. She had bat's wings, and (if it must be told) cloven hoofs. And, to make her personality entirely clear, her nature was indicated in the inscription beneath her, which read, "The Little Blond Nightmare."

Daunt glared at the thing in silence until it had entered his soul, then said, with conviction:

"The man who thought *that* up should be able to cook!"

He said it aloud, which is a way men have who incline largely to their own company, and he received a reply. For, from somewhere within the little dark doorway of the place, an incisive, high-pitched voice, like the voice of a small girl speaking through her nose, called out:

"Red bloaters! Baked ham! And what is probably the best coffee on earth! Come in, kind gentlemen, and rest your bones!"

The Reverend McGregor Daunt started violently throughout his plump length. Daily, he received invitations from restaurant keepers, but this was like none of them. The voice had an elfish, bird-like quality, as of something not human. The words, too, were at once cleanly cut and distinct, yet subtly wrong in intonation. Daunt stood a moment irresolute at the threshold. Perhaps an inner prophetic sense warned him that, stepping through the dark doorway, he was entering upon a more outrageous problem than any he had yet tackled. He hesitated; then, tapping firmly upon the step with his cane, went in.

2

"CUSTOMERS! WAKE UP, mama!"

The clergyman careened around so sharply that he nearly overbalanced. The screech had been in his very ear. Then he perceived.

At a small high desk, to the left of him as he entered, was seated a woman. A notable woman. Save for the accident of having been born thirty centuries or so too late, she would have made a fit spouse for Goliath. She filled all the space behind the desk, and threatened to overflow into the rest of the room. Her chin ran down in billows, her lap in terraces. Her great head, which had been reposing against the high back of the chair, was leonine. Daunt regretted—though the thought did not occur to him until afterward—not having entered in time to hear her snore. Such a woman surely must have roared in her sleep; and she had been asleep, for she was chubbily knuckling her eyes. Even the parrot's shrill efforts had hardly awakened her.

The parrot—a large, green-and-gold bird—was perched upon her pillow-like breast. He continued his alarm, spitting the words out at the side of his beak, until the large woman silenced his clamor by the rather severe expedient of gently throttling him with thumb and forefinger of one hand. In a contralto voice, smooth as honey, she explained the maneuver to Daunt, who perhaps appeared slightly shocked by it.

"He'd go on shrieking 'customers' all afternoon if I didn't choke him off; but that fixes him. You see, we had a monkey once, that a sea captain gave us, and one day the monkey tried to wring his neck. Ever since, all I've had to do to stop his racket is tickle his throat a little. He thinks it's the monkey come back to finish him."

"A useful bird, doubtless," Daunt commented, stiffly.

The fat woman nodded, rather vigorously for so vast a personage. In spite of her size, there was a deal of feminine charm about her. Her eyes, soft, gray and kindly, twinkled as she talked, in a manner which might have moved some men to reflect that, buried beneath the pyramid of her flesh, was a nice woman—a nice, *young* woman. She could hardly have been more than thirty.

"I was having my nap. Fat folks must sleep, you know!" She laughed, with a very pleasant trill. "When customers come in, Napoleon wakes me up. Did he tell you about our coffee?"

"And ham, and bloaters—red bloaters, if I recall correctly," Daunt affirmed, remembering that he was hungry.

"Red Holland bloaters," she nodded. "But we stand or fall by our coffee. I make it myself. Just sit at a table—any one of them."

She jumped down from her high seat, with a lightness that was astounding. As she tripped off agilely toward the kitchen, Daunt almost committed the naive discourtesy of gazing after her open-mouthed. Fat and flabby, she yet had the step of a girl. She stimulated his curiosity.

"An unusual woman," the clergyman commented, with his old trick of thinking aloud.

"A damned remarkable woman!" affirmed a deep voice, near him.

Daunt started, and for the first time—so engrossed had he

been in the proprietress and her feathered advertising manager, which had ridden off perched complacently on her shoulder—he looked about the room. It was a room requiring deliberate effort if one was to observe it accurately. Save for a soft diffusion of daylight from the doorway, and two small windows in front, darkness was held at bay only by a few oil lamps, depending from brackets on the walls. Each lamp was assisted in the unequal struggle by the tops of the small oaken tables, rubbed to a glistening polish, and by the immaculately white surface of the wooden floor. Narrow paths of pleasant brown radiance traveled across some of the tables toward certain lamps, as if to emphasize the cooperation of lamps and tables in the common effort. It was somewhat past the usual lunch period, and the man who had replied to Daunt was the only person in the room. He sat at one of the farther tables, in such a position as to intercept one path of light while another reflected upward upon his face.

He was a broad little man, very square of shoulder, with dark, staring eyes, reminiscent of the shiny, button eyes of a rag doll. A grizzled, closely-cropped mustache perched on his upper lip, like something which did not rightly belong there, having perhaps been lent by the hair of his head for temporary facial adornment.

"A remarkable woman—and a fine woman," he emphasized, hospitably kicking the chair at the side of the table opposite him, so that Daunt could seat himself. "I shouldn't mind marrying that woman."

As he sat down, Daunt manifested a tiny degree of polite interest—not that the fat woman or the broad-shouldered man concerned him in the slightest, but they seemed rather curious specimens of that human race whom the reverend gentleman delighted to study like bugs on a pin.

"Is that consummation to be expected?" he inquired.

The broad little man spat furtively out of a corner of his mouth, making the brass spittoon between tables by a narrow margin.

"I ain't spoken to her about it," he declared.

He shut his mouth decidedly, as if all had been said on the subject that needed saying. He turned his face away from Daunt, toward the wall, and was silent for so long that the visitor thought best, in the interests of scientific investigation, to venture a further remark.

"You can't very well marry her without speaking to her about it, can you?" he asked, with ponderous humor.

The little man turned his face back. One of his eyebrows arched itself appreciably higher than the other, and he stared at the Reverend McGregor Daunt with an expression which might have been taken for resentment. At length, he spoke.

"That's none of your damned business!" was what he said.

"Well, I'm blessed!" exploded the clergyman, returning the little man's stare in high indignation; but his companion looked away again and once more seemed to commune with his own thoughts. So deeply was he engrossed, and so impersonal was his attitude, that Daunt's anger began to melt into quickened interest in the usual character of the situation. He was occupied with the thought of this when the little man coolly glanced at him once more, and resumed his effort at speech.

"Name's Mogadore," he said, tersely. "Lucy Mogadore. Husband was a lake captain. Damned fine man but no brains. Ought to have been a street car conductor. Takes brains to run a ship. The ship ain't got none—somebody has to have. Got in a storm, he did, and she's been a widow for seven years. Started this hotel on the strength of her coffee. There *ain't* no better coffee. It's that coffee keeps me from suicide!"

He rose, at that, and made a movement toward his throat, so sudden and violent that Daunt half rose, too, with the interested speculation that, the effect of some previous cup of coffee having worn off, his informant was about to take forcible leave of this life. But the little man was reaching for his mouth, not his throat. He grasped his top row of teeth, and abruptly removed them, in entirety. A glass of water, before unnoticed by the clergyman, stood at the side of the table, against the wall. The little man dropped his teeth, with a splash, into the water. That done, he walked off, toward the rear of the room. In a moment, he could be heard ascending an unseen flight of stairs; immediately thereafter his feet were pattering about overhead.

For several minutes, Daunt stared in silence at the place where he had disappeared. Then he shook himself, like a man rousing from sleep.

"That," he observed, aloud, "is the queerest performance I ever witnessed in my life!"

The fat woman, entering with a tray, was in time to catch the sense if not the words of this remark.

"He *is* an odd one, isn't he?" she agreed, cheerfully. "It'll be five years in September since he came here. Five years is a long time, but I can't make him out yet. He's got a heart of gold, though. If you don't like this coffee, don't pay for it, sir; and don't ever speak to me again!"

Still feeling contrary, Daunt nearly resolved to take her at her word. But after the first long, satisfying draft—a draft which he prolonged because he lacked the heart to interrupt his palate—he sighed, and no longer made resolves about the coffee.

"I'll get you another cup, sir," she suggested.

"In a minute! I'm going to sip the rest of this cup slowly, and prolong it with the bloaters. It should not be hurried over. You said that unpleasant little man has a kind heart?"

Mrs. Mogadore seated herself, majestically, upon the chair which the man in question had lately vacated.

"But for Mr. Donegan, sir, you would not be enjoying that coffee. I should not be here. I don't know where I *should* be, sir, but it wouldn't be in this place. He came to me right after I started here, sir—him and the parrot. He gave me the parrot and taught it to talk up my coffee. But where they come from I don't know. He's never said. You'll learn, after you know him better, sir, that he's not a man to answer questions he don't want to answer."

"I noticed that."

"He's queer; but a heart of gold, sir. When everything was in, and the business starting very nicely, I found I was short six hundred dollars of paying for what I had. Not much, you may say, but they were going to shut up my doors. He lent it to me, did Mr. Donegan. 'You needn't thank me, Mrs. Mogadore,' were his very words. 'Pay me when you are able.'"

She sighed.

"A heart of gold, sir! But who'd ever know it to hear him talk? And the way he can paint! You noticed our signboard, sir?"

Daunt nodded; he had been intending to lead the conversation toward the signboard.

"He painted that, sir—right out of his head! Don't ask me

what it means—he never said; but it's wonderful! 'It will bring you custom, Mrs. Mogadore,' were his very words. He says painting signs ain't his line, but he makes a living at it, nowadays; and a good living it is, because people like his ideas. You've seen that laundry wagon, 'We wash everything except the baby?'—and the big moving van, 'The earth moves, so does Slavinsky?' He painted those signs, sir. He's a wonderful man. And a heart of gold!"

When the Reverend McGregor Daunt left the hospitable precincts of "The Little Blond Nightmare" that afternoon, he was imbued with the conviction that here was a couple who might be worth studying, when no problem more sinister demanded attention. They had lived under the same roof for five years, in mutual admiration, and were not even engaged. This was a minor mystery; the meaning of the bizarre sign over the door was another. Both cried aloud to be solved. Even without such incentives, he would have returned occasionally, for the sake of the coffee; for Gaston in all his excellence could not touch the nut-brown beverage. But coffee and mysteries taken together brought the reverend gentleman back not occasionally but on most of his visits to town. Lake captains and others, the transient guests, came and went, but the Reverend McGregor Daunt finally fitted in as a fourth, with the man, the woman, and the parrot.

A queer place, in its way, he considered "The Little Blond Nightmare"; but a place of only minor mystery. Its quiet, dusky interior carried no sinister suggestions. The sole human touch in a street composed otherwise of blind warehouse walls, it was homely and odd and inoffensively hospitable. Daunt would have scouted the idea of a tragic problem—a police problem—

there. Which indicates that even clergymen, with their professional instinct for occult matters, can not poke their measuring rods far into the future.

3

THOUGH DAUNT BECAME a regular visitor to the little hotel, there were, of course, some days that he missed even when in town; not that the coffee had lost its enticement, but he had other obligations. One of these days was that on which Slavinsky's empty van toppled into the railroad excavation, only a square down the alley from "The Little Blond Nightmare," seriously injuring the two men on the driver's seat. With any kind of luck, Daunt told himself, he might have come up McGuire Court on that particular day, and have witnessed the drunken driver turn too sharply as he crossed the tracks. It must have been a sight worth seeing; one doubly illustrating the legend painted by Donegan on the side of the van, that "The Earth Moves, So Does Slavinsky." The clergyman sighingly directed his steps, the following day, so as to pass the place, but, as he had feared, the wrecked vehicle had been removed. Only some shattered windshield glass remained. He sighed more profoundly, and proceeded to lunch. Life at best is so humdrum that the loss of even an obvious, physical thrill is to be deplored.

But a thrill of another sort awaited him. Though he found that charming mountain of flesh, Lucy Mogadore, stationed as always at the receipt of custom, she was not seated in the attitude usual to her when the luncheon guests had departed. Her mighty arms were folded on the desk. Her face was hidden in them. Napoleon, hopping about from chair to desk and back again, uttered weird, incoherent chuckles probably meant for sympathy. For Mrs. Mogadore was crying; not noisily or lightly as lesser folk weep; but with profound bosom-racking sobs of anguish. Daunt stood aloof. He regarded tears as annoying and unnecessary symptoms of the feminine temperament.

"Mrs. Mogadore!" he exclaimed, disapprovingly.

She looked up, and nearly overthrew the desk in the enthusiasm of her welcome.

"Mr. Daunt, sir! I know it in my heart, Mr. Daunt—something terrible has happened!"

He brightened, hopefully, and began searching for words to calm such gigantic perturbation. He had not found them when the fat woman, hopping lightly from her seat, seized him by the arm and began urging him toward the rear of the restaurant.

"This way, Mr. Daunt. See for yourself. There!"

They stopped before the table at which the Reverend McGregor Daunt had first met Mr. Donegan. In a way, Daunt regarded that part of the restaurant as dedicated to the little man with the staring eyes. He gazed at the cleanly polished table; the glass of water next the wall; the vacant chairs. The teeth were in the glass, and to them Mrs. Mogadore pointed, tragically.

"They've been there, just that way, ever since he left them yesterday noon. His door is bolted on the inside. I've tried the handle and called him, but he doesn't answer. Something terrible has happened. I know it!"

"You're sure the door is bolted?" Daunt suggested, with rapidly rising interest.

"I've tried the key, sir; and besides, he always bolts it. He's a queer man. When he first came to me, he said, 'Mrs. Mogadore, I'm a man that loves privacy. I haven't had a chance at it for years, so I'm going to have it strong now. I'll take the room,' he said, 'but no one must come into it, now or any time. I'll do my own cleaning and make the bed. It'll be kept in good condition. There won't be nothing unlawful going on in it. But I must have privacy.' Those were his very words. And not in five years time has anybody been in that room saving himself, unless it was through the window, and there ain't even a toe-hold for a squirrel on the outside wall. When we had the monkey, he used to climb in through some of the other windows, but never through that one. Shall we go up, Mr. Daunt?"

The clergyman considered. He tried to be careful at all times not to usurp the functions of the police though he *had* made glaring exceptions to the rule and successfully reconciled them with his conscience. Besides, he found it useful to be friendly with the force.

"We will not go up," he concluded. "You will wait here, Mrs. Mogadore, while I find a policeman."

Leaving "The Little Blond Nightmare" at his best speed, he hurried up Starling Street, reckoning that on this thoroughfare or the one connecting with it he should be likely to meet that tall and efficient member of the department known to his intimates as "Lanky" Kerns. Kerns had been on the beat a day or so before. Very likely he would be the one to handle the initial stages of this problem—if it turned out to be a problem at all.

Just around the corner of the busier street, Daunt caught the glint of blue in the distance—blue which vibrated, as its owner swung the regulation baton. He saw what he had hoped to see: the spare, athletic figure and the Lincolnian features of "Lanky" Kerns.

By the time they were back at the little hotel, Kerns was in possession of the details. "The Little Blond Nightmare," it seemed, was no strange place to him. He, too, spent much of his bachelor leisure there, and strongly favored Lucy Mogadore's coffee.

Reaching the second floor, with Mrs. Mogadore, tearful again, regarding proceedings from the end of the hallway, the policeman, after calling without response, set at once about his task of breaking down the door. He backed a step or two, and, with a sudden lunge, brought his weight against it. It creaked; but there was no other result.

"Must be a heavy bolt. I'll try again."

"It's a very heavy bolt," the fat woman volunteered. She had stopped sobbing and had come nearer, to watch the attack. "Mr. Donegan bought it special and put it up himself."

"He certainly must have something in there he doesn't want seen," commented the policeman.

He backed the full width of the hall; breathed deeply, crashed sidewise into the door. There was the wrench of something uprooted from seasoned timbers which sought in vain to hold it.

"Bolt screws torn out. Shall we go in together, Reverend?"

Daunt had made up his mind what would be within that room. There were but two exits to it: the locked and bolted door, and the window, topping a sheer brick wall which overhung the inset entrance to the place and offered no rest for a human foot nearer than the remote cobblestones of the street. The spirit of the man who had locked himself in the room might no longer be within. His body, however—so the clergyman reasoned—could hardly be elsewhere.

They went in quickly, as if trying to rush whatever horror

might be awaiting them. They stopped, as suddenly, just within the doorway.

The room was papered with circus posters, which were screamingly evident on walls and ceiling. Posters everywhere; but no one in the room.

"Well, I'll be hanged!" exclaimed the policeman.

Then he laughed, grimly, and in two long strides reached the tightly shut door of a closet on the far side. Mrs. Mogadore screamed. Kerns wrenched the door open and jumped back, as if expecting something to fall out. Some articles of masculine wearing apparel were within; that was all. The policeman turned again, with a peculiarly blank expression of countenance, and walked thoughtfully to the violated door of the room. He examined the bolt, with interest.

"Nothing phony about it," was his verdict. "If ever a door was bolted on the inside, that one was."

After the instant of painful expectancy while the closet was giving up its commonplace secret, Daunt stooped to examine an irregular stain on the rug.

"I should call that blood," he declared.

He was interrupted by a sibilant and incoherent sound from Mrs. Mogadore. She was pointing, with rounded eyes and rigid frame, to something on the floor in one of the corners opposite the window. It was a long knife, very keen and shiny, with a hard wood handle. The two men bent over it, without picking it up.

"We'll leave it there for the fingerprint man," the policeman said. "This is a detective case, all right. What's that on the blade?"

"I know—blood," the fat woman put in, soberly. "The stain

on the rug, too, Mr. Daunt. He's been killed. But where is he?"

She was answered by a raucous shriek from the hallway; a shriek so prolonged that the three of them had time, during its continuance, to turn sharply, like automatons, toward the open door of the room. Mrs. Mogadore spoke first.

"I declare, he startled me!" she laughed, shakily, with hand on heart. "He seems to know when I'm excited, and makes the most abominable noises!"

And the parrot, Napoleon, climbed to her shoulder, without losing an iota of his dignity.

"That bird could enter this room with the door bolted," Daunt suggested, his voice still rather uncertain. "You notice the window is open."

Mrs. Mogadore nodded.

"Since you mention it, Mr. Daunt, he does visit around the neighborhood once in a while. He was out yesterday afternoon. But I don't think he flew away with poor Mr. Donegan! I must go back to the restaurant," she finished. "Hold tight, Napoleon!"

As soon as her light footsteps were audible descending the stairs, "Lanky" Kerns turned to the clergyman with a smile.

"Help yourself, Reverend!" he invited, heartily. "I know you'd rather do detective work than preach—and this is your case, anyway. Of course, I'll have to call in the department; but they know you, and they won't mind you going right ahead with your examination."

The Reverend McGregor nodded, slowly and meditatively.

"Thank you, Kerns, I will. I shall not spoil any clues. What do you consider the most valuable clue here?" he asked speculatively, looking keenly at the tall policeman.

"The knife, I should say."

The clergyman shook his head.

"There is a more distinctive clue in this room—one that sets this particular problem all by itself. A really unique clue is a precious thing, Kerns."

"You mean the posters, Reverend?" the lanky policeman inquired, respectfully.

The clergyman nodded.

"You have been inside a number of rooms in your time. Did you ever find one papered with circus posters?"

The policeman shook his head. His mentor continued, pointing about the room after the manner of a college professor lecturing his class.

"Circus posters on the four walls; circus posters on the ceiling. He might have run out of them before the job was complete, you would say, and have used race track posters, or something advertising the pure food show; or he might have had to repeat himself. But no! They are all circus posters, and, though some of them feature the same performers, they seem different views. What do you make of it?"

The policeman circled slowly about the room, examining its garish paperings. Their name was various, as well as legion. One wall was covered by an enormous atrocity, spread at right angles upon the adjoining wall and folded for a few inches along the ceiling. Most of the works of art, however, were smaller; some of them so diminutive, by comparison, that they probably were reduced copies of original posters. There was no narrow-minded specialization as to subject matter: a few of the posters featured equestrians, others jocularly blazoned the merits of famous clowns, each in its own way and with all possible pictorial eloquence showed forth some one of the many sides of circus talent. Strong men. Ladies who tied themselves into knots. Intellectual elephants. Japanese who could not have bobbed their hair without sacrificing a livelihood, since they slid twice daily by that hair down a cable, while the reserved seats and the general admissioners applauded. There was a brilliant tribute to the man who rode a motorcycle upside down inside a cage; a picture of his fellow-worker, of the trim, lightly-running bicycle, who shot down an inclined plane into a tank of fire. The room was a marvelous representation, within a small space, of the many-faced life of a circus. The posters themselves were not art, but their selection was; for they had been arranged to make the very most of their possibilities. Within this small room at the sign of "The Little Blond Nightmare" lived the atmosphere of the Big Top; and the breath of life had been blown into it by a few square feet of paper, splashed with printers' ink.

"I should say that the man who pasted those things up was crazy about circuses," the policeman observed, at last.

"Anything else?"

"He's probably an old circus man. But I can't see how that helps us with his disappearance."

"It does not," the clergyman returned, crisply. "Except for one possibility—that they are hiding something."

"Covering something else, you mean?"

"Not just that. I fancy you could strip these posters off without finding anything more criminal than the original wall paper. That might be criminal enough, if it matched the paper in the hallway, but still it has nothing to do with Donegan. We will look at the window."

It seemed just a window, with nothing unique about it; but Daunt, scrutinizing the sill closely, uttered an exclamation:

"Blood stains!"

"That settles how he went out of the room," the policeman commented, with satisfaction.

"It settles *where* he went out," Daunt corrected. "Perhaps you will be kind enough to wait here a moment. I should like to look at the street. I may make a guess then as to where he went *after* he went out."

Daunt darted out, with the enthusiasm of a rather stiff hound chasing a rabbit. Once in the street, below Mr. Donegan's window, he circled in and out and back and forth over the cobblestones in much the fashion of the same canine trying to recover a lost scent. For the street bore not a semblance of a blood stain. It was a clear afternoon, with exceptionally good visibility. The sun was shining on both the wall of "The Little Blond Nightmare" and the rounded stones below. But though Daunt conjectured up a number of imaginative pictures of the probable course of a body leaving the window sill, then examined the various spots where such a body might have landed, he found nothing. He was obliged to mount the stairs again, with the conviction that whatever clues there were began and ended in Mr. Donegan's room.

Daunt's return to that room was deliberate rather than silent. Anyone within it must have been able to hear his footsteps distinctly, as he mounted the stairs in his stiff-legged fashion, then stumped along the hallway, tapping with his cane as he came. Which perhaps explains why Lucy Mogadore, with the parrot still on her shoulder, emerged from her lodger's room and met the little clergyman at the entrance. He was so much astonished at her presence there, instead of in the restaurant where she had been a few minutes before, that he merely stared when she passed him smilingly and descended the stairs. His thoughts were working on the main problem; so he dismissed this minor puzzle as of no importance, and hastened into the room to go on with what he had in mind.

"I have one theory, Kerns," he observed; "just one, but it is worth following up. I shall take a few minutes collecting data for it before you call your detectives."

The policeman nodded, and returned—with a rather embarrassed air, it seemed—to his own investigations. He had worked before with Daunt. The vicissitudes common to the force in a great city had brought him once by promotion to the detective ranks, then had reduced him again to a beat. He now awaited the next turn of fortune's wheel. Perhaps this case would be the lever to revolve it.

Daunt produced a notebook from his pocket, and made a slow tour of the walls, carefully writing down the essentials of each poster. He took particular pains to be accurate as to names of performers. Where these were duplicated, he recorded that fact. Their rank in their respective troupes, where that was shown, he noted, also. When he replaced the book, it contained as clear a picture of the remarkable papering of the room as could be painted with words. By this time Kerns had left, to notify the detective force. Daunt walked out, slowly, spending the minimum of words on Mrs. Mogadore as he passed through the restaurant. He was ready to start his independent investigation. The odd but apparently harmless adventure of "The Little Blond Nightmare" had developed into a problem.

4

THE FIRST STEP in the investigation of that problem was rather tame. It occurred in a large room in the manse at the rear of his church, which apartment the Reverend McGregor Daunt was wont to term his "City Study." He preferred the hunting lodge as a place to think; but at times the distance from town to that quiet spot made it inconvenient. In a way, this study was in the city, beyond doubt, for the church edifice fronted on one of the busiest downtown streets; but the atmosphere of the room was one of seclusion, rather than of urban noise and bustle. The very door which opened into the "City Study" was tucked away at the end of a narrow brick footpath between the church and the skyscraper next to it. Once inside that doorway, the clergyman was in his castle. He was surrounded there by books—armies of volumes which beleaguered the study on all sides. The windows, which might have been useful in the early days before neighboring buildings shut off their light, had been blocked by the bookcases. Their place was taken by an impartial skylight and by the electric fixtures. On the one side the small door, on the other a fireplace and a door into the living quarters of the manse, still held the books at bay. Elsewhere, they were in possession. The Reverend McGregor even found it necessary to remove several of them tenderly from the large table in the center of the study before he could lay out some sheets of paper upon that flat surface, and begin his investigations of "The Little Blond Nightmare's" mystery.

Beside the sheets of paper he laid his little notebook; with that, a symmetrically sharpened lead pencil. He picked up the pencil again, and began tapping a tune with it upon his teeth, at the same time staring ferociously at the paper. Half an hour went by. The paper remained blank. The Reverend McGregor Daunt, having thought out the first step of his investigation, reached for a telephone directory. He rather favored doing business by telephone, where that was feasible. It obviated the bother of a personal interview.

The number he called was that of the largest theatrical agency in the city. He apologized to the pleasant young woman who answered. He knew this was a theatrical agency; that it had nothing much to do, as a rule, with circus people; but possibly she could tell him…. And he read her the list of names from his notebook.

She did tell him. She was a well-informed young woman. Among those names, she said, were many who had performed for years with a certain mammoth circus. She thought that some of the others had left that great organization, but they might once have been with it. Yes, she could inquire where the circus was now, and she would be glad to telephone him.

That night, a fast train bound westward carried with it the Reverend McGregor Daunt, the preacher who seldom preached, the theologian who studied everything except theology, and who was now on the heels of a clue which he believed the police department had overlooked.

The considerable city at which he arrived in the morning happened to be a two-day stand, and this was the second day; so Daunt taxied directly to the principal hotel, where the circus stars were likely to be found. Here he was halted, momentarily. They were not at that hotel. Because of some disagreement with the management on a previous visit, they had patronized a rival hostelry. Though the clerk at the desk was ready enough in his information, Daunt registered a black mark against the record on this case of one McGregor Daunt, Investigator. That was what came of being too sure of one's reasoning. A man of plodding mind—a professional detective, for instance—would have saved time by asking the taxi driver where the circus stars were staying.

Daunt was crestfallen, but not completely humiliated. He managed to enter the second hotel with proper dignity. Stumping in to the accompaniment of his heavy cane, he unconsciously demanded respect; but he was not prepared for just the quality of respect he received.

For a large, mustached man, of quite impressive appearance himself, rushed forward from the depths of the lobby and grasped the little clergyman warmly by the hand.

"Ah, Monsieur Daunt!" he exclaimed. "I am Prallaire, the manager. I welcome monsieur! Mademoiselle Coligny awaits. She commands me to show monsieur to her suite immediately."

The Reverend McGregor Daunt felt his senses reel, ever so slightly.

"Mademoiselle Coligny?" he repeated.

"The eminent equestrienne, monsieur. Famed on four continents. She who is the entertainer and friend of royalty. She informed me that monsieur had arrived on the eight o'clock train, and intended visiting mademoiselle."

"I do not know the lady! I have her name here, but she can hardly have heard of me!" Daunt protested, stiffly.

The manager achieved a French shrug of his shoulders, and lifted his eyebrows.

"Nevertheless, mademoiselle commands! Shall I show monsieur up?"

Daunt nodded. After all, he wished to speak with the circus stars—one, or more, as might be necessary. This one would do as well as any for a start. But he felt like a man who casts a line into the sea, intending to fish, and finds suddenly that the fish has taken charge of the affair. It is possible for one to be too heartily and unexpectedly welcomed.

A few minutes more—in which brief space on the elevator and through the hallways of an upper floor, he tried a number of conjectures as to Mlle. Coligny's identity—and the door of her suite opened, in response to the manager's knock. Mlle. Coligny stood before him.

Daunt took the athletic hand of a straight, slim woman, with confident eyes, who seemed much older in years and experience than in body. She was smiling—enjoying his evident discomfiture; but there was reserve and no hint of discourtesy in her smile. Though the Reverend McGregor responded to the smile, his response was a matter of technique, so to speak. One of his most cherished theories had to do with the necessity for cheerfulness under trying conditions. The present condition was distinctly trying. For he did not recognize the lady.

"I fear you have the advantage of me, Mademoiselle Coligny," he said, with dignity. "I believe I have never met you."

She laughed, quietly but with enjoyment.

"I'm sure you haven't, Mr. Daunt; and I never saw you before in my life. Won't you come in?"

He did so; but his advance was so obviously a victory over

what seemed his better judgment that she laughed again. This time, he did not respond. He was becoming annoyed.

"The manager stated you were expecting me," he remarked.

"I was, Mr. Daunt. You must have been delayed. I have been expecting you for nearly fifteen minutes. If you will give the maid your hat and coat and step into the next room, you will see my reason."

Though his back was turned to her as he strode obediently through the arched doorway, he felt certain she was laughing at him, and his face became pink. He turned his head sharply from side to side—a man very much on guard. Consequently he was not taken quite unawares when "Lanky" Kerns, rising from a chair which had been out of sight around an angle of the doorway, confronted him with extended hand.

"Not offended, I hope, Reverend? Too good a chance to miss, you know. I got here a little before you did, so fixed it up with the Madame to spring a surprise. It's all right?"

Before Daunt could reply, Mademoiselle Coligny, who had followed, took up the explanation.

"It is I with whom he 'fixed it up,' Mr. Daunt. Am I forgiven, too?"

"They let me go back into plain clothes for this job." The tall policeman seemed anxious to finish all of his explaining before the victim of his joke could speak. "You passed within a foot of me in the Pullman, and never saw me. That gave me the idea. I kept out of your way and wired a taxi driver I know to find where the circus folks were staying, and he was ready to shoot me up here as soon as the train got in. I was first man off. You took longer than I counted on, at that."

"Congratulations, Kerns." The clergyman nodded gravely.

"And you, Mademoiselle Coligny. You did it well. I suppose, Kerns, you have our little problem all settled?"

"Well, no." The policeman tucked his big hands into his trousers pockets and gazed moodily at his boots. "I don't mind telling you, Reverend, that I felt rather chesty about picking up that hint you dropped about the posters. You'd be up here to question the circus people, I figured, so I'd beat you to it. But if they can't tell you any more than the madame told me, the lead won't help either of us." He grinned, sheepishly. "If I make good on this case, they've promised to keep me in plain clothes right along. But things aren't looking any too rosy."

They were seated now, at the equestrienne's invitation—she with her back to the light, in accordance with feminine instinct. Daunt looked quizzically at the gloomy policeman, and, faintly smiling, put a question to him.

"You say that you acted on my hint, Kerns. What did you ask Mademoiselle Coligny?"

"Why, I asked her about Donegan—told her what happened and described him. She couldn't remember anyone like that who was with the circus five years ago. Then I brought along a copy of the fingerprints on the knife. That mayn't do much good—and it may. I've had a little experience in the print department, you know."

"You are trying to find those who were named on the posters?" Daunt inquired.

The lanky policeman nodded. Daunt drew forth his inseparable notebook.

"The person you need to find is not named on any of those posters. That person's name has been very carefully omitted. Now, I claim the right to do a little mystifying. You had your joke on me, Kerns. You helped him in it, Mademoiselle. Will you help me in my little mystery?"

"With anything in my power," the circus star promised, readily.

"All I wish is an answer to a question—or possibly two questions. I am going to write one out, and request you, Mademoiselle, to write your answer in my note book. That will help the mystery. It will save my making notes, too. Is that fair?"

The policeman nodded. Daunt wrote busily for a moment, and passed the note book, with a pencil, to his hostess. She glanced at it, and gave a start.

"Why, Mr. Daunt!" she exclaimed.

The clergyman smiled.

"You catch my meaning?" he suggested.

She nodded.

"You have the solution, Mr. Daunt. I'm sure of it!"

"Will you note down the name for me? I am relying on you, Mademoiselle, not to give any hint of this to Mr. Kerns. I shall take pleasure in unfolding it to him at the proper time."

She nodded again, without looking up.

"As it happens, I can give you the name and the present address," she observed, writing. "We circus people keep track of one another, you know. Remembering addresses is one of the best things I do."

She finished the information and extended the note book toward Daunt. He had put out his hand for it, when a thought seemed to strike her. Her face darkened. She withdrew the book again.

"Before I give you this woman's name and address, tell me what is likely to happen to her," she demanded.

The clergyman met her gaze, frankly.

"That is beyond my power," he answered.

"Will she be executed? Or sent to prison?"

"I do not know."

She opened the note book impulsively to the sheet on which she had just written, and, jerking out that sheet, crumpled it in her hand.

"Here is your book, Mr. Daunt. You very nearly trapped me. But one circus performer will not willingly turn informer on another. I shall make a point of warning the others against you. Mary, will you show the gentlemen out?"

"Well, I'll be hornswoggled!" exploded the policeman, when they stood in the hallway, on the outside of Mademoiselle Coligny's closed door. "It wouldn't have been any use to argue with her. And they're so darned strict with us that if I'd forced the paper from her I'd have been in trouble up to my neck!"

"That comes from my notebook hobby," the clergyman commented. "I might easily have taken her aside and let her tell me the name before she had had time to think matters over. This same thing happened to me once before. Fortunately, I use thinner leaves now in the book—and I gave her a hard pencil."

Kerns stared at him.

"You don't mean to tell me—"

Daunt nodded.

"The name and address are quite clearly traced on the sheet next the one she tore out. I have just read them. Now they are traced on my mind, too. The mademoiselle was fussed, Kerns. Even a bright woman overlooks things when she's fussed. We are fortunate, too, in the fact that, being a lady of considerable bodily vigor, she presses hard on her pencil. I held my breath for fear she would tear out two leaves—but it did not occur to her."

"I may as well go back home," the policeman said, with a sigh. "Let me know if I can get any information for you, Reverend. You seem to have the case sewed up, and I'm as much in the dark as ever. I'm about as useful around here as nothing at all."

They had emerged from the hotel into the street. The Reverend McGregor Daunt shook his head.

"Your one defect, Kerns, is a certain element of puritanical gloom. You run to meet discouragement half way. As it happens, you have become necessary to this little investigation. If our subject shows fight, those fingerprints may be invaluable. We will finish the case together. When it is over, I shall drop out, and leave the glory to you."

"I don't like it, Reverend," the policeman protested. "I'm not entitled to credit for your work. It isn't right."

"It is essential," Daunt declared, firmly. "A clergyman may practice detective work for a hobby, but he must keep out of the papers. We will breakfast, Kerns; then we will take train for Chicago, in accordance with the directions Mademoiselle Coligny so kindly but unintentionally gave me."

They had been in the train for some time when "Lanky" Kerns roused from a doze to say to his companion:

"By the way, Reverend—those fingerprints. They were all on the blade of the knife—on both sides of it. None on the handle, at all."

"Yes—they would be on the blade," Daunt agreed, absently.

Puzzled, the policeman shook his head, but, after a moment, gave up the riddle and composed himself for another nap. He was just achieving sleep when the clergyman spoke again.

"You have a second defect, Kerns—lack of imagination. Cultivate imagination. Without it, one invariably becomes stodgy."

Kerns waited expectantly for more: but the Reverend McGregor Daunt, having delivered himself of this pearl of wisdom, perched his hat at the bottom of his broad forehead so as to shade his eyes, and shortly began to snore.

5

IT WAS THREE hours later, almost to the minute, before the clergyman again brought up the problem of "The Little Blond Nightmare." Having reached the appointed city, and even the neighborhood to which they were bound, they were walking slowly before a line of brick terraces, all exactly alike, all narrow-chested and shabby, but not all of them occupied.

"I should say the lady in the case has not done very well, of late years," Daunt commented. "Number thirty-five is the third from the end. By the way, the lady's name is Mrs. Patrick James. You may possibly recognize her."

"Have I ever seen her?" Kerns demanded, astonished.

"Probably not. My suggestion is just a long shot guess. We'll see how it comes out. A plain wooden door without glass— that is fortunate!"

Neither Daunt's first knock, which was quiet and courteous, nor his more emphatic second, brought results. All was silent. Kerns stepped back for a glance at the single front window, and immediately resumed his place on the door sill.

"The way these doors are set in helps our game," he observed. "Keep close, and she can't look us over through the window. I'm going to try an old trick, Reverend!" He raised his voice, and called, sharply: "Special Delivery!"

"That often gets them," he commented, in lower tones.

There was a shuffling on the other side. The door opened. Only an inch—just enough for a pair of sharp blue eyes to peer out—but that was enough, with the aid of a sudden shove, for

Kerns to wedge his shoe into the opening. He pushed harder, and the defiant little figure within suddenly stepped aside, permitting the door to swing.

"Two strong men against a woman; a sick woman, at that!" she cried, shrilly. "Very manly, gentlemen! Very honorable! You trick me into opening, then you enter by force. I never saw you before, you two, and I don't think I've lost much by not knowing you!"

She was a tiny woman, unusual in her diminutive size, and in the venom with which she seemed to barb her words, so that each syllable pricked like a thorn. Her skin, very delicate and white, contrasted with the flushed cheeks. Her blue eyes shot out hostility. Even the crisp flaxen ringlets of her hair, fine and tightly curled, seemed to bristle.

"Now you are here, what do you intend to do?" she continued. "Eject me from my palatial abode? Perhaps you wish to search me, too? You are not satisfied that I should be dying alone here; you wish to push me into the grave a little faster! Every man's house is his castle, but a woman's house is nothing—less than nothing, gentlemen! She is dust under your feet. Why not take my life at once if that will make you happier? Here, gentlemen—permit me to offer you a weapon. I am armed, you see, and you might be injured if you attacked me. Allow me, gentlemen; allow me!"

From somewhere under the loose kimono she wore, she produced a knife, as if by sleight-of-hand. Holding it by the extreme tip of the blade, she offered it to her visitors. Kerns was fairly nonplussed. He glanced from the knife to the little woman and back again, and seemed to be attempting speech, though no words came. Daunt, however, gravely accepted the weapon. He examined it minutely, with a care which seemed to arouse the little woman's curiosity.

"You seem interested in my knife," she observed, bitterly. "Do you care to stab me? You may as well take my life as my home!"

The clergyman looked at her—a deliberate, keen scrutiny. She met his gaze, defiantly. He continued to eye her, in silence, until apprehension crept across her thin features—as delicately expressive as the strings of a harp.

"I believe you misunderstand our visit, madam," he said, coldly. "Why do you think we are here?"

"You are come from the landlord," she answered.

He shook his head, gravely.

"We know nothing about your relations with the landlord—except what we may judge from your actions. We are here to interview you about the murder of a man named Donegan, in Cleveland."

She trembled, slightly. Her eyes widened. That was all, for a moment. Then she whispered, softly and thickly, as if to herself:

"Dead? Oh, I knew it! I knew it!"

Her face contorted, suddenly. She reached into the folds of the loose kimono she was wearing, and something gleamed in the gray light. Kerns leapt upon her.

"Quick, Reverend! Hold her hands!"

She was twisting in his grasp like a cat, struggling to complete her stroke with the knife she had aimed at her own breast. He foiled the effort, but could not capture the elusive, supple wrist. Daunt caught the upper part of her arm, and forced her hand back, until the knife fell with a clatter to the floor.

"Search her, Reverend!" Kerns requested, curtly.

"There are no more! I give you my word of honor there are

no more on me!"

"I believe, you, madam," the clergyman declared. "I shall not search you. Your word of honor is sufficient." He paused, eying her thoughtfully. "Besides, you have no reason to kill yourself. I used the word 'murder,' merely to see how you would react to it. I do not know that Mr. Donegan is dead."

"You don't—know?" She was looking at him with the wistful anxiety of a child.

"I am not even sure that he is badly injured. He may not be injured at all, for aught I know to the contrary."

"Oh!"

She was standing against the dingy wall, hiding for the moment a place where the paper had peeled off and exposed the plaster beneath. The policeman facing her at arm's length, held both of her wrists in one of his large hands. She seemed helpless, but, as Daunt finished speaking, she gave a curious, snakelike wriggle, and another knife fell to the floor. She smiled—an oddly roguish, juvenile smile for so violent a small person. It was as if the reaction from her shock of a minute before had brought to the surface another part of her nature—a simple, childlike part which could not conceal its naïve relief.

"Now I really haven't any more!" she laughed, mischievously. "I'm not altogether a rough-neck, gentlemen, if I *have* come to this. If you accept my word of honor that way, I'll show you I have as much honor as anyone."

Daunt nodded without ceasing the intent scrutiny with which he had first cowed her.

"Shall we seat ourselves in the next room?" he suggested. "We have not come here with the bare intention of handcuffing you and taking you into custody. Indeed, that may not be necessary.

I think we shall understand one another much better if we talk matters over. Kerns, if you will release Mrs. James now, I will be responsible for her."

Again she smiled; this time with a keenness in her blue eyes which matched Daunt's intensity.

"Thank you," she said, simply.

She led the way into what evidently was the living-room: a very shabby living-room, furnished with a table and chairs which must have been rickety enough when new. She motioned them to seats, and took her place in a creaking arm chair, like a diminutive and pathetic little queen, robbed of her throne. Daunt's quick eye, roving about the room, noted its one distinctive furnishing: a large board of soft wood, roughened by what seemed innumerable tiny scratches. This board was nailed firmly to the wall opposite that end of the room where the little woman sat. She noted the direction of his glance, and nodded, as if in confirmation of what he was thinking.

"If you've come to arrest me for what I did, you know how I use that board. One never quite breaks away from one's hobby. I'll show you!" With her quick intuition, she had seen the puzzled expression of the policeman's face. "Don't be frightened! I could kill you both if I wished, but I shan't even try. I'm resigned to my fate."

Before even the physically alert Kerns could stop her, she had pulled open a drawer in her end of the table. Something flashed and whirled through the air, reaching its mark with a crisp *"chug."* Something else followed, so swiftly as to seem an elongation of the first missile. A third whizzed over their heads; a fourth; a, fifth. The little lady stopped, smilingly, her hand pressed to her heart.

"I haven't much strength left," she explained; "but my aim's still good. You won't find an inch deviation in any of them."

She spoke truth. In the center of the board quivered a large knife. Spaced at even distances from it, so as to form a square, were the four others. They were as accurately spaced as if she had walked to the board and stuck them in their places.

She remained, quietly smiling, with the air of a triumphant conjurer, whose trick has captured his audience. The two men stared at the board, until the knives had stopped quivering. Suddenly, Kerns slapped his knee.

"By George, that's how she got him!" he exclaimed. "Through the window!"

Daunt nodded.

"It was the only way that answered all the conditions. Now you can guess what was in the note I handed Mademoiselle Coligny. I requested the name of any knife-thrower who had been with the circus about the time Donegan came to Cleveland."

Little Mrs. James confirmed his words with a violent inclination of her head.

"Did you just make a guess and hit it like that?" she asked, incredulously. "Didn't he tell you that I stuck him through the window?"

"He told us nothing, madame," Daunt answered.

"You don't even know how I came to do it?"

The clergyman shook his head.

She laughed—a high soprano trill, with childish ripples and gurgles.

"Oh, I'm willing enough to tell you! I thought, of course, you knew, since you've been able to find me. You know he's my husband, I suppose, and that his name is really 'James?'"

"We did not *know* it," corrected the Reverend McGregor.

"Why, I shall have to begin at the beginning and tell you everything!"

The policeman half-rose from his chair, stared at her, then gave a start, as if a wasp, unseen and previously unfelt, had stung him.

"Well, I'll be jiggered!" he said, with feeling.

Daunt glanced at him, amusedly.

"You see it?" he asked.

"I knew her face looked familiar, just as you said," the policeman declared. "I've only this minute figured out why."

Daunt nodded. "Tell your story, Mrs. James. I am curious to hear it."

"There's not much story to it. We disagreed—and we separated—that was all," she sighed. "That was all—it was enough. We're both temperamental. I still love him, yet I tried to knife him. I'm a curious sort of person. He said so when he left me, and I guess he was right. He said other people would be satisfied to throw knives at him in the circus, but that I even threw them at home. Well, I did. I admit it. I did."

"You made a target of him in your circus act?" the clergyman prompted.

"Of everything but him. He stood against a board, and I threw all around him without hitting him—outlined him in knives. He used to be an acrobat—one of the Five Flying Ferrins. You've heard of them, of course. They're still doing their act, but not one of the original five is in it now. James had a fall one day—knocked out his whole upper row of teeth. While he was getting well he acted as my target, and it went so big that we kept it up. He didn't leave me flat when he went. I had lots of money. But I lost it all."

She gazed dreamily at the board with its five knives symmetrically placed, but soon shook off the thoughtful mood, with a queer little bob of her head, and flashed a smile at Daunt.

"Ever see the Big Top in a tornado? You'd think nothing could blow away a tent like that, with all its ropes and stakes. But once let the wind really get under it, and you can look for it somewhere beyond the next town." She laughed, ruefully. "My money was like that. The wind got under it. First, I lost my job—hadn't the heart to go it without James. Then I speculated—that was the wind that blew away my money. I took in sewing after that, but it didn't go very big. And though I'd promised James on my word of honor I'd never trouble him again, and he had promised me the same—both of us being temperamental people, you know—I set to work to find him. It was the only thing I had left to do. You understand, don't you?"

This time it was the tall policeman who answered.

"We understand, ma'am," he assured her.

"I found out where he was. And I went to Cleveland. I went straight to the little hotel, and there was that sign board staring me in the face!"

Kerns seemed anxious to keep up his end of the interview; but here he made an unfortunate remark.

"It is a good likeness, ma'am. I was wondering where I'd seen you before, and it came to me suddenly that it was on that board."

The little woman favored him with a level glance.

"You can't see my feet now, of course, since I have shoes on," she remarked cuttingly. "I suppose, though, you noticed my horns and my bat's wings, so you can take the hoofs for granted."

"I meant the face, ma'am," he hastened to add, in some confusion.

"Oh, the face." She paused abruptly, but smiled again in a moment. "It's all right. I know how you meant it. But you've no idea how I felt when I came on that sign board all of a sudden. James always was a clever artist—it was a passion with him. And he's a peculiar man. Who'd have thought he would put up a thing like that, just because he had had a fight with me? I was so furious I hardly knew what I was doing. I stared at it, and then I looked up and caught sight of him sitting at the window. He hadn't seen me. You know what I did?"

Daunt nodded, soberly.

"Yes, we know," he replied.

"I always carry a knife about with me. I shouldn't, but I do. I'm peculiar, too! I let him have it. And he fell. I think he caught sight of me just as he went down."

The clergyman was leaning forward, with half-closed eyes and compressed lips.

"Did he fall out of the window?" he asked, casually.

"Why, no. He fell back into the room. I didn't wait, because there was a moving van at the end of the street, and I was afraid the driver had seen me. I just went crazy with fear, and ran. I took the next train back, and thought no one would ever find me. But I haven't had a minute's peace since. I didn't want to hurt him. I just did it before I had a chance to think. I love him—really I do!"

She hid her face impulsively in her arms, folded on the table. Her blonde curls quivered, and she sobbed quietly. The Reverend McGregor Daunt regarded her with critical eyes.

"You have not told us where to find Mr. James," he prompted.

She looked up, instantly.

"Don't *you* know where to find him?" she demanded.

"We are relying on you for that information."

"Wasn't he in his room?" Her blue eyes were rounded with wonder, which, if it was feigned, was very well feigned.

Daunt shook his head, without taking his keen gaze from her face.

"He fell back into the room," she said, slowly, as if trying to remember the incident exactly as it had occurred. "He looked at me, just as he fell. Then I grew frightened, and ran."

"You saw nothing of him after that?"

"Nothing whatever."

The clergyman's eyes wandered. They rested upon the "Little Blond Nightmare," who, tiny and childishly feminine, sat very still in her chair, looking frightened; upon the amazed Kerns. Daunt seemed to inspect anew the poor furnishings of the place, and the disreputable wall paper, and to take fresh interest in the target board, with its five skilfully placed knives. At last his roving gaze met that of the policeman.

"I thought our search was ended, Kerns. It seems to be just fairly begun."

"If *she* doesn't know where he is, who in blazes does know?" the officer ruminated.

"You state the problem well. Who does know? Who, indeed?"

He stopped. A slow smile crept over his plump face.

"Do you remember, Kerns, I hazarded a long-shot guess as we stood before the door of this house? I guessed that you might find Mrs. James' face familiar, and you did? That guess was based on my judgment as to Mr. Donegan's—Mr. James'—vindictiveness; also, my knowledge of his skill in the painting line. If he had had a falling out with this lady—which seemed probable—he would very likely have pilloried her on that sign, which obviously is someone's portrait. And he would do the likeness fairly well. You say he used to be an acrobat, Mrs. James?"

The little lady inclined her head.

"A good one?"

"One of the best," she affirmed, with a touch of pride.

"Kerns, we will return to Cleveland. We will inquire at the hospitals. I am ready for another long-shot guess—that the solution of this problem was presented to me in advance of the problem itself, if I had had the wit to see it."

"The hospitals have been canvassed," Kerns declared doggedly.

"Nevertheless, we will inquire. And take Mrs. James along," he added.

She seemed willing. Indeed, when the Reverend McGregor pointed out, a few minutes later, that she might be sacrificing some of her legal rights by going without due process of law, she replied:

"I still love him. I should like to help find him."

"How could he get to the hospital?" the policeman demanded, suddenly. "The door was bolted on the inside. There was blood in the room, but none on the street."

The clergyman smiled sardonically.

"You are about to win permanent promotion to the detective service, Kerns, by solving the inexplicable. I am hungry. When Mrs. James is ready, we will all repair to a restaurant. Doubtless we can arrange with the next-door neighbor to hold off the landlord, should he come within the next few days. You are on the eve of a triumph, Kerns!"

The policeman sighed perversely, but offered no reply. Indeed, his only original remark of the evening was presented at the restaurant, where he took occasion to observe that the coffee, though good, could not compare with Lucy Mogadores'; an observation with which Daunt acquiesced in thoughtful silence. The little lady, meanwhile, was trying pathetically to satisfy what seemed a ravenous hunger, and still dine daintily.

Much later, when they were on the train, and Mrs. James had retired to her berth, leaving the men to linger a while in the smoker, Kerns referred to his charge's appetite.

"Of course, I'm not a doctor," he prefaced his remark. "But I should say that what chiefly was the matter with her is starvation."

The clergyman nodded.

"I am a doctor, though not in practice; and I agree with you."

The next morning bore out that diagnosis. When they descended from the train in Cleveland, and the morning sunlight turned Mrs. James' rather too blonde hair to gold, she had lost the haunted, saddened expression which had lurked in her face even when she was laughing gaily. Being fed, she was entirely the buoyant self she had tried to be when hungry. The policeman was not unaffected by her loveliness.

"Dash it all, I like her!" he declared, privately, to Daunt. "I hope we shan't have to jug her."

"She has temperament," the clergyman commented, without enthusiasm. "Her type has a peculiarly fascinating effect upon the opposite sex. I am about to base an interesting experiment, Kerns, on the theory that a man who has loved her will continue to experience that emotion in spite of whatever may have occurred."

"But if he's dead, his love won't do much good," Kerns returned, gloomily.

Daunt looked at him steadily for a moment.

"He is not dead," was his retort, at length.

To this the policeman was very slow in replying; so slow, in fact, that the three of them were entering one of the large Cleveland hospitals before he again alluded to the subject.

"I'll say this for you, Reverend: you seem sure of yourself. But how you can be sure is beyond me. You not only say he isn't dead, but you even know the hospital. I've been with you ever since we hit Cleveland this morning, but I didn't know he was in a hospital, let alone which one."

"You may recall, Kerns," the clergyman returned, calmly, "that I said the solution of this problem was given me before the problem itself—if I had had wit to recognize it as the solution. I recognize it now, so am able to use the knowledge that was mine all the while. Did you ever consider that the Problem of the Universe may be in our grasp, in much the same way? The elements for its solution may be already in our possession—if only we could recognize them! You and Mrs. James will remain below in the lobby, while I go up."

It was not yet the hour at which the public were admitted; but Daunt's name had weight with the nurse in charge at the door. She gave him a card to the floor supervisor. He was ushered into a small ward containing two beds, each bed with a bandaged masculine countenance on its pillow. Both countenances were turned toward the door as Daunt entered. He advanced to the left-hand bed.

"Good morning, Mr. Donegan," he began formally.

To his astonishment, the countenance in the other bed replied. It was a rather rough-looking countenance, with a square jaw and prominent yellow teeth.

"Can that stuff, guvnor!" it advised. "Yer in wrong. Where d'ye get that talk? That's my pal, Bill Jenkins, that I've knowed since him and me was kids. Yer barkin' up the wrong tree."

The clergyman turned and looked down with interest at the square-jawed countenance.

"Not Mr. Donegan?" he marveled, softly. "I could have sworn that I knew him, but I must have been mistaken."

The face in the right-hand bed grinned with a sort of savage amiability.

"Mistakes will happen, guvnor," it conceded.

"They will, indeed," sighed the Reverend McGregor. "You will pardon the error, will you not, Mr. Jenkins?"

"He ain't talking," the square-jawed one volunteered. "Him and me was knocked out when our truck was wrecked, and it hurt his windpipe some. He won't hold that break you made agin you."

Dejectedly the clergyman walked doorward.

"I regret that Mr. Donnegan isn't here," he concluded. "But I must not stay. There is a woman below inquiring for Mr. Bill Jenkins, and I fear I am taking time which really belongs to her."

Half-way through the door by the time he had finished speaking, he was interrupted by a phenomenon from the left-hand bed. The owner of that countenance abruptly sat up. Despite that interruption of his power of utterance, due to wind-pipe complications, he addressed the Reverend McGregor.

"Hey, wait a minute!" he called in a queer mouthing voice. "What kind of a woman?"

The clergyman turned innocently, with no expression of surprise.

"A small woman with curly blonde hair and blue eyes," he replied. "I happened to overhear her name. It is Mrs. James. Is that the information you wish, Mr. Jenkins?"

"Good God!" Bill Jenkins groaned; then— "Mr. Daunt!"

"Yes?"

"I'm Donegan."

The Reverend McGregor came back into the room, and let the door shut itself.

"I was aware of it," he said, quietly.

"Is she really downstairs? If she is, I'm going outa that window there."

Daunt sat down on the edge of the bed occupied by the square-jawed man, who relapsed into astounded silence, and gazed thoughtfully at Donegan.

"I wondered what ailed your speech. It's the loss of your teeth," he observed, at length. "She is in the lobby, Mr. Donegan. But I should not recommend your climbing out of that window. She will come up when I send for her, and not a minute before. That being so, can you find it in your conscience to check a few of the conclusions I have arrived at?"

Donegan returned the clergyman's look with intense earnestness.

"If you'll keep her away, Reverend, I'll tell you anything you want to know," he promised. "I'll tell you everything that happened, from first to last."

"On the contrary, I will tell you." The Reverend McGregor held up a plump, short-fingered hand. "Let me check off what happened, point by point. You can tell me where I am wrong. In the first place, Mrs. James threw a knife which struck you, though not in a vital spot."

"Fleshy part of the arm," the patient interrupted.

"Ah! That accounts for the blood. We will call that Point Number One. Point Number Two: you thought she was coming upstairs to finish the job, and you looked for some means of instant escape. You were desperate."

"I'll say I was," Donegan interrupted.

"A large moving van was coming up the street. Being a former acrobat, you saw a possibility which never would have occurred to most men. You jumped for the top of the van, as it passed beneath your window. I have that right?"

"I don't need to tell you anything," the little man declared, admiringly.

"Point Number Three—this is where I need a little help. I know the driver of the truck dumped both you and himself into the railroad excavation, but I am not quite clear as to why he did so. The paper stated that he was drunk. Is that the reason?"

Donegan had no opportunity to offer the explanation of Point Number Three. It came instead, promptly and profanely, from the bed on the right.

"Drunk my eye! Goshawmighty, I leave it to yer, guvnor. Yer driving yer truck, not paying no attention to nobody, and all of a sudden a bloody fool drops square onto your head outa the sky. Wouldn't you damn near twist the wheel off? I leave it to yer?"

"It was my mistake," Donegan apologized. "I landed on top of the van, but of course people would have seen me there and wondered. So I crawled to the front and tried to drop down beside him on the seat. But just then the van lurched."

Daunt nodded.

"I see. I suppose they thought at the hospital that you received your arm injury, as well as the cuts in your face, from windshield glass. And you arranged it with our friend here to identify you as Bill Jenkins if you were inquired for?"

"I'm a married man myself, guvnor, and I don't hold no grudges," the square-jawed one put in.

The clergyman nodded at this excellent declaration, but made no reply in words. Instead, he stumped back and forth between the two narrow beds, thinking. At length he turned abruptly to the left-hand bed.

"Donegan, do you know why your wife came to Cleveland the other day?"

"She came to do for me," the little man replied, with conviction.

"She came to make up with you. Though I have no interest in love, I am willing to tell you that. After all these years, in which you two fools, both in love with each other but both too proud to take the first step, had lived apart, she dropped her pride and came. And what did she find? A scurrilous libel on a signboard. Except for her sake, Donegan, I am rather sorry she did not kill you. You deserved it. As it is, she is heart-broken for what she did, and still ready to make up. She will never throw another knife at you without your consent. I am going now, and I would advise your friend to pretend sleep when she comes up."

As he left the room, the Reverend McGregor looked back; and what he saw justified his thrill of satisfaction, at the successful conclusion of his experiment in the emotion known as "love." For Mr. Patrick James, alias Donegan, had hidden his face in the pillow.

"I was correct," the little clergyman assured himself. "No man who ever had loved her could really cease to love her."

6

"IN ONE WAY—IN just one way—I am disappointed," the Reverend McGregor Daunt said confidentially some time afterward, to Detective Kerns. The clergyman had run into town from his hunting lodge, and they were sipping incomparable coffee at the sign of "The Ancient Mariner," formerly "The Little Blond Nightmare."

"Of course, I am pleased to see them reconciled. But before I became acquainted with the lady in the case, I had surmised that Donegan would sometime marry Lucy Mogadore. Mrs. Mogadore is a remarkable woman, who makes exceptionally fine coffee. She should not be a widow."

At that, the Lincolnian features of Mr. Kerns relaxed, and he permitted himself a sincere and hearty guffaw. He even went so far as to poke the Reverend McGregor Daunt facetiously between the third and fourth buttons (counting downward) of his ample vest—a liberty at which the clergyman stiffened, noticeably.

"That's one point you didn't get. Reverend. You're clever, and I give you credit; but you missed that one. Even though you nearly caught us together in Donegan's room the day we started on the case, still you didn't tumble. That's what it is to be a confirmed old bach!"

He laughed again, and tried to catch the eye of Lucy Mogadore, as she sat at her desk; but she and the parrot both seemed asleep. So he continued.

"Lucy and me have been engaged this six months, and I

haven't let on to a soul. I've even called her 'Mrs. Mogadore,' and she's called me 'Mr. Kerns,' so no one would get wise. When you told me that man Donegan, or James, or whatever his name is, said he might tie up with her, I had a job not to bust right out with the truth. He never had a chance in the world. She was grateful to him. She wishes him and Mrs. James all kinds of luck in the circus business they've gone back to. But gratitude and good wishes ain't love. We expect to stand up in front of you, Reverend, about the middle of June."

The yellow light of the oil lamps reflected from the brown of the table at which they were sitting. It was the table which had once been favored by the man with the removable teeth. The teeth were gone. There was not even a glass of water against the wall. But Lucy Mogadore slumbered serenely at the receipt of custom, near the door, with the parrot blinking on her breast. As Detective Kerns, recently promoted, finished his remarks, the parrot screeched. Perhaps premonitions of a change in his many-yeared and placid existence troubled him; perhaps it was his stomach. Whatever it was, he awoke the mistress of the hotel, who, half turning her impressive head, smiled fondly in the direction of the occupied table, then went to sleep again.

The Loud Voice of Time

*This is the third of the McGregor Daunt
stories. In the present tale, Mr. Suter's unique
clergyman-detective solves an apparently
unsolvable murder mystery. We won't say that
it's the best so far; but we'll bet that you do.*

1

SUAVE YET UNSMILING, Chief of Police Maximilian ignored his stout visitor for the moment, and appeared absorbed in the structure of his lightly held cigarette. Such was the Chief's courtesy of manner, however, that his attitude carried no offense. He had turned his eyes inward—that was all. His dark, perfectly groomed face retained its expression of polite interest. Trim, lithe, with the hint of easy muscular co-ordination beneath all his movements, he symbolized the quiet adequacy of his administration. He was not young, yet his grey hairs hinted at wisdom rather than age. "The Wisest Police Chief," a student of big city politics had called him in a magazine. He continued to deserve the title, always without fuss; and always suave, though never smiling.

A shade of impatience crossed the flabby, rather arrogant face of the fat man. Unlike the Chief, he smiled; but there was less of courtesy in his smile than in Maximilian's grave suavity. The fat man wore his smile like a mask. Occasionally the mask slipped away for the space of a breath, and disclosed unpleasant things.

"Is there anything else I should tell you about this here affair?" he clacked, with a hint of insistence in his thick voice.

The Chief looked up.

"Ah, yes. Anything else that you should tell me?" he echoed. "Have you told me anything, Mr. Bartram?"

"I told you everything that happened: how I am threatened with death; how I have one letter every week for five weeks; how—"

Maximilian lifted a protesting finger; as one, touching a push-button very lightly, stops a noisy piece of mechanism. He eyed his silenced visitor whimsically, though still without smiling.

"Everything—except the two items of information that might lead to a clue. You have not told me the contents of the letters, nor what in your past life has brought them upon you."

"There is nothing in my past life."

"It is your present life, then?" The Chief of Police lifted courteous eyebrows. "One's neck is seldom threatened without cause, Mr. Bartram; unless it might be by practical jokers, and I take it you consider this something more than a joke. You are no longer a young man."

"What's that got to do with it?" exploded the fat man. His perpetual smile was nearly erased. What of it remained served merely to crinkle his upper lip into a snarl, revealing two or three carefully whitened teeth. He was something of a dandy, this Anselm Bartram; an old dandy, always immaculate, whose manicurist hated him.

"When one is young, one makes love without offence— unless it be to the wives of others. Older men must be more careful."

Bartram rose podgily, quivering with rage.

"Did I come here to be insulted, or did I come to get police protection? Ain't I entitled to protection?"

Once more, the Chief suppressed him without words, speaking only when all was quiet, except the fat man's wheezy breathing.

"We have our channels of information, Mr. Bartram. They are more effective than you may imagine. Often, our results are astonishing. If I should mention certain indiscretions of which the police have knowledge in the lives of our foremost citizens, you would be astounded."

Bartram had seated himself again. He was too fat to remain standing for long. He leaned across the Chief's desk, and his smile returned.

"Yes?" he purred, encouragingly.

"To speak of only one of them—" The Chief eyed his guest narrowly, still with that curious expression of grave whimsicality. "We have been interested for some months in an affair between a very wealthy widower of this community and a young girl. You know the man intimately, Mr. Bartram. There is no doubt of his intentions. They are not honorable. Yet the police are hardly in a position to interfere. The girl resides—"

Bartram's fat lips drooled with eagerness. He dabbed them absent-mindedly with a perfumed handkerchief, the while he grinned into the Chief's face.

"You recall the old house in the 'Y' between Walnut Street and the beginning of Payne Avenue? She lives just east of it, on Walnut."

The fat man jumped to his feet.

"Damn you!" he said, earnestly; but Maximilian, giving him no opportunity to proceed, went on:

" 'Thou art the man,' Mr. Bartram—if you will pardon my quoting Scripture. Very possibly, this is only one of your little affairs. It chances to be one that has come to my notice. I mention it in connection with my suggestion that these letters—these threats—may have to do with something in your present life. It happens occasionally that a young lady has male relatives—or even an honorable lover—in whose eyes conduct of a certain character is objectionable."

"Look here, you!" Bartram, swaying a little with the force of his indignation, shook a thick forefinger under the Chief's placid nose. "When I want to be preached at, I go to church. I drop a bill in the collection plate, and that pays for what I get. If I feel like taking the preacher's advice, I take it. Generally, I don't feel that way. But I ain't calling on no damned policeman for advice on my personal affairs, not any time! Maybe I should have that written out and sent to you, with my compliments, so you would be sure to get it?" He paused, as if in realization of the Chief's faintly sardonic expression, and added: "I called for protection, not advice."

"Protection! Are you willing to pay for it?"

The fat man started, then winked, appreciatively.

"Sure I'm willing to pay for it! How much?"

Maximilian waved him back to his chair, and continued, without changing expression.

"American cities—large cities, Mr. Bartram—are not run scientifically. We have yet to learn how. Our cities are usually short of funds. Occasionally, the shortage becomes acute, and extreme measures have to be taken. Within the last two months, I have been obliged to lay off a considerable part of my force, through lack of money to pay them. When I spoke of pay, I referred to some of these men, who have found no other employment, and would be glad of work in their line. I could recommend quite a number of them, say from one to a dozen, whom you could hire to protect you."

"One to a dozen!" Bartram closed his small eyes, speculatively. "They're regular policemen?"

"In everything except uniforms. Of course, they could not wear those."

"Will you boss 'em? I'll pay you for it. Good pay."

The Chief shook his head.

"I have my salary. But I will keep an eye on them, for the credit of the Department."

Bartram rose, and extended his hand; but the Chief was busily lighting another cigarette. The fat man smiled broadly, and shrugged his shoulders.

"I'm counting on you to get in touch with those men right away, Chief. Get the whole dozen—six for day and six for night. I ain't broke. I guess no black hand artist is going to feed the daisies with me while I've got the money to buy police protection! Call me up and tell me when the first shift is coming. I'll be home."

His hand was on the dull brass door knob, when the Chief recalled him.

"This protection you are buying may not save you, Mr. Bartram."

The fat man stopped in his tracks. He regarded Maximilian reproachfully.

"What d'ye mean, not save me?"

"Because you are buying merely physical protection—police technique. The man who threatens you—if there is a man threatening—may have brains to cut under that."

"You mean I should buy something else?" Bartram demanded, his flashy face turning pale.

"There is nothing else to buy. When you have hired these policemen, you will have taken all the orthodox measures for safety. The protection a private agency might give you would be merely the same thing under another name."

The fat man returned to the chair he had just vacated, and sat down, with the air of one intending to remain. He wiped his forehead, and breathed heavily. His tone, when he spoke, seemed compounded curiously of fear and determination.

"While I'm here, I'm safe, anyhow," he remarked, succinctly.

But the Chief's abstraction had come back upon him. Again he was gazing at his cigarette. In a moment he rose from his chair, with an apparent weariness which sat queerly upon his alert personality.

"Mr. Bartram, you will excuse me for a few minutes... a few minutes only... I will return."

Just beyond the desk, a door was ajar. Through this doorway the Chief slipped with tottering haste. There was nothing in the bare little room adjoining his office but a plain chair and a table, upon which lay two or three orderly piles of paper. Maximilian had had the little room fitted up a few months before. It afforded a handy means of escape, when he wished to work or think in private while a conference was in progress.

But his need now was for neither thought nor work. He literally fell into the chair. His limbs became rigid. He clenched his hands on the chair arms. His lips, compressed until they were white, told of an inward upheaval which intensified until it became nearly too great for flesh to bear. Then, in a few minutes, the tension passed. He was again master of himself.

He went back to the room where the fat man awaited him.

"I have a suggestion for you, Mr. Bartram."

"Something I can do to protect myself from the murderer?"

"Something that may possibly be worth your while. Of course, I can promise nothing. You have not honored me with your complete confidence, and, very likely, even if you had, I could do no more than I have done. You remember my surmise that this affair might demand something more than physical protection?"

"I'll say I remember it. That's why I'm sitting right here. You kinda got me worried," the fat man confessed.

"Have you, by any chance, heard of McGregor Daunt?"

Bartram shrugged his thick shoulders.

"You mean the crazy preacher that hires his preaching done, and has a hunting-lodge somewhere where he don't hunt? I read about him once in the Sunday paper."

"I am glad you know of him," Maximilian remarked, dryly. "If being different from other men is to be crazy, he is very crazy indeed. His mind works along lines of its own, and, fortunately, he is extremely wealthy, so that he can permit it to do so. In several instances, Mr. Bartram, he has succeeded where the police have failed."

"You think maybe if I hire him he can protect me where the police can't?" the fat man inquired, with fresh interest.

The Chief regarded him, speculatively.

"I am not sure, Mr. Bartram. You speak of hiring. It will be well if you do not mention that to him. You see, he is possibly a richer man than you. My thought is that there may be something in your case which may interest him. If that is so, his original mind may cut to the very bottom of your problem, and—it may be—save your life. Very likely he will not care to bother with you at all; but it is worth trying."

Bartram had caught, breathlessly, at one of the Chief's phrases.

"You—you think my life is in danger?"

"You seem to know of some secret reason why it should be."

The fat man considered, staring hard at his coarse, carefully manicured hands. His thoughts seemed unpleasant, but they came quickly to a point.

"Suppose you tell my chauffeur where to find this here preacher," he suggested, rising. "I ain't got no memory for things like that."

"Gladly."

The Chief of Police ushered him out, with a suggestion of old-world ceremoniousness, yet also with something of the air with which one opens the door to eject a filthy beast. At a nod from his master, Bartram's chauffeur, who looked like a rising young minister, left the expensive car about which he was loitering, and sprang up the broad steps of the police station to receive his instructions.

They proved unnecessary. Daunt's dislike of publicity was intense, but no man whose eccentric habits are combined with success in a sensational hobby can remain unknown. That he was likely to be found either in his city manse, connected with the church, or at his so-called hunting-lodge, the chauffeur was aware. Maximilian nodded satisfaction, and promised to telephone at once to the special guards.

"Home first, George. Then find out where this here preacher is, and take me there," the fat man directed.

On the way to his Euclid Avenue mansion, however, Bartram changed his mind.

"We'll go to-morrow," he told the bespectacled chauffeur, as he stepped from his machine. "It's too late now. Nearly five o'clock."

In the stately residence which his riches had bought from an old family of declining fortunes, the fat man ruled with an expansive smile and a heavy hand. He ruled alone. The trail of his presence was over the place in cringing male attendants, and servant maids who valued liberal wages above their reputations. He was cunning; thus far the police had found no handle with which to grasp him. Yet such is the irony of life that of late he had lived in his own house with dread, and had even reached the point of having his meals served in his private suite on the second floor, lest the big dining-room, whose windows fronted on a side lawn, might expose him to danger.

He was about to sit down thus to his dinner when a trivial incident changed his mind once more. The incident had to do with his coat. Purporting to dine privately in his shirt sleeves, he was about to remove that article of apparel, when he chanced to slide his hand into the right side pocket. He drew forth a short note. It was written in ink on a piece of common scratch paper.

Between the time that he jerked the bell pull and the prompt response of a servant, Bartram paced jerkily about the floor, and repeated over and over to himself:

"Where did this one come from? Right in my own coat pocket! Oh, my God!"

"Tell George we start for that place right after dinner," he instructed the maid. "And I want dinner right away."

After which he continued to pace the floor.

2

THE REVEREND MCGREGOR DAUNT awoke with a start from soft, sticky slumber—for it was a hot night even at the hunting-lodge—and discovered that he had fallen asleep in a rocking-chair on his own broad porch. The small voices of the summer evening serenaded him from the woods surrounding the lodge. He was conscious of crickets, rustling leaves, the sighing of the wind among the trees; comfortably conscious, for such sounds as these soothed him pleasantly into the speculative kind of thought he enjoyed. In his time, the Reverend McGregor Daunt had been a fair doctor, an original type of lawyer, a decidedly eccentric clergyman. Though still the latter by profession, he preferred to look upon himself merely as a thinker—one who contemplated men and considered them, coldly and scientifically. He had fallen asleep while thinking thus, and now he was wide awake, yet it was still too hot for going to bed. So he determined to continue his train of solitary thought. But just then he heard a man swearing in the woods.

"Damn you, boy, I don't think you know the way!" the man was saying, irascibly. "You say it's a mile, and you make me walk five."

He was answered by an impertinent youthful voice:

"Aw, dry up, mister! You're almost there now."

Upon which a third voice cut in, indignantly:

"You keep a civil tongue in your head, boy, or I'll bat you one in the ear! D'ye know who you're talking to?"

"Tell him who I am, George, and you're fired!" interrupted the first voice, sharply.

There was silence at this, except for the swish of footsteps approaching through the long grass; but in a few minutes the boy spoke again:

"There's where the old guy lives. Now say I don't know the way! So long, mister."

This was followed by the sound of cheery whistling, rapidly receding, and two figures appeared in the little rim of moonlight to the left of the lodge.

Thus did Mr. Anselm Bartram call that evening upon the Reverend McGregor Daunt. The fat man had been obliged to leave his car at a farmhouse on the road, a mile away, and to take his choice of riding horseback through the woods with his chauffeur and the farmer's boy for a guide, or of walking. He had chosen what seemed to him the lesser evil. Though not a good walker, he was at least fairly experienced in that method of locomotion, and it appealed to him strongly in preference to the other.

Daunt's reception of his visitors was not enthusiastic. He disliked visitors in general, and he had not listened for five minutes to the fat man (George having been left at the fringe of the woods by his master) before the sentiment became specific.

"I do not care to go into your problem," he declared, with cold finality. "I am working on one or two little matters of an abstract nature just now, and they afford me all the mental exercise I require."

"But this is important," the fat man protested earnestly.

"Not to me."

Bartram mopped the sweat from his forehead. It was a hot night to be pleading, as it were, for one's life.

"I wonder whether you understand, Reverend Daunt, that these here letters say that the fellow that wrote them is going to kill me," he suggested, desperately.

"Have you the letters with you?" the Reverend McGregor asked, without interest.

"I burned them. I don't keep things like that."

"Ah, well, it does not matter. Very likely, I should not read them, anyway. After you are killed, I may possibly go into the problem; but only if the murderer shows originality in his work."

"My God!" the fat man exclaimed.

"Most crime," the clergyman continued, gently rocking in his chair, "is commonplace. It evinces little imagination and no originality. Its consideration must be distasteful even to an intelligent police officer, though of course he is obliged to handle it, in the line of duty. I am not connected with the police. I am merely a speculative thinker. Only the occasional crime—the rare, unlikely crime—is worthy of speculative thought. Your case seems not to be of that character. All that it demands, I should say, is police protection."

"You think police protection will save my life, then?" Bartram demanded, eagerly.

"Very likely not. A determined murderer with brains can usually circumvent the police, insofar as the commission of the crime is concerned. I think you would do well, Mr. Bartram, to put your house in order. But your problem is not one for me—as yet."

"Look here, I come all this way through the woods—and

I'm no walker, Reverend Daunt, far from it—and I even sent the boy back who showed us the way. That's how sure I was—"

Daunt interrupted him.

"As to that, I trust that I am not wanting in common hospitality, Mr. Bartram. You and your man will remain for the night, and breakfast with me in the morning. You should be reasonably safe. It would be annoying if the writer of these letters should follow you through the woods, to settle with you here; but I hardly expect that."

It very evidently had seemed to Mr. Bartram that a man of his wealth would be a welcome guest at the clergyman's hunting lodge, whether previously announced or not; however, he now drew a relieved breath. Only one such breath, though. His next was devoted to explaining further the object of his visit.

"You see, Mr. Daunt, I'm making something of a mystery out of this," he began. "I ain't telling just what was in these letters. If it would help you to find the writer, I should tell, oh, yes. But it wouldn't. It's too, as you might say, general, don't you see?"

The Reverend McGregor Daunt quietly but firmly turned his back, and took a determined step toward the front door of the lodge.

"You might call your man, unless you wish him to spend the night in the woods," he suggested. "I have several guest rooms, which are kept ready for occupancy. I will show you to these, and while you are retiring will indulge in a little solitary reflection here on the porch."

The fat man sighed, but meekly called to George, and the two of them followed their host into the lodge. Switching on the lights, Daunt led the way upstairs.

"Breakfast will be ready shortly after eight o'clock," he announced; and returned to his chair on the porch.

When the subject matter of the speculative clergyman's thoughts was unexciting, and the hour late, reflection sometimes gave way to sleep. It was so on this night. For greater comfort, he leaned far back in the congenial rocker, and stretched his short legs to the utmost. His head presently lolled, and he gazed more or less thoughtfully into the moonlit sky. He was himself bathed in a little pool of moonlight—a rather conspicuous object on the broad porch—when sleep overtook him.

He had descended into slumber gently, almost imperceptibly. He came out of it with a start. Something violent had awakened him. Instinct, rather than reason, suggested what it was. Instinct, too, prompted him to throw himself out of the moonlit pool. He retreated through the front doorway, and listened.

Ten minutes later, still listening, he shook his head, closed the door, and locked it. Then an idea struck him. He reopened the door, and, standing on the porch but in shadow, spoke loudly and clearly into the night:

"It may interest you to know, whoever you are, that you have been shooting at the Reverend McGregor Daunt."

There was no response, so he locked the door again, and went to his bedroom.

He stood a few minutes in the darkness of his casement window, gazing sleepily at the fringe of woods, moonlit as to its outer trees, but impenetrably black beyond them. He wondered whether Bartram's mysterious enemy might be lurking in that darkness. If so, he hoped to be spared the annoyance of a murder there at the lodge, with its inevitable publicity. But the prospect seemed remote. He yawned, and went to bed.

As he fell asleep, he was debating whether it really had been the report of a revolver, coupled with the whiz of a bullet past his head, which had aroused him on the porch. That was a matter which could be investigated in the morning. The whole incident might have been the figment of a dream.

Suddenly, he was awake again. What had awakened him was not a dream, he was sure. It was a scream, high and wild, and scarcely human in its tones. Before he could stumble in the darkness to the door of his room, the scream was repeated twice. It came from somewhere in the lodge—somewhere close at hand.

He flung the door open, and reached for the electric switch, which was beside it.

"I wouldn't throw the light on, sir," counselled the voice of the dignified chauffeur.

Daunt perceived the man's figure in the darkness. He was already struggling with the door of Bartram's room.

"What was it?" demanded the clergyman.

"The master, sir. I'm afraid they've got him."

"Who have?"

"I don't know, sir. Someone—or something's—been after him for weeks. He didn't tell us, but we've got eyes. Have you a key to this door, sir?"

"I think it is being unlocked from within," Daunt returned.

The door opened. Anselm Bartram stepped into the hall, flung both arms above his head, and fell in a heap on the floor.

"They've done for him!" groaned the chauffeur.

But something in the manner of that heavy fall had awakened Daunt's medical memory.

"Shut the room doors and turn on the hall light," he directed. "You might also pull down the window shade at the end of the hall."

The fat man, with closed eyes, was breathing stertorously. His host knelt and made a swift examination. Soon, he rose, observing:

"I thought so. Men who are wounded sometimes throw up both arms at the time and topple over, but they do not do so for five minutes after they are wounded. They may fall then, but they will omit that little demonstration with the arms."

"How bad is he hurt, sir?" the chauffeur inquired, anxiously bending over his prostrate employer.

"Rather badly, I should say—in his sensibilities. He is quite conscious. In a few minutes, doubtless, he will explain the situation. Am I taking too much for granted, Mr. Bartram?"

The fat man opened his eyes, and glared about him wildly.

"The face! The face at the window!" he croaked.

Daunt stared; then, turning suddenly, opened the door of Bartram's room and peered in. He closed the door almost immediately, nodding with satisfaction.

"That is possible; physically possible, though not probable. The moon is shining brightly into both windows, and if someone had climbed up by the vines you might easily have seen him. Did you recognize the face?"

The fat man struggled to a sitting position on the floor. A long shiver passed through him. He stared about him like a frightened child, his mouth trembling and his fat cheeks aquiver. After a period of hesitation, he nodded.

"You recognized it? Who was it?" prompted Daunt.

"My wife!"

The answer seemed torn from Bartram, against his will. The chauffeur backed away, with rounded eyes, and crossed himself. Glancing at him, Daunt inquired, sharply:

"What's the matter with you?"

"Mrs. Bartram died five years ago," the man whispered, shuddering.

The clergyman nodded understandingly, after the fashion of a doctor noting certain well-defined symptoms. He helped the fat man to his feet.

"Your nerves are rather tangled, Mr. Bartram," he observed, in the orthodox medical manner. "Nerves and a nightmare make an unpleasant combination. Perhaps you will remain here while I go downstairs and mix a sleeping potion for you. We will put you back to bed, then, and I will guarantee that you see nothing further before morning."

When the mixture had been prepared, Daunt did not immediately return upstairs. Instead, he procured an electric lantern from his desk, and, wrapping his dressing-gown about him, stepped out into the garden, through the rear doorway of the lodge. He proceeded around the corner of the house, and turned the flashlight on a flower bed which lay beneath Bartram's windows. In the soft earth at one corner of the bed were two footprints.

Thoughtfully, the clergyman retraced his steps to the rear, and, this time skirting the building on its shadowed side, gained the front porch. Most of the steps, also that part of the porch where he had been sitting earlier in the evening, were in shadow. He pondered a moment, then swept the light transversely and vertically along the clapboards behind his rocking chair. Abruptly, he shut off the lantern, and turned away. He had found a fresh bullet hole.

Once more on the second floor of the lodge, Daunt administered the prescribed medicine to his guest—now reasonably well persuaded that he had been dreaming—and put the fat man back to bed. He pocketed the key, and tapped at the door of the chauffeur's room.

"Give Mr. Bartram ten minutes to turn in, George," he directed, "then stretch yourself out on the couch in his room."

With that, Daunt returned to bed, and resumed his interrupted sleep, and this time it was favored, along with that of his guests, for he awoke to find that Stubbs, the manservant, who regularly brought bountiful breakfast supplies each morning from the city, already had arrived, and that Bartram was walking about the lawn with his chauffeur.

Catching sight of his host, the fat man greeted him.

"Nightmare's a fearful thing, Mr. Daunt," he remarked, with feeling. "Sorry I disturbed you, but you know how it is. I'm going to double the police guard when I get back to town."

3

WITHIN FORTY-EIGHT HOURS of the fat man's visit, a business matter demanded McGregor Daunt's presence in the city for a few days, so that he was in his study when a 'phone call came from Police Headquarters. Daunt recognized the genial voice of his friend, Chief of Detectives Kerns.

"I have an impossible murder, Reverend—something that couldn't have been done, yet it was done. Care to get into it?"

Memories of past cases stirred enticingly in the clergyman's mind. Kerns had never led him into anything commonplace. But there was that item of business....

He nibbled at the bait.

"Was it absolutely impossible, Kerns?" he inquired.

"Absolutely, Reverend. Couldn't have been done at all, in the way it seems to have been pulled off. Yet there the poor devil is, as dead as Caesar. You'll enjoy looking over the ground for yourself."

Daunt considered. The situation seemed tempting.

"Perhaps I might spare a little time," he concluded.

"Be right over after you," the detective promised.

On the point of ringing off, a perfunctory question occurred to Daunt.

"By the way, who was murdered?" he asked.

"Anselm Bartram, on Euclid Avenue—the sporty old millionaire, you know."

The clergyman hung up, with a sigh. So it had come to this, after all! He regretted the matter, of course—even though his impression of Bartram had been far from favorable. He sighed again; then brightened. Kerns had called it an impossible murder. That sounded like a difficult problem. Perhaps there was a pleasant side to the crime, too. His rotund face bore an expression approaching happy expectation when he met the tall detective at the door.

"Reverend, I believe you enjoy murders," Kerns remarked, with a smiling glance at his too-eager companion.

Daunt shook his head, gravely.

"No, Kerns. You misunderstood my attitude. I deplore all crime. The news of a crime invariably inclines me toward sadness. If I seem to plunge with too much gusto into the intellectual aspect of the situation, it is because I seek relief from the melancholy it has forced upon me."

"Well, you'll find some real intellectual stuff in this one," the detective assured him. "I can't get up much sympathy for the old rounder. He caught what was coming to him, and the city would be better off if he'd caught it sooner. But I'll say this— if he had wanted to die in a way that would keep us guessing, he couldn't have planned it better. Here we are at the house, Reverend. You see those fellows standing around?"

Daunt glanced at fully a dozen men, who seemed stationed at regular intervals in the spacious grounds of the mansion.

"Policemen in plain clothes," he appraised. "Bartram told me he had hired them, but I hardly expected to see so many."

"I know he went out to see you. Since then, he doubled the guards. Not only that, but he made himself a prisoner in his upstairs suite of rooms. He sent for the Chief, just an hour or so before the murder, and the Chief had to go up to his room."

"Why did he send for the Chief?"

"Wanted still more guards. He had worked himself up into an absolute blue funk."

"Suppose we circle outside the house before going in," the clergyman suggested.

It was a compact, stately house, which gained its ample roominess by its height of three stories. A lofty pillared porch extended across the front and along the westerly side, reaching to within a short distance of the second-story windows. Daunt stopped and surveyed this with interest, seeing which, the detective smiled.

"I might as well tell you, Reverend, that all the windows on the second floor, including those in Bartram's private suite, and also the door to his suite, were shut and locked. And there's another thing, too—" He jerked his finger toward the base of the building. "Bartram had a liking for flower beds, just as you have out at the lodge. You'll notice that the house is practically surrounded by them. You'll be looking for footprints in the soft ground, but if you'll take my word for it, I can save you that time. There aren't any."

Daunt nodded.

"Anything else."

"Bartram was not killed from a distance. He was hanged—in a very peculiar and original fashion. He has been cut down, of course, but nothing else has been changed. The body is there for your inspection."

Within the broad, high-ceilinged hall downstairs, another man was stationed. Kerns nodded to him, and turned to the clergyman.

"Their time will be up tonight, so I just left them on. There are three downstairs, as well as the guards outside, and another three upstairs. One man was posted right outside the door to Bartram's suite. When the Chief left Bartram this morning he made the rounds. Every man was on the job. I don't see how a flea could have broken into the suite without being seen."

The clergyman nodded again, mentally checking off the points his companion had made.

"Can you determine the time of the murder?" he inquired.

"I can, Reverend. That's another of the unique features of this crime. We have so much definite information, yet we really don't know a thing. You'll remember that Bartram sent for the Chief this morning? Well, after the Chief returned to his office, Bartram called him up, speaking from the 'phone in his suite. I dropped in at headquarters just as they were finishing their talk. That was at five minutes to eleven. You see, I was in a bit of a hurry, and pulled out my watch—which was lucky, for that was the latest Bartram was known to be alive. At twelve, or there-abouts, one of the servants brought up his lunch, and couldn't make him hear her knock. The guards tried, too. Finally, they broke down the door, and there he was—hanging."

Daunt had been listening, closely.

"No possibility of suicide?" he suggested.

"We'll go up, and you can have a look at him," the detective evaded.

The uniformed policeman at the entrance of the suite saw them coming, and opened the door. Daunt glanced about him, as they crossed the threshold of the first room.

"This was his private library," Kerns informed him. "Just beyond is his den, with the bedroom opening out of that."

The clergyman hastily examined the contents of the single ornate bookcase.

"Maupassant in translation," he noted. "Balzac's 'Droll Stories'; the unexpurgated 'Arabian Nights.' You will observe, Kerns, that this was the man's private reading—the key to his character. I saw Dickens, Scott, and Thackeray—probably uncut—in the hall library downstairs. He bought them because it was the thing to do—but these he read."

"The door into the den was open," interjected Kerns.

Daunt nodded.

"Where is the body?"

"On the couch in the den, Reverend."

Before crossing to the silent figure which lay, with face turned to the wall, on a gorgeous oriental couch, the clergyman paused just within the doorway and looked about him.

This place, which had been Bartram's den, was large enough to have constituted another man's drawing-room. Yet it was so over-furnished as to appear small. The furnishings had one note in common—they were the costliest obtainable. An ebony table sank its massive claw feet into a delirious but unquestionably expensive Eastern rug. Upon the table—curious phenomena of life in the presence of death—fat goldfish swam about placidly in a cutglass bowl. Chairs of the thickly cushioned type, finished in silken oriental stuffs, crowded the floor. In one corner was a floor lamp, which Daunt examined before he came to the corpse. It was of bronze—two lovers, naked, and in each others' arms. She held the light laughingly above his head, while he embraced her. Its beams fell upon her bronze companion and, flowing downward, lighted up the purple cheek of the fat man as he lay upon the couch.

At last Daunt stood before the real object of his visit. He looked down at the figure silently for a while, then kneeling, examined the hands, which were tied together behind. The cord which fastened them, too long for its purpose, had been carried up the back and secured to a silken kerchief, bound about the lower part of the face. The clergyman looked up at his companion.

"May I disturb these fastenings?" he inquired.

Kerns nodded.

"The coroner has made his preliminary examination. He said you could do anything you pleased. He left things pretty much as they were for your benefit."

Daunt untied the cord from the handkerchief, and releasing the knot which held the latter, drew it from the face. Something dropped with a rustle from the gaping mouth. The clergyman reached over, and picked it up.

"A folded newspaper, used as a gag," he noted. "It was tied in by means of the handkerchief, then the handkerchief was connected with the cord which bound the hands. Why do you suppose that was done, Kerns?"

"The coroner and I made the same guess," the tall detective answered. "For some reason, the murderer wanted to show that this was not a case of suicide. Bartram might possibly have bound his own hands behind him; he couldn't possibly have tied them to the knot of the handkerchief. That's our reasoning."

"It covers the facts. But why did the murderer wish to display his handiwork?"

Kerns shrugged his shoulders.

"You tell me, Reverend. I can't figure it out."

"Suppose we reconstruct the scene, as far as possible. That is always a helpful plan."

While he spoke, the clergyman examined a lower fastening, which bound the ankles of the quiet figure tightly together; but he did not disturb it. He stepped backward then, slowly, with his eyes on the rug, and next studied the lofty ceiling, attached to which, through a bright new screw-eye, was a light but closely-woven rope. This rope was cut, and the other portion of it, somewhat loosened, had been suffered to remain about the corpse's neck. Before finishing his examination, Daunt returned to the figure on the sofa and carefully scrutinized the face. Then, it appeared, he was ready to speak.

"I think we can begin by assuming a visitor—a deadly visitor. Suppose, for convenience, we call him 'Smith.'"

"One name's as good as another, when we don't even know what he looked like," Kerns observed.

"Don't we know?" The clergyman gazed about him, meditatively. "I should say that he has left a description of himself—rather general, but accurate as far as it goes. For one thing, he is a smoker. Bartram smoked, too, of course. But on this occasion, and in the short interval since the room must have been cleaned by the maid, I question whether he could have left all the cigarette ashes we see here. Smith sat, probably, in this easy chair on the left, near which most of the ashes have fallen. Here is another chair drawn up to face it, with a few ashes on the right-hand arm. Bartram sat there. You will notice, by the way, that none of the cigarette stubs are lying about. Smith took them with him. He is a careful man."

The detective nodded, silently, and Daunt continued.

"Smith brings with him a few stage properties: a large screw-eye, a pocket drill, probably a pair of pliers. He has a coil of rope, too, possibly wound around his waist, where it can be concealed beneath his coat. It is ordinary sash-cord. Very likely, he bought a morning paper, too, on his way here. He would hardly risk a slight derangement of his plans by the chance that Bartram might not have a paper."

"He used one of Bartram's scarfs to tie the gag in," Kerns objected.

"By which he proved his quickness of wit. He did well, certainly, to use such devices as came to hand in the room. Still, he is likely to have brought a plain neckerchief with him. He would hardly overlook the possible need for it."

The clergyman stepped over to a slightly-built, ebony chair— the only fragile chair in the room—and examined it with interest.

"I noticed this when we came in," he observed. "This chair and the table give us some valuable data on Mr. Smith. After a conversation with Bartram—a rather long conversation, which must have vitally interested both parties to it—he gagged Bartram and tied him hand and foot."

"Why didn't someone hear Bartram, Reverend?" the detective put in. "You don't suppose he kept quiet while all this was being done to him?"

"I cannot tell. Neither can I say how Smith entered in the first place. I am enumerating now the items we know. Take the tale he has written here, for instance." With one plump finger he traced certain recent marks on the table's polished surface. "This is where he placed the chair on the table. He used the little ebony chair, and scratched it quite badly in standing on it." As he spoke, he placed the fragile chair on the table. "If my reasoning seems far-fetched, check it by this. Do you recognize it, Kerns?"

Examining closely the tiny particles which Daunt had pinched up from the chair's wooden seat, the detective suddenly brightened.

"I get you, Reverend; He put the chair on the table, and stood on it to drill the hole in the ceiling, and some of the bits of wood and plaster fell on the chair. There's some on the table, too."

The clergyman nodded.

"We can reconstruct that part of the scene quite vividly. And we can draw from it the inference that Smith is a tall man— else he could not have reached that lofty ceiling, even with the help of chair and table together. Also, he is rather slightly built. A heavy man could not have trusted his weight to the chair. Now, how did Smith conduct his main performance?"

He replaced the light chair on the rug, and sitting coolly upon the corner of the sofa, looked about him.

"I think I see. Yes—there are the tracks which the feet of the table made on the rug. Do you follow, Kerns?"

"Not quite, Reverend," the detective confessed.

"Smith had the loop ready, and his victim bound and gagged. All that remained was to stand Bartram on the table, and slip the noose around his neck, then to pull the table from beneath the screw-eye. The soft slippers Bartram wore made the task a little easier."

Kerns' eye followed the gesture toward the corpse's feet, and he shuddered; but his companion had already risen and, with the air of having secured all necessary information from his surroundings, was on his way out of the room. At the door, he paused.

"I presume you have heard about the threatening letters, Kerns. Have any of them been found?"

"None, Reverend. He seems to have burned them all."

"Who discovered the body?"

"Inspector Baines—he is the man out in the hall."

"And he telephoned headquarters from the house?"

"That was the way of it, Reverend."

Daunt grunted and, without apparent interest in whatever clues might remain in the suite, made his way to the hall door. Here again he paused.

"I should like to talk to the cook."

By racing ahead, the detective had this functionary awaiting Daunt in the hall when the latter had descended the stairs in his usual leisurely fashion. She was distinctly unlike the chef found in many homes of wealth—a tall, maturely cheerful woman, with iron-gray hair and the direct glance of an expert confident of her skill.

"Two meals were sent up to Mr. Bartram today?" the clergyman inquired.

"Breakfast and lunch, sir. But the lunch was not served, for reasons which you know."

Daunt nodded. In a household most of the members of which were red-eyed and excited with the shock of tragedy, this woman seemed entirely self-possessed.

"Of what did these meals consist?" he pursued.

"Breakfast was half a grape fruit, kept overnight on ice, and champagne. For lunch, more champagne, and a steak. He always ate lightly in the morning, but he made up for it at noon and night, sir."

"And the steak was delivered this morning?"

"Ordered by 'phone from the Gibbons-Pinkett Company this morning, and delivered within half an hour, sir. That was the only order I sent in. Everything else was in the house."

The clergyman turned to Kerns.

"I should like a few minutes with Chief Maximilian. On the way to headquarters we can stop at the telephone office and you can get me a list of the calls they have charged against Bartram's number for the past week. Get it by days."

The detective appeared mystified, but nodded acquiescence.

Within half an hour they had procured the information desired and were in the presence of the suave but unsmiling Chief of Police, whose manner bore the imprint of sternly repressed pain behind its quiet efficiency.

"You are exceedingly kind to interest yourself in the case, Mr. Daunt," he acknowledged, warmly, waving his visitors to chairs. "Perhaps you know that Bartram came to me for protection just before he visited you. He called me up again this morning, and begged me to come to him at once. He was afraid to leave his home even for the trip to headquarters. You see the man's frame of mind! Of course, I went; and I had hardly returned to the office when he called me again from his private suite, suggesting further means of protection. I take it, Mr. Daunt, that you would like the gist of the talk I had with him this morning?"

Daunt regarded the Chief reflectively—almost absent-mindedly.

"You are a busy man, Chief Maximilian; so am I. If I should say that your conversation with Bartram had to do with additional measures of protection, would that be correct?"

"Entirely so."

"And in which room of his suite did you have your interview?"

"In his library."

The clergyman rose.

"I need nothing further. You have been very kind to present so unique a case for my consideration. I thank you." He turned to the detective. "I thank you, too, Kerns; but I regret that I must decline absolutely to have anything further to do with this case."

4

———

IN THE FACE of persuasion amounting to entreaty, the Reverend McGregor Daunt remained reasonably good-natured, but firm. He cared to have no more to do with the Bartram murder case. He did not wish to offer an explanation. By the next day he had repulsed his friend Kerns in three personal interviews and perhaps half a dozen times over the telephone, so that when the Chief of Detectives called again at the city study on the afternoon of that second day, Daunt's disposition had grown somewhat frayed.

"I told you I was through, Kerns," he said, acidly. "You saw everything that I saw. Up to a certain stage, I expounded my reasoning to you, point by point; and you are aware what I did after that. As far as I am concerned, the case is finished."

The detective laughed.

"That's what I've come to tell you, Reverend," he returned, with his usual good humor. "It's finished with us, too. We've found our man!"

He paused to allow his words effect, but Daunt regarded him enigmatically.

"You remember the threatening letters, Reverend? That was where luck played into our hands. The murderer wrote one final letter, and in some way it was delayed in delivery. It didn't reach Bartram's place till this morning."

"You caught him from the letter?" the clergyman inquired, with a slight show of interest.

"We caught him from the letter. How do you think we did it, Reverend?"

Daunt shook his head.

"I have no idea," he admitted, and the detective chuckled.

"Once in a while we get a mental flash," he laughed. "This one was simple. I started with the assumption that mail men are not such dumb brutes as some folks give them credit for being. The handwriting on this letter was very odd, and it didn't seem to be disguised. If the writer was a regular resident, I thought possibly one of the mail men might recognize it. I got them together at the Central Post Office and, sure enough, one of them did!"

The clergyman extended his hand.

"Clever work, Kerns!" he congratulated. "Who is the man?"

"Walter Graves—the brother of a girl old Bartram was trying to get. Bartram was a devil, you know—a low, dirty devil, if he *is* dead!"

"How did your man break into the suite and out again?"

The detective smiled, ruefully.

"He won't tell, Reverend. In fact, he hasn't confessed, by any means. He owns up to the letters, but he won't admit killing Bartram."

Daunt arose with an abrupt air of determination, and put on his derby.

"You understand, Kerns, that I have declined to have anything further to do with solving this case?"

"I ought to understand it."

"That decision stands. Nevertheless, I should like to talk with your prisoner."

"I hoped you would say that, Reverend," his friend declared,

116 / J. Paul Suter

heartily. "You won't obligate yourself in the least by talking to him; and maybe you can secure a confession where we can't."

The interest which the Reverend McGregor Daunt manifested in men had little to do with their external personalities. He was concerned with the inter-play of motive and action, the curious complexities and subtleties of the brain. Whether the one within whom the internal drama was staged appeared fair to the eyes or not was of small moment to him.

Yet he started slightly when Kerns' prisoner was brought into the private room at the jail where the interview had been arranged. The detective withdrew and Daunt was left alone with a clear-eyed, faintly-smiling young man, far removed from the type that might be expected to kill its fellow.

Despite himself, the clergyman was interested in the young man's appearance. In a voice unusually gentle for him he invited the other to sit down.

"Tell me why you did it, Graves," he directed, with purposeful abruptness.

The prisoner's mouth tightened. Without accepting the invitation, he returned Daunt's scrutiny squarely and replied:

"I didn't kill him, sir."

"I referred to the writing of the letters. I am aware that you did not murder Bartram," the clergyman persisted.

The young man sat down. His blue eyes widened.

"How do you know that?" he demanded.

"Because I know who did kill him."

For a moment the two men looked at each other without speaking; Daunt with an amused smile as he noted the blank amazement on his companion's face. Then the clergyman continued:

"I wish to learn why you wrote a series of threatening letters to Bartram, and why you shot at me as I sat on the front porch of my lodge, and why you climbed up my vines to look into the window at my guest."

"I didn't look in. I just showed him something," the young man defended.

"He took it for Mrs. Bartram's dead face."

The young man smiled.

"I hoped he'd do that. It was her death mask I showed him."

"Ah!" The clergyman nodded with the satisfaction of one to whom moot points are becoming clear. "You obtained that from a confederate in the household—the same one who planted your letters for you."

"Yes, sir."

"I shall not ask you her name. It is immaterial. You sent some of the letters by mail, too—for the sake of variety, I suppose. And you made the mistake of writing one letter too many and sending that by mail."

The prisoner appeared to be thinking, with bowed head. Daunt watched him and waited. Presently he was rewarded, for young Graves looked up with the air of a man who has made his resolution.

"Look here, sir! I'm in a pretty tight fix, and you knowing who killed Bartram won't help me any unless you tell. The police won't believe me if I tell them what you said. I don't think you're trying to double-cross me. Just to show you I don't, I'm going to give you what I know and take a chance on you doing the square thing."

Daunt merely nodded, non-committally, and the young man went on:

"This Bartram is better dead than alive, and I don't care who hears me say it. If there's one girl in the town that he has driven to the streets, there's twenty. They say he killed his wife, too, but it never could be fixed on him. Well, when he began to rush my sister, I figured I was due to get into the game. He was rich. He could show her a good time. The women seemed to fall for him—you know how it is. I might have beat him up, or warned him to lay off, but that wouldn't have done any good. He'd have had me pinched. So I hit on the idea of those letters to scare him off."

"Did you intend to kill him?"

"Not at first—no, sir! That's straight. I thought he'd quit and let sister alone. When he didn't, I made the letters stronger, and I got this—this friend of mine—to stick some of them around where he'd see them and they'd frighten him. They were letters he wouldn't want to show to anyone else—I saw to that. Oh, I was working up to it, all right! If he hadn't been killed, and had kept running around with my sister, he'd have lived about another week. You get the idea, don't you?"

"I still fail to understand why you took a shot at me," Daunt replied, obstinately.

The young man smiled, ingenuously.

"Oh, well, sir, you see, I didn't know it was you. I thought it was Bartram. And I wasn't trying to hit you, anyway. Why, the way you sat there, with the moonlight shining on the top of your head, I couldn't have missed! This friend of mine told me Bartram was going out to your lodge, and I jumped into my little bus and followed. I thought that out there in the woods I might scare him so that he really would quit my sister. I tried to do a good job, first taking a shot at him, then letting him have a peek at that death mask in the moonlight. But I made the mistake of following that up with a good, strong letter through the mail. I never figured they'd know my handwriting well enough to trace me from it."

The clergyman rose.

"I think, Graves, you have told me everything I need to know. What you have said does not affect the murder problem—you could not possibly have committed that; but you have cleared up one or two minor points."

"I'll keep mum about what you told me, if you say so, sir," the young man offered. "But don't let them lock me up here very long."

With the door half opened, Daunt turned, and shook his head.

"No! Tell the police what I have said."

5

ALL OF THAT afternoon the Reverend McGregor Daunt was restless. He paced back and forth within the confines of the city study, occasionally stepped into the little courtyard between study and manse, and examined the stone flagging, or the aged lichens crawling up the church edifice, with the grave, inconsequential scrutiny of a man whose mind is elsewhere. Once or twice he walked as far as the rear door of the manse, but he turned each time without entering, and retraced slow steps to the study.

His business in the city was done. In the natural course of his habits, he would have returned to the hunting lodge, for it was ideal woodland weather. No one had made an engagement with him for any purpose. Yet he was expecting a visitor.

He was in the study in the late afternoon when lagging footsteps sounded on the flagstones outside. Someone had turned from the busy street upon which the church faced to the narrow walk under the high, stained-glass windows. The footsteps stopped just outside the study door. Daunt opened the door.

"Come in, Chief Maximilian," he said.

The Chief of Police entered. His face was worn and very pale. He walked heavily to the nearest chair, and sat down in silence, without invitation. Daunt, still standing, regarded him keenly.

"You are not well," he observed.

The Chief nodded, wearily.

"It is true. I am not well," he assented, dully.

"I have had the advantage of medical training. If you will excuse me for a few minutes while I step over to the manse—"

But the clergyman's visitor held up a thin hand, imperatively.

"I wish no stimulant," he declared. "I am here for a purpose, and I shall have strength to carry it out. Am I mistaken, Mr. Daunt, in assuming that you expected me?"

"You are not mistaken," the clergyman confirmed, seating himself.

"You would expect me. Naturally, you would. Yet may I ask another question? Suppose I had not come; what would you have done?"

"Nothing," Daunt replied, unhesitatingly.

"Neither now nor later?"

"Neither now nor later. You will remember that I declined the case."

The Chief's chin sank upon his breast. Evidently he was fighting for self-control. He looked up again, and his eye met his host's, frankly.

"This is not a painful occasion for me, Mr. Daunt. It is rather one of satisfaction. Yet, I am laboring under a nervous strain, and a physical, as well. You can ease me greatly by taking the initiative. Before I give you the reasons for my action, will you tell me how your own conclusions were arrived at?"

Daunt regarded his visitor quizzically.

"I am willing," he acceded. "Let me begin by asking you a question. Chief Maximilian, in your school days, were you ever confronted by a problem in which the statement of the proposition actually contained its own solution?"

"I think so."

"This was some such problem." The clergyman leaned

forward with the zest which was always his when a feat of reasoning from effect to cause presented itself. "Suppose I state the proposition. Here is a man, enclosed in a suite of rooms, with all entrances locked on the inside." He drew such an imaginary enclosure with his finger on his broad thigh. "There seems one way by which a visitor might enter—through the door. He might have a key, or pick the lock. But that way is rendered impossible by the guards on duty outside the door, as well as around the house in which the suite is situated. Now, in spite of these conditions, someone enters and kills the man in the suite. Does that state the proposition as it came to me?"

The Chief nodded.

"That states it," Daunt continued, "but, as stated, it is manifestly impossible. Therefore it must be misstated—but in what respect?" He tapped the imaginary plan on his thigh for emphasis. "The entrances, locked on the inside, are noted immediately after the crime. That part of the statement must be correct. It is evident, too, that the possibility of a man concealed in the rooms, who commits the crime and then breaks his way out, is likewise out of the question. The guards have been on duty continuously, and the door and windows are still locked. Who, then, did the thing?" He paused, and smiled at his visitor—the satisfied smile of an analyst who has reached his impersonal conclusion. "Who could it be but the last man known to visit the suite—the man who, without concealment or suspicion, walked out in the full sight of the guards?" Still smiling, he waved an admonishing finger. "You were open to criticism there, Chief Maximilian. Speaking as a critic of crime, to whom murder is an intellectual problem, I am bound to declare that your execution of this lacked the expert touch.

You should have unlocked one window on the inside, then have called away your guards, after you had left the suite, for a brief consultation on the opposite side of the house. That would have left a means of escape for a mythical murderer concealed in Bartram's rooms."

The Chief nodded, thoughtfully.

"I am not an expert," he admitted. "Yet I confess that I thought this job well done. Indeed, I was anxious to call you in, so that its merit might be proved. Had I taken those precautions would you have solved the problem?"

"Not so easily." The clergyman looked down at his imaginary design and wrinkled his broad forehead. "Yet there were two indications which would at least have aroused my suspicions. You recall that I inquired in which room of Bartram's suite you held your interview with him, and you said it was the library?"

"I shrank instinctively from mentioning the den. It was a weakness," Maximilian confessed.

"Precisely. But all of the cigarette ashes were in the den. There *were* none whatever in the library. When a man begins to lie about a crime, that is strong evidence against him. Then there was the matter of the telephone."

The Chief started.

"You caught that?"

"It was simple. But two outgoing calls were made from the Bartram residence on the morning of the crime. Respecting one of these, the cook—quite without realizing—supplied me valuable information. She phoned to order the meat for lunch. The other call came from your own men when they discovered the body. Yet you stated that Bartram called you twice that morning from his suite. I suppose that when Kerns entered your office, after you had returned from Bartram's, it occurred to you to take up the receiver and finish an imaginary conversation with the man you had just killed?"

Without wincing, the Chief nodded.

"It occurred to me, as you say. I see now that it was a mistake. I wished a few days respite to clear up my affairs—so I tried to delay the inevitable disclosure."

"It was a mistake only because fate turned against you. Had there been several other calls from the Bartram house that morning—as there easily might have been—and had I been unable to trace them, your spurious call would have appeared genuine."

Daunt paused, and as his visitor said nothing, continued:

"The solution of the problem was inherent in the initial proposition, as you perceive."

"One thing I don't perceive." The Chief's spare, nervous hands clenched and unclenched. "You had the solution. I was utterly at your mercy. Yet you declined to go on with the case, and you kept your counsel."

The clergyman smiled again; this time, the cold, sardonic smile which was peculiarly his.

"You forget that I am not a detective. I am merely a connoisseur in crime. When a criminal achievement presents distinctive features, I dabble in it for the intellectual pleasure it affords me. Justice, as it is known among men, is a relative term. It is one thing here in America, and quite another among the Turks. What is absolute justice? Neither you nor I can say! Why should I give you up to the combination of sublime ethics and third-class legislation which happens to be this year's fashion in justice, when, by merely holding my peace, I might receive some other problem of genuine interest from you? You are not an ordinary man. Your motive for this crime was not ordinary, I am sure. I shall be pleased to hear it, and you need fear no disclosure from me."

"No, I need not." The Chief turned his dark eyes on Daunt with an expression which the clergyman could not fathom. It was fearless—fearless beyond question; but the courage it contained had in it the very essence of despair. For one in whom emotional responses were seldom profound, the Reverend McGregor was strangely affected by that glance.

"I need fear no disclosure you may make," Maximilian repeated; "but I am here to explain my side of the case to you. I admire you, Mr. Daunt. Yours is a type of brain unlike any other I have come upon. I think you will be interested in the motive behind this crime of mine. May I ask whether you were aware of Bartram's character?"

"To some extent."

"I had interested myself in the man for some years. I hoped—and several others in the department joined me in that hope—that he would put himself into the power of the law. He was too cunning for us; but I can say this to you, that for more than one young woman in this city whose right to innocence and happiness should have been above question, he was ruin. We saw the trail of his filth, but were powerless to curb him. Wealth, coupled with the devilish subtlety of the serpent, can go a long way in any American city, Mr. Daunt."

"I grant that he is better dead," the clergyman admitted, judicially.

Maximilian nodded his acknowledgment.

"You will understand my feelings when he came to me. I had

no sympathy for him, yet duty obliged me to give him what protection I could. I obeyed that duty. Whether we could have saved him, I do not know. It is doubtful. But on the evening of the day he came, I had a personal experience which affected this case profoundly." He paused, almost imperceptibly, then went on: "It was my visit to a specialist—the climax of many such. On that visit, Mr. Daunt, I was sentenced to death."

Daunt had the curious impression of watching a man who, walking along a narrow and precipitous place, had lost his balance, then caught himself before he could topple over. The Chief continued slowly, gazing at the study wall as if it were transparent, and all space stretched beyond it.

"A doctor's sentence of death is unlike a judge's. *That* may be commuted. For the sentence which I have received there is no commutation. Wherever I may go, I shall carry my executioner with me. My body has come to the end of its days. It is the voice of Time which pronounces the sentence—the loud voice of Time, ticking off its seconds. What I have done is due largely to the fact that I hear this voice so distinctly."

He shrugged his shoulders.

"Well, there is not much more to my story, Mr. Daunt. I lay awake that night. All night a certain conclusion was hounding at me at every twist and turn of my mind, yet I was unwilling to turn and face it. Early in the morning, Bartram telephoned me from a pay station. He was on his way home from your lodge, and he wished to make sure the guards would be on duty when he arrived. He told me of his night's experience. I saw then that the matter had become pressing. Someone undoubtedly intended to kill him soon, and his death would mean not only his own obliteration, but a ruined life for the man who brought it about. Now, Mr. Daunt, please attend to me closely! Just at this point I wish you to see with my eyes."

His slender body quivered, but the emotion it masked was rigorously suppressed.

"Here was I, under sentence of death. Another man, unknown to me, was on the verge of a crime which might place him also under that sentence, which at the least would ruin his life. And this was the irony of it—that the wiping out of the thing he meant to kill would be a service to humanity!"

He pressed thumb and forefinger together, like one crushing out a noxious insect.

"I had already determined not to await fulfilment of the doctor's sentence. Why should I die in slow agony when a bullet would end the hopeless affair in a moment? I meant to kill myself, and—mark this!—I determined now to make my death count for something; not just to die, but to die to some purpose; to rid the city which I guard of a devilish influence, and at the same time avert the wreck of someone's life. I don't condone murder. I have not turned against the law. But that was my determination, and I have no regrets."

He met his host's eye without defiance, yet with no hint of apology. The clergyman gazed at him thoughtfully for a space before replying.

"It is not my office to judge you, Chief Maximilian," he said at last. "For what you did you will answer elsewhere. Neither would I appear to put the mere intellectual problem above the moral issues involved, and yet...."

"You wish more light on certain points?" the Chief suggested, calmly.

"On two points. Whether or not I approve your motive, I at

least understand it. But I cannot understand how you applied the gag and the ropes to Bartram without a struggle—though you evidently did so. And I am curious as to the reason for your means of death. Why did you hang him? Was it in the nature of an execution?"

Chief Maximilian nodded.

"I conceived it as exactly that," he confirmed. "An eminently just execution for sins which our imperfect laws as yet cannot touch. I was at pains to explain it to Bartram. That clears up your first point, too, Mr. Daunt. For, as the purpose of my visit became clear, he was literally paralyzed with fear. I expected that. I could read the man's cowardly soul. I gagged him, bound him, lifted him to the noose, without his making an effort to prevent me. I might then have contrived some sort of drop, of perhaps a foot at least, to make the end quicker, but I felt that slow strangling might be more merciful."

"I do not quite see that," the clergyman commented.

"Not physically merciful." The Chief of Police rose, with the definiteness of one who has accomplished his purpose. "Physically painful, I grant you. But spiritually merciful. His was a black soul. His mind was too paralyzed with fear for real repentance. Yet you know the saying of the Church, 'Between the bridge and the river there is time for an act of real contrition.' Who knows what may have passed through his mind in the brief interval while he was hanging there before life left him? At least, I gave the opportunity.... I must go," he said, abruptly. "Several matters remain to be looked to. That young man Graves must be cleared. And I am determined, too, to tell Kerns everything. He could have solved this mystery, I think, if he had been willing to suspect me.... Mr. Daunt—" He eyed the clergyman whimsically. "I have enjoyed your exposition of this case. I should like to study your methods in future cases. But that can't be, can it? Will you take the hand of one in farewell whom the law will proclaim a murderer?"

Daunt grasped the extended hand. He looked into the level eyes—eyes from which all hope was gone, but which were quite unafraid.

The Chief walked heavily to the door and opened it without turning again. His host followed him and stood at the threshold. He watched the slender figure, very erect but a trifle tottering in its gait, pass slowly through the stone flagged courtyard and out of sight around the corner of the church.

The Cat Mocker

*The following story of the Reverend McGregor
Daunt,* Black Mask's *clergyman-detective,
has such a simple solution that—that if Mr.
Suter were not such a good workman, you would
have no trouble in guessing the ending.*

1

——

ON ALMOST ANY fine day, from the library window of his hunting lodge—where he thought but did not hunt—the Reverend McGregor Daunt could see General Pendergast's Angora stalking her prey. The great orange animal went through her routine with a certain degree of art. Spotting some tree in which the birds were twittering, she would approach stealthily, blending her body with grass and underbrush; climb the tree, pausing motionless every few seconds with her baleful eye on the unsuspecting birds; slowly, very slowly, creep to a spot a little higher on the bough than the bird she was stalking; then spring. Nearly always she reached the final stage without being discovered; and always she missed the bird. For she carried with her her own undoing, in the shape of a tiny silver bell hung to her collar. Creeping, she could keep the bell silent, but it invariably twinkled its warning when she sprang. The clergyman watched her with fascination. In his more idle speculative moments, he would make mental bets with himself, at long odds, that once at least she would reach her objective. But the short end of the bet always lost. The little bell never failed.

General Pendergast, whose country home a quarter of a mile away was the nearest house to the hunting lodge, was the president of a securities company in the city. He lived at Pengrove the retired life of an elderly widower, with his only daughter, Natalie. Once or twice in the course of a month, Daunt would glimpse the General—a tall, erect figure with white hair and bristling white mustache—cutting through the trees on a morning constitutional. More often, Natalie appeared, in quest of the Angora. Though expensively dressed, she was small and dumpy, this daughter of the General. She had none of her father's air of distinction. So Daunt, who speculated about everyone he saw, concluded that she must resemble her mother. They considerately avoided the lodge, and the clergyman, who had taken to that retired spot to escape from human society, was not at all likely to make advances.

One member of society, however, always found a welcome at the lodge, whether he came merely to chat, or—his more frequent mission—to bring a problem for Daunt's speculative mind to chew on. Chief of Detectives Kerns was that member.

Kerns usually took the path through the woods which led to the front door of the lodge. That path connected with the main road, a mile away. There was no reason why anyone, coming from the city, should approach from another direction.

Yet on a certain July evening, the clergyman was sitting at his library window—the same window from which he watched Pendergast's Angora in the daytime—when he perceived the detective's tall figure striding toward the lodge from the side opposite the woodland path.

Kerns was hurrying. He emerged from the well of blackness which was the woods, into the little pool of light from the library window. The light illumined his face for just the fraction of a second necessary for Daunt to identify him; and he was out of the pool again, on his way to the front porch. He had lifted the knocker but once when Daunt opened the door. For the clergyman had responded promptly. Something indefinable in the flash of Kern's face, out of the dark and back into it, had enjoined haste.

The detective stepped in, with his usual good-natured smile.

"Didn't expect me, eh, Reverend? I've just come from Pendergast's place. Someone stole his cat and his daughter."

The clergyman motioned his friend to a seat in the library, with its comfortable smell of old books. He himself took a Morris chair. He was partial to Morris chairs. Their soft cushions bolstered up one's ideas, while their arms, hard and straight, were conducive to similar qualities of thought. In solving criminal problems, one must think straight, and not let softness and mercy blind the judgment.

"His cat and daughter!" Daunt exclaimed, puzzled. "Why the daughter?"

"I don't quite get you, Reverend," the detective confessed.

The clergyman smiled.

"Never mind," he said. "My remark was prompted by my having seen both the daughter and the cat."

"I thought maybe you'd know them. You like queer problems, Reverend, and this one is queer. Ever see the Pendergast place?"

Daunt shook his head.

"We can go over there after a bit, if you think it worth while. It's a big, old house—a porch all around it, and shrubbery around that. The shrubbery near the front door is where the cat disappeared. She was sitting on the porch when, without any warning, she jumped into a hole in the shrubbery. That was curtains, for her. They searched the grounds and went under the porch, but she wasn't seen again. She wasn't *seen*—but here is where the thing begins to sound queer. She wore a bell, I understand."

"A small silver bell," the clergyman confirmed.

"Well, every night since she went they heard that bell in the shrubbery. They'd hear it, and they'd look for the cat with lanterns. No use. Not a sign of her. When they started to look, the bell would stop, but it always seemed to be in exactly the place where she had jumped. Of course, Miss Pendergast nearly went crazy. It was her cat. When the bell was heard she would rout her father out and they would simply go through the place with a fine-tooth comb. And then, night before last, the girl took the jump herself—and disappeared, exactly as the cat had done. There you have it, Reverend. The General has been looking for her ever since."

"And has found nothing?"

Kerns smiled with satisfaction at the effect he had produced upon his usually cynical friend.

"Nothing is the word, Reverend. You can make it just as emphatic as you wish. He hasn't found the least trace of anything wrong in the shrubbery. He has been looking two days for her in the daylight without coming on even a footprint. The way General Pendergast puts it is that you wouldn't think a mouse could have disappeared and left as little trace as there is. I haven't been over the place myself in the daytime, but it certainly looks like a first-class mystery."

"You have not been over it in the daytime? Why not?" demanded the clergyman.

"I wasn't called in till this evening, Reverend. It was not General Pendergast who called me then, but Mr. Robertson, the chairman of the company. Pendergast hated to tell the police. Didn't want the publicity. Kept believing the girl would turn up. But Mr. Robertson said the General would go insane if his daughter wasn't found mighty soon, so he let us know."

Daunt looked at his watch, then deliberately walked to the hallway and put on the wide-brimmed hat which was his invariable headgear, summer or winter. He started in silence for the front door, hesitated, and returned to pick out a heavy cane from a number in the umbrella rack. Thus equipped, he was ready.

"Half-past nine," he announced.

"You have your flashlight, Kerns?"

"Never without it, Reverend."

"Then suppose we go."

2

IT WAS A dark night, dark with a clear, transparent blackness, which seemed to promise a vista ahead yet really revealed nothing, like an impressionistic painting in oil. The two men walked rapidly in the little circle of the electric lamp; Kerns with a long, easy stride, Daunt stiffly, yet with enough speed to keep abreast of his friend. The detective had something of a woodsman's instinct. He retraced unerringly the way he had come from the Pendergast place. A sharp ten minutes of dodging in and out among tree-trunks whose tops were lost in the darkness above, and they broke into a space of smooth lawn, at the far side of which was the house.

"You can get a pretty good general impression of the shrubbery from here, Reverend," the detective observed.

Daunt paused, and gazed with interest at the place. He liked to gather his first impression of a house from a distance. Distance emphasizes the big structural features which, because of their very largeness, might be overlooked on close inspection. In this instance, the big feature was the shrubbery. The little paths of light from the many windows of the house undulated and rippled on the luxuriant growth, which seemed broader than the rest of the place and in all ways more notable. Daunt was impressed with the curious idea that the shrubbery had been there before the house and had merely withdrawn for a time from the center of the plot, and that it would close in and take the whole by right of ownership after the house was gone. He shivered, then glanced aside quickly to note whether his companion had observed him.

"It's all right, Reverend," chuckled the detective. "I feel the same way myself. There's something darned queer about this place. If I was asked to pick a house, from all those I've ever seen, where a girl or a cat or anything else could disappear and never be heard of again, this one would do as well as any I know of. How about it?"

"It *is* a striking place," the clergyman agreed, thoughtfully, "Shall we go on?"

They reached the wide steps. Kerns, beginning to mount them, turned.

"It was right here, Reverend...."

He stopped abruptly, and whirled toward the other side of the steps. They were in the center of a sudden circle of light, behind which was a tall figure in the darkness.

"I am sure I beg your pardon, gentlemen," said the figure, urbanely. "I had no wish to startle you. I was looking into the shrubbery, and straightened when I heard your voices."

"My friend, the Reverend McGregor Daunt, General," Kerns introduced, recovering. "You remember, I promised to bring him over, if he would come."

"Ah, Mr. Daunt, I appreciate this, from my heart. We hardly dared hope for your help on our poor little mystery. It will be very simple to you, I have no doubt."

Daunt regretted that the window blinds, which rolled from the bottom, were drawn up just enough to cast the base of the shrubbery into darkness. He would have preferred a clear view of the General's countenance at the outset. All that he could see was that the keen-visaged old man behind the electric lantern had scrutinized his own face closely in the brief interval which courtesy allowed before the light was lowered.

"What you saw in the shrubbery was best visible without light, I take it?" the clergyman suggested, quietly. "If your lantern was on as we approached, I must have been very unobservant."

The General laughed easily.

"On the contrary, you have employed your eyes to good purpose, Mr. Daunt. I used the light only to guide me about the lawn. Perhaps I am illogical—I certainly cannot defend my position with argument—but I feel that the mystery of the shrubbery is something that mere light will not solve. My dear girl disappeared into the darkness. We shall find her—if we find her at all—by examining the darkness. I have spent most of my nights in this place since she went."

Daunt took the flashlight from the detective's hand and directed it toward the spot where General Pendergast apparently had been searching.

"You seem to have something of a hole here, under the shrubbery," he observed.

"You are right, Mr. Daunt." The General pointed his own light. "It connects with that into which Natalie jumped. Do you care to examine it?"

"In the daylight."

The clergyman snapped off the light and handed it back.

"Were you present when the cat jumped into the bushes?" he inquired.

"My daughter and myself were on the porch."

"The animal sprang suddenly, I understand?"

"Very suddenly, Mr. Daunt. Bobbo was asleep on the porch, between my daughter's chair and mine, when, with no previous warning, he launched himself directly into the shrubbery.

His action was so strange that it startled us both. Natalie called him, and, when he did not come, and we could not even hear his bell, she went into the house for the flashlight. We looked into the shrubbery quite thoroughly that night, but saw nothing."

"You heard his bell as he sprang?" the clergyman persisted.

"I think so. Of course, one cannot be sure about such a point."

"You heard the bell, I am told, on nights subsequent to the cat's disappearance?"

"That is the simple truth, Mr. Daunt." The white-haired man bent his head gravely. "I cannot account for the fact; but it stands as a fact, nevertheless. We have heard that bell since poor Bobbo went. Each time we heard it we searched the shrubbery. We found nothing."

As his host finished, Daunt started up the steps; so abruptly that he was at the top, and a short distance to the side of them on the porch, before the others followed. He halted then, and peered with interest into the blackness of the shrubbery, as seen from above. Dense as a tropical jungle, and higher than a man, it felt its way hungrily with thick tendrils over the railing into the porch itself. A few of the weaker tentacles, not yet long enough to reach the dignity of the upper rail, twisted upon the porch floor, where they writhed when stepped upon. The growth crawled out into the grounds well beyond the line of the steps, and blotted out with its blackness all of the upper part of the lawn. The window blinds, partly lifted, helped in the eerie effect, by sending little glistening streams of light along the top of the shrubbery, but keeping all below that in darkness.

"Do these shrubs extend entirely around the house?" Daunt demanded of his host, who had followed him.

"Entirely, Mr. Daunt, except for the front and rear steps."

"There is a cellar?"

"A large one, beneath the whole of the house. We already have examined the stones of the foundation walls, if that is in your mind. They appear perfectly firm."

The clergyman grunted. Out of the corner of his eye he was studying the General with interest. Though bearing up under an evident nervous strain, the old man was repressing his emotions admirably; so much so, in fact, that at times he appeared almost calloused to his loss.

"Suppose we sit here on the porch, General Pendergast, while you tell me all you can about your daughter's disappearance. Let me sit farthest from the door, Kerns, with the General between us."

When they were seated, Daunt had contrived to place himself in shadow. An oblique ray of light from the library window illumined his host's face. The detective, nearest the doorway, seemed framed in its warm yellow; but his back was to the light.

"Your daughter was at this part of the porch when she leaped into the shrubbery?" began Daunt.

The General nodded, without speaking.

"Was she seated or standing?"

The old man hesitated a moment, and answered:

"She was standing, Mr. Daunt. She had just come upon the porch. I was smoking in this very chair, and hardly noticed her presence for a minute or two, but my impression is that she stood there, listening. Then the bell tinkled in the shrubbery. We heard it, just as we had done on other nights since Bobbo disappeared. Before I realized what she was doing, Natalie had run to the side of the steps and jumped directly into the shrubbery, in the spot from which the tinkle seemed to come."

With a sudden gesture, as of one throwing off restraint, he hid his face in his hands; but Daunt was inexorable.

"Did she appear to you to sink into the shrubbery?" he persisted.

The old man rose abruptly, and took two steps toward the edge of the porch, almost as if he meant to throw himself over; but he wheeled again and faced the clergyman.

"Mr. Daunt!" he began in a whisper. "I have not spoken about this to anyone. I had not meant to tell you. But you should know; yes, I believe that I am doing right to tell you. I am as sure, Mr. Daunt, as I am that you face me this minute, that my daughter did not jump into the shrubbery. She ran to the edge of the porch—the very edge—and something reached up and pulled her down!"

The detective half rose, with a muttered exclamation; but Daunt asked quietly:

"Did you see this?"

"She was between me and the hole in the shrubbery. I saw nothing. But there is a difference, Mr. Daunt, between the attitude of one who jumps and one who is dragged down."

Very deliberately the clergyman pulled himself to his feet. He reached silently for the flashlight in Kerns' hands, and snapped it on as he walked to the edge of the broad porch. The opening in the shrubbery led obliquely downward at his feet. He knelt and thrust the light into it.

"See anything, Reverend?" Kerns asked, with interest. "I looked that hole over pretty carefully, and as far as I can see it ends at the foundation wall."

Daunt did not reply, but as he rose and dusted his knees, his eyes shone with an excitement unusual for him. He turned to the General.

"Are you sure that your daughter disappeared exactly at this spot?" he inquired.

"Quite sure, Mr. Daunt."

"She was dragged into this hole?"

"That is my judgment. In my own mind I am sure of it."

"You were not astonished, I take it, that she seemed to be dragged rather than to fall?"

The old man stared at his questioner.

"Do you mean that I expected her to be dragged into the shrubbery?"

"Your statements have given me that impression," the clergyman acquiesced.

The old man staggered backward. The light from the doorway fell across his face and showed it to be distorted. He appeared to have forgotten his guests, and to be talking to himself, in low tones charged with grief.

"I wonder whether I did expect it? If I did, how could I have been so careless? How could I have let her out of my sight?"

He stopped abruptly and turned with dignity to Daunt.

"You are very keen, Mr. Daunt. You have seen something which I had not confessed, even to myself. You are right. Somewhere in my mind there must have been the expectation that that accursed thing in the shrubbery would take her, in spite of all I could do."

The clergyman eyed him narrowly.

"What thing?" he demanded.

3

THE GENERAL LAUGHED—A dry, mirthless laugh.

"I don't know that I can make you understand," he said. "This is an old house, Mr. Daunt, and I am an old man. Old houses have their tales and old men believe them."

He sank heavily into a chair.

"Four long-lived generations have occupied this house. Natalie and I are the last of the old family. We are steeped in tradition—both of us. Yet I believe we had forgotten the thing I am about to tell you, until—until this."

He waved a hand toward the hole in the shrubbery.

"The man who built this house—my great-grandfather—came here more than a hundred years ago, in the old Indian days. When you go through the house, you will see that the beams are held together with wooden pins, after the fashion of those times. He was a hard man, this ancestor of mine. He brought with him his wife, a small son, and a negro servant; and tradition declares, that he abused them with the ingenuity of a fiend. The wife—my great-grandmother—had a cat to which she was attached. Not content with treating her and his little son with the utmost cruelty, my ancestor deliberately tortured the poor beast before their eyes. He cut away parts of the animal, piecemeal—always giving his amputations time to heal so that the victim would not die. He had a devilish faculty, Mr. Daunt, of imitating the call of a cat, combined with a sort of hypnotic influence—if I can call it so. To this day, there are men with that faculty—especially in the South. They are known as 'cat mockers.' He could force the unfortunate beast to come to him against its will."

Daunt nodded.

"I have seen men with that power," he observed.

"You will understand, then, that there may be a basis of truth in this story, strange though it is. In our day, this ancestor of mine would be adjudged insane and committed to an asylum, but such measures were not feasible then. He had his way, and terrorized his little household for years. But the end came."

He gazed silently for a time at the dark mass of shrubbery at his feet. His guests waited. There was no sound but a subdued cricket chorus from somewhere at the side of the house.

"It came through the cat," he resumed. "For years he had tortured it with impunity. He carefully avoided any retaliation from the beast. But one day it seized his hand in its mouth— the very hand that held the dissecting knife. That was the finish. Blood poisoning set in. He died—raving."

The old man gazed sombrely at the dark expanse of lawn, stretching in front of the house and on the visible part of the sides, to the blacker rim of the woods. His eyes returned to Daunt. As the light from the doorway glanced across them, they seemed to hide a question. But the clergyman sat motionless, his own face in shadow, and waited until his host resumed.

"If you are a materialist, Mr. Daunt—one of those who scoff at every possibility beyond the five senses—you will have small patience with what I have left to tell. I intend to tell it, nevertheless. This part of the tradition is necessary to an understanding of the present situation."

He paused again, meaningly, but Daunt maintained his stony silence.

"According to the body, this ancestor of mine was dead. His interment was the first in the private burial plot of my family, which is in the woods not far from the rear of the house. I suppose that my great-grandmother—poor woman—felt that she was rid of a curse—of a blight upon her life. In due time she married again. They say that her second husband was an excellent man. It seemed that the happiness she had lacked was to be hers at last—though late. Then, one night, the poor, miserable animal which had been tortured, but which still survived, disappeared—into that shrubbery!"

He seized the arm of the clergyman's chair.

"Mr. Daunt! Within a week—within a week, mind you— the lady herself was gone. She was seen to enter the shrubbery. She never emerged. No trace of her could be discovered, but three months later her body—terribly mutilated but not in the least decomposed—was found, early one morning, there on the lawn."

He stopped, quivering with emotion; but Daunt, cold and apparently unmoved by the vibrant appeal in the General's voice, merely nodded, as if checking off the story in his mind. The old man waited, then, tempering his voice to a whisper, added impressively:

"The tradition does not stop there, Mr. Daunt. The cat wore a little bell. And the story declares that the final tragedy was preceded by a sound in the bushes like the tinkling of a bell; and that the unfortunate lady entered the shrubbery by compulsion, because something dragged her into it!"

"Does that conclude the tradition?" the clergyman inquired unemotionally.

"Save for this—there is a further tradition that something—

some unspeakable thing—has had its abode ever since in the shrubbery. It is invisible. For long periods its presence may be utterly unsuspected. It may even skip entire generations. But when it is ready to strike, it manifests itself by a tinkling sound."

Kerns had been listening silently but alertly. Now he spoke.

"Has anyone else died in this manner, General Pendergast?"

"One other—a little girl, a child of three, in my grandfather's time. As far as known, no death of an animal preceded her. But her body was found, similarly mutilated."

"Have you yourself ever heard the tinkling in the shrubbery before the events of the last week?" continued the detective.

"Frankly, I do not know. I am not a superstitious man, Mr. Kerns. Though I have known this family tradition ever since my boyhood, it made no impression on me until Natalie's disappearance. Granting that such a sound has actual existence, I may have heard it and given it no attention."

Daunt roused, suddenly, from the study into which he had fallen.

"Do you expect to be at your office in the morning, General Pendergast?" he inquired irrelevantly.

"I do not, Mr. Daunt. I cannot give my mind to anything but this." With a wave of his hand he indicated the besieging shrubbery, and they understood him to refer to what it symbolized. "I have not had a thought for business since my dear girl disappeared. It is a rather important time with my company. The annual audit, which is due, has been postponed to my return; and my absence is delaying the final stage of a large issue of bonds. I should be there. But it is quite impossible, Mr. Daunt."

The clergyman rose crisply.

"There is nothing more to be done on the porch; nothing more tonight," he observed. "Have the servants been questioned?"

"Our menage is small, Mr. Daunt. My daughter acted as housekeeper, and we have only one servant—a foreign girl. Shall I waken her?"

"You talked with her, Kerns?"

"Pumped her to the limit, Reverend. And got mighty little."

"She will be in bed, I suppose. I see no reason for rousing her," the clergyman decided. "Are you going back to headquarters tonight, Kerns?"

"I don't have to, Reverend."

"You had best go. When you arrive in town, telephone Mr. Robertson. If he has retired, get him up. Tell him that this problem is by no means solved. Urge him to go ahead with the audit and whatever other business is awaiting the General's return. I am quite sure that this is desirable, as matters will be far more serious here before they are better."

"Mr. Daunt!" the General exclaimed, in dismay; but his guest silenced him with the assumption of dignity he could always use effectively.

"I am sorry if I seem to talk in riddles, General Pendergast. I am not yet able to give you reasons; but I can see the possibility of much worse things ahead for you. You must stay in this house. You will do well, indeed, to avoid the porch, even in daylight. I shall remain with you for the night."

The old man seemed rather taken aback.

"You wish to spend the night here?"

"I can sleep on a sofa. In fact, that will be preferable. And I shall turn in in my clothes. I am with you in the capacity of a guard."

"That's more my line than yours, Reverend," the detective protested. "Better let me take you over to the manse and come back here. You can call up Robertson yourself."

The clergyman smiled, a trifle sardonically.

"In the event that something invisible, which manifested its presence by tinkling a bell, should try to pass you, to attack the General upstairs, how would you conduct yourself, Kerns?"

Kerns grinned, though not without a trace of worry in his lean face.

"You don't expect anything like that, Reverend?"

"I expect the unexpected; whether it will be like that or totally unlike it, I am unable to say."

Once more, the clergyman turned to his host, and there was an authoritative ring to his voice which admitted no contradiction.

"I am in charge of this case now, General Pendergast, and it seems best for me to stay with you tonight. I insist on sleeping downstairs. Let us consider that point settled. Before turning in, however, I should like to be taken through the upper rooms, so as to have my bearings in case of an emergency. We can gather a blanket or two upstairs."

4

LEFT TO HIMSELF after bidding the General good-night, Daunt arranged his blankets upon the comfortable sofa in the library which had been assigned him, but did not at once occupy that place of repose. Instead, he made a slow and painstaking inspection of the massively furnished room. Half-a-dozen papers, left rather untidily on the mahogany table, caught his eye, and he examined them without scruple. They proved to be stock-market reports. He wandered past the bookcases on the inside wall, opposite the long windows, and indulged in little grunts of appreciation at sight of the carefully selected volumes. Some of the books were undoubtedly old. Very likely, they had descended to the General from his ancestors; a few, perhaps, from the very ancestor whose sinister character formed the basis for the family legend. At the thought, however, the clergyman chuckled, and passed on to the more modern books. They, too, were discriminatingly chosen. General Pendergast evidently was a connoisseur. If his forebears had been blessed with taste as to the printed page, he was following worthily in their steps.

Having finished with the library and made sure that the windows were locked, Daunt sauntered on to the hospitable living-room, in whose broad fireplace a garrulous log crackled. With his back to the log and his hands outstretched behind him to catch something of its comfortable glow, he stood for a space in thought. He liked to think with his back to a fire. The heat thus directed did not assault his face violently, but enveloped him gradually in its mellow flood and trickled urbanely through the crevices of his soul. Reluctantly, he left the living-room. There were other rooms he wished to patrol. But he glanced back at the fireplace with regret as he passed into the dining-room, on his way to the kitchen.

He glanced back; and stopped, with a shiver of absolute amazement. Lying on its side on the mantel, in plain sight, was a little silver bell!

Daunt returned to the mantel and picked up the bell. Here was an instance in which his score as a keen observer—and probably Kerns', also—had been nil. The very obviousness of the little object had served to hide it. He examined it carefully, and replaced it on the mantel. When he resumed the tour of the lower rooms it was with a mind in which a new and significant clue had been planted.

Nothing in dining-room or kitchen seemed notable. As a matter of routine he examined them, as also the scullery off the kitchen and several closets. At length, he walked back slowly to the library. There the long windows intrigued him for a time. He peered through them thoughtfully at the dark army of the shrubbery, undulating and shivering in the night breeze. Finally he decided to go to bed.

But he had omitted to turn off the lights in the other rooms, and he walked back through them crisply, finishing with the electric lamp in the library. Not until everything was in darkness did he produce from the pocket of his overcoat—thrown upon a chair—a flashlight and a revolver which Kerns had privately lent him. To find them required some fumbling. The task would have been easier before the light was off; but he did not turn it on again.

With his shoes and coat removed, he threw himself emphatically upon the sofa. Several sighs, almost vulgarly hearty, testified to the conclusion that he was eager to exchange the cares of waking life for sleep's comfortable oblivion. The sighs were accompanied by a prolonged settling-down motion, which made the springs of the sofa groan audibly. A few minutes later, he began to snore. Ten more minutes passed, or thereabouts. The snoring grew gentler; his heavy breathing toned down so as to be no longer noticeable. Then, with extreme care not to make a sound, he sat up, keenly awake, having advertised to any possible listener that he was sound asleep.

He remained sitting for some time on the sofa's edge, listening closely. Outside, the night was growing more boisterous. Though the cricket chorus at the side of the house continued, augmented by additional talent from the front lawn, the wind was beginning to overrule both parties. In the shrubbery it seemed especially active. It growled menacingly among the lower growth, probably made vocal through cracks in the foundation. It slapped the floor of the porch with twigs. It even employed one of the longer tentacles as its instrument to reach entirely across the porch and tap one of the dark library windows. That, at least, was how Daunt explained the tapping to himself. It made him nervous.

For another reason, too, the wind annoyed him: it was likely to stifle some sound from within the house; some sound which it would be particularly important for him to hear. He held his breath and listened intently for anything of the sort. There seemed nothing. Except for the ticking, sharp or sedate, of the several clocks posted throughout the lower rooms, the house was silent. With this fact made sure beyond reasonable doubt, the clergyman rose and started toward the front stair-way, which ascended from a little hall between library and living-room.

Half-way up the stairs, which he was climbing by touch without using the flashlight, he stopped and again listened. Nothing was to be heard. The General and his one servant probably were asleep. So he continued to the top, and there paused once more, to make sure which was the room he meant to examine first.

It was the second from the head of the stairs: Natalie Pend-ergast's room.

Daunt grunted with satisfaction to note that the door of this room was ajar. Had it been locked, and no key within reach, that simple obstacle would have blocked his investigation quite effectually. Though Stubbs, his manservant, having been a burglar in his younger days, probably could have opened a door without the formality of unlocking it, the clergyman did not count breaking and entering among his own rather varied accomplishments. He delayed a few seconds before pushing open the door, to consider that defect in his preparation for a career, and to note mentally that a few confidential lessons from Stubbs might not come amiss.

He did not use the flashlight. It seemed safer, on the whole, to slip into the room past the partly opened door, and make sure in the darkness that no one occupied the bed. This was quickly done. Like most stout men, the clergyman was light on his feet, and even a shallow sleeper, had there been any, would not have been aroused by his careful approach. But the bed was vacant. Daunt passed his hand across it, to confirm the opinion of his eyes, and felt free to slip on the pocket light.

He directed the beam dancingly about the room, like an army of will-o'-the-wisps, and swiftly registered the impression of a neat and comfortable apartment, pleasantly feminine in its touches, and furnished in excellent taste.

He peered hopefully into the large closet which, to Miss Pendergast, probably was one of the apartment's chief advantages. A few pieces, chiefly lingerie, were here. He snapped off the flashlight and slipped back into the hall.

The General's room adjoined his daughter's. Daunt avoided that. But he pushed open the door of the opposite room, and continued his search. Large and airy, this room must have been distinctly cheerful on sunny woodland days. It possessed a spacious closet, too; but what he sought was not there.

Several other apartments were examined, hastily but thoroughly, as also a large hall closet. The clergyman hesitated before the door which had been pointed out to him as the servant's, and at length decided not to enter. He had no personal scruples on the subject; but if the girl should happen to awaken and scream, beyond doubt the situation would become compromising. Even in late middle life, a wealthy bachelor must not let professional zeal fog his discretion. He saw nothing to gain by the examination of that room, anyway.

He had gone thoroughly through the sleeping quarters, also into every closet, upstairs and down. There remained the General's bedroom, where the old gentleman probably was asleep. This was a more ticklish job. As he stood before the door, Daunt weighed the issues carefully. Age sleeps lightly. Without such an examination, however, his data would be incomplete.

Very gently he turned the handle, then applied a gradual pressure. The door remained firm. It was locked on the inside.

For a little while, the Reverend McGregor Daunt, thinker, stood in the thick darkness of the hallway, baffled by a locked door. He reflected that for Stubbs the situation would have been easy. Presumably his own brains were of better quality than Stubbs'. Why could he not solve this very minor problem?

Thus goaded, his mind put forth an idea. It was simple. A lesser mind would have had it at the start. He merely returned to the last room examined, and removed the key from the lock of that door. Confronting the General's quarters again, he carefully thrust in the key.

Strange what foibles may lurk in the best brain—even the brain of a McGregor Daunt! As the key encountered a slight resistance, which yielded to the clergyman's pressure, he suddenly glimpsed the meaning of that resistance, and the danger of discovery it put him in. But the glimpse came too late. Even as he drew his own key back, the one on the other side, which he had thoughtlessly forced out, fell with a clatter.

At that, Daunt's mental processes resumed their wonted speed. He glided swiftly in the darkness to the head of the stairs, descended a few steps, and waited.

There was no sound from the General's room; no sound in the house except the staccato voices of the clocks. When this silence persisted, the clergyman returned, as quietly as he had left it, to his host's door, ascertained that the key he had tried did indeed fit the lock, and very carefully opened the door.

His precautions upon entering this room were even greater than they had been elsewhere. He wished to search the apartment—particularly its clothes-closet—but he did not wish to arouse the General. An awakening would involve embarrassing explanations. Ordinarily, one does not prowl in the room of one's host after the latter has retired. Daunt did not even look directly at the old man on the bed. Sometimes the magnetic power of the eye, unaided, will awaken a sleeper. There was enough dim light in the room from the windy night outside to enable him to avoid objects of furniture and find his way to the closet.

Here again a door had to be noiselessly opened. He achieved that feat, and directed a carefully guarded beam from his light around the closet's interior. This was the last stronghold. Unless he found what he sought here, but one conclusion was possible. His hand worked swiftly but thoroughly among the various articles of clothes. In a moment, he snapped off the light. Nothing was hanging there but the General's apparel.

He returned as he had come to the door of the room. There something prompted him to glance back at the sleeper. The bed was in deep shadow, but the old man, with his white hair and face, lay distinct, even against the snowy sheets. Daunt listened for his breathing. The clergyman's training as a doctor, before he had entered the ministry, persisted in such things as this. He listened; then, with sudden apprehension, stepped to the side of the bed and turned on the flashlight.

He had not been mistaken: General Pendergast was dead.

5

ON HIS WAY back downstairs Daunt no longer relied on the flashlight. He turned on the chandeliers, until the big house was bright. In the presence of death, even a philosopher prefers light to darkness.

There was a telephone in the library. With the usual difficulties attendant upon a suburban exchange—difficulties which somewhat sharpened his never-too-tolerant temper—he secured the operator's attention; and, after a much longer delay, he got through to Kerns. That genial representative of the law, rudely aroused from his sleep, at first could not grasp the full force of what he was told.

"Dead?" he repeated, vaguely. "Who killed him?"

"I did," the clergyman declared, calmly.

Whether literally true or not, this statement was dynamic in bringing Kerns suddenly to a condition of wakefulness.

"Good Lord, Reverend!" was his astounded rejoinder; but Daunt inquired, evenly:

"Have the accountants begun the audit of Pendergast's company?"

"They'll begin in the morning. I got Robertson at his club, and he worked fast."

Daunt glanced at the substantial grandfather's clock in a corner of the library.

"It is only a little after twelve. They are wasting eight or nine hours," he said. "Get Robertson again. Have them start tonight, with a full force of men, and run day and night shifts. Send the police and the coroner out here when you can do so conveniently, but attend to the audit first. And, Kerns—"

"Yes, Reverend?" responded the detective's puzzled voice.

"Though I should like to await the accountant's findings, a few hours may mean everything. This is one of the instances where a long shot is justified. You will do well, I think, to start the police at once after Miss Pendergast."

Kerns' amazement came almost palpably over the wire.

"I don't get that, Reverend. Darned if I do!"

But the clergyman disregarded his friend's evident state of shock. He went on, thoughtfully:

"I can give you one or two leads which may be of value. Miss Pendergast is short, rather stout, and sallow of complexion. Send out here for her photograph when you have opportunity. She probably has with her a large orange Angora cat."

The detective whistled.

"You don't mean the cat that disappeared, Reverend?"

"Don't ask what I mean," Daunt admonished him. "Take the facts and use them. You will look for the lady—" He hesitated.

"Yes," came over the wire, eagerly.

"Look for her preferably in some country whose extradition treaties with the United States do not cover embezzlement. That will be another lead, in case you fail to pick up her trail at the seaboard."

The detective sighed, so heartily that even the telephone conveyed it.

"All right, Reverend. All right! We'll do exactly as you say. We always do, whether we can see through it or not. Maybe I shan't rout out the coroner before morning, as long as you think it's all right. He likes his sleep. When you get around to explaining how you worked this all out, I'll be sitting at your feet!"

With the telephone call accomplished and half the night still before him, the clergyman indulged in a little diversion which, though not strictly necessary to the case, still seemed to have possibilities. He unlocked the massive front door, and proceeded to make a flashlight tour of the shrubbery.

Now that a dead man was in the house, encompassed by the dark and luxuriant vegetation, the bushes seemed more sinister than ever. Daunt was not nervous, but he was highly imaginative. He recalled vividly all the details of the grim tradition connected with the shrubbery. Whatever fancies he had were not permitted to hamper his examination of the curious growth. He poked his flashlight calmly enough into the various holes and tortuous tunnels. But he knew himself to be unnecessarily alert. It was almost as if an inner part of his mind, more in tune with the powers of darkness than his normal self, continued to be aware of some reason why the shrubbery was not safe. He ignored these dim apprehensions, and proceeded slowly on his rounds until he had completed the circumference of the house. Nevertheless, he experienced an odd sense of relief when he was once more within the walls of the library; even though a dead man, and a sleeping girl unaware of the dead man, shared the ancient mansion with him.

There was no further need for his remaining awake, nor even a further excuse. So he went slowly through the lower rooms and turned off all the lights, ending with the lamp in the library. Then he stretched out on the blanketed sofa, and composed himself at last for sleep.

But the lights in the upper hall remained shining brightly.

6

TWICE IN THE succeeding three days the telephone of the hunting lodge, where the Reverend McGregor Daunt thought but did not hunt, injected the excited voice of Detective Kerns into the quiet of that peaceful refuge. The first call Daunt received with interest. It apprised him of the arrest in Paris, France, of Miss Natalie Pendergast. Having delivered his information, Kerns proffered a request; but the clergyman denied it, flatly.

"I am not yet ready to talk to you, Kerns," he declared, with cold finality.

The second call might have been dubbed a request, too, though it was more of an entreaty.

"We can't hold her much longer, Reverend," the detective expostulated. "She's playing the innocent dodge, and Paris is simply burning up the cable. What charge can we place against her?"

"Embezzlement—or receiving stolen property," his friend returned, calmly.

"Embezzlement of what?"

"I cannot say."

Though the detective's voice was fairly tearful, this was all the imperturbable clergyman would vouchsafe. But Daunt was not so well satisfied with the situation as his telephonic answers seemed to indicate. He paced the thick rug of his library much more than was customary with him. He opened books, read a few pages, and sighingly replaced them. He even took a walk through the woods to the Pendergast place, and surveyed it thoughtfully from the edge of the trees; but he did not approach nearer. Viewing the scene of his deductions seemed to fortify his patience, for he was much calmer on his return. He went so far as to smile grimly when the third day passed and the phone did not ring again.

The call which he knew in his heart was inevitable came on the morning of the fourth day. Kerns' voice was different in its very first tones. It conveyed not excitement only, but jubilant admiration.

"You've scored, Reverend! Guess what the accountants have found?"

"They have found a shortage," answered the clergyman, with conviction.

"It's a shortage, all right. Three hundred thousand, and so cleverly covered up that they didn't even suspect it till this morning. It was in the issue of bonds. Pendergast had duplicate sets made by the original engravers, who never suspected a thing, and—"

Daunt interrupted.

"I have no interest in the details. I am not an accountant. Do you care to check my reasoning through?"

Kerns did. He made the assurance so emphatic that even the icy clergyman showed a grain of appreciation.

"Thank you, Kerns. Drop in at the lodge, and we will walk over to the Pendergast place together. I can explain best on the ground."

Kerns was at the lodge within an hour. Knowing his friend's dislike for more than a slight flavor of complimentary adjectives, he was sparing with his remarks; and Daunt, for his part, seemed inclined to marshal his thoughts in silence. But when their brisk walk had taken them through the woods, and they were approaching the mansion itself, the clergyman spoke.

"Have you ever reflected, Kerns, on the impotence of spirits? So far as our knowledge goes, the mind without the body is quite destitute of power. Virtually all demonstrations of the supernatural rely upon physical instruments—the body of the medium, for example."

The detective looked at his friend in perplexed amazement.

"Do you mean to tell me this thing was supernatural, Reverend?" he demanded.

"I was speaking in parables. I am the spirit, Kerns; yourself and the police force—including the Paris police—are the body. No matter how keenly I might have reasoned, without the physical instrument I should have been helpless. You may tell them from me that their work has been clever. Did they find my hint as to the extradition treaties of value?"

"I don't think they used that, Reverend. They didn't need to. What you told us about the cat was plenty. A woman carrying a big orange cat with her on a steamer—even if she has it in a grip—is pretty easy meat for the police."

The clergyman nodded appreciatively.

"I suppose so. There is far too much of a tendency to belittle the police. They perform, purely as a matter of routine, miracles of efficiency which would baffle the most advanced theorist. Here we are at the shrubbery, Kerns—the starting-point of my investigation. You recall that evening we sat on the porch with Mr. Pendergast?"

"That's one night I'm not likely to forget, Reverend," the detective declared emphatically. "I don't mind saying that he had the shivers playing tag up and down my back."

Daunt mounted the steps and stopped just above the hole in the shrubbery, which was beside them. Using his cane for a probe, he began poking into the hole.

"Come here, Kerns," he directed, with a curious smile. "The sun is shining into this hole. You will observe the little green filaments across the opening, within a foot of the top. They are practically undisturbed. The few that do not stretch across, I have just broken, myself. Do you know, Kerns, what I should have done had I been in Pendergast's place? I should have broken all of those filaments. Yes, I am sure that I should not have overlooked that point."

The detective peered into the hole with an expression of deep perplexity on his face. Before he had time to reply, his friend went on, airily:

"That was one of the two major slips which he made. The other was more important—much more important. He was so thoughtless as to mention in the same breath the bond issue, and the fact that this mystery of his had postponed the audit. He supplied a motive, Kerns. Have you a key?"

"I have, Reverend."

"I suppose the body has been disposed of?"

"The coroner has removed it to a vault."

As Kerns was fitting the key to the lock, his friend suddenly shot a question at him.

"No doubt you have been investigating Pendergast. Did he play the market?"

Kerns straightened, with a sharp intake of breath.

"How in thunder did you know that, Reverend? He not only played it, but he was in bad. That's where part of the money went. The girl had put the rest into a Paris bank."

The clergyman smiled with smug satisfaction.

"I have seldom seen a more complete case. We have not merely the physical crime itself, but the very psychology of crime. First, the comparatively small peculation, to cover a stock market debt; after that deeper thievery. The father and the daughter were very closely thrown together. Beyond a doubt, they were in each other's confidence. When one fell, both fell. You cannot conceive a character so odd, Kerns, but that somewhere, among the infinite variety of mankind, is a living individual to fit your conception. Here was an old man whose career, to a certain point, had been honorable and brilliant. And then it twisted into an exceedingly strange and crooked bypath. Was it heredity asserting itself—perhaps from that sinister figure he called the 'Cat Mocker'?"

"Did such a man really exist Reverend?" the detective inquired.

"I believe so. The legend is not altogether new to me. It has a basis in fact."

They had entered the silent house. Daunt broke off suddenly, and, going to the mantel picked up the little silver bell. He tinkled it to the detective's amazement, as he continued into the library. There he opened the windows, threw back the shutters and drew himself up a chair.

"I can recommend the sofa, Kerns," he remarked lightly. "It is still covered with my blankets. This bell"—he tinkled it again— "is in the nature of a confirmation. It represents one of those odd slips which you, as a detective, have often noticed. The criminal is painstaking and thorough in all things but one— and that one damns him. You must bear in mind, Kerns, that Miss Pendergast probably left at least a week before the date which the General gave for her disappearance. She insisted on taking the cat along—a woman's fancy. At the last minute, she must have removed the bell, and carelessly thrown it on the mantel. No one noticed. But my finding of it went far to tear down the General's story. If you wish another item of interest, Kerns, may I suggest that you go upstairs to Miss Pendergast's room, which is the one directly above this, and look into her clothes-closet? Report your results to me. I feel in the humor to give you an object-lesson."

The detective good-naturedly shrugged his shoulders, and started on the quest.

"Well?" Daunt prompted sharply, on Kerns' return.

"I found some lingerie, Reverend, and a pair of shoes. Want me to name the articles?"

"What you have found has no bearing on the matter," declared the clergyman, rather hastily. "I am interested in what you failed to find; what I, also, failed to find, in a careful search of the entire house. The lady dressed expensively, Kerns. Even granting that she may have given away her cast-off clothes, she would have at least one cloak in the house, and I should say that she must have possessed a traveling bag. Yet I found neither. Can it be that when the hidden monster in the shrubbery dragged her down, she took along her cloak and bag?"

The detective returned Daunt's quizzical smile with a puzzled grin.

"It seems pretty positive, Reverend."

"Not positive, but evidential. The small items all point in one direction—"

"Look here, Reverend." Kerns sat heavily upon the sofa, with the air of a man determined to clear his mind of all lingering doubts. "Was Pendergast's story a lie, from start to finish?"

If he expected a downright answer he was to be disappointed; for Daunt slowly and smilingly shook his head.

"You are discourteous, Kerns. The word is too ugly. Call the story rather a work of art, evolved by a man who, having lived all his life in the midst of this shrubbery, knew the depressing and fantastic influence of the place. The same tale, told elsewhere, would have been absurd on its face. Yet, when he told it here, he made you believe it."

"I guess he did," the detective admitted, ruefully.

"He was wise enough to perceive the advantage the place gave him; and cunning enough to take the tradition, which he knew we could check up, and merely bring it down to date to serve his purpose. It was fine work, Kerns. I felt that his acting did not quite ring true, yet it was excellently conceived. He needed to gain time. That was his sole object. Time for his daughter to lose herself in Europe before the audit took place. But for these few little oversights, he might have won."

"What I don't see is where he was getting off," objected Kerns. "He seems to have held the bag."

"I believe he contemplated that. Though his daughter probably expected him to join her, he was willing to sacrifice himself to gain liberty and financial independence for her. He was a desperate man, I think, since he was risking all, and was prepared to kill me, if necessary. I used every precaution, that one night I was in this house. What was the coroner's verdict, Kerns?"

"Heart disease, Reverend. I knew you didn't mean it when you said you'd killed him."

They had reached the edge of the woods, when Daunt stopped and looked back.

"A strange setting for a strange drama!" he remarked, thoughtfully. "I did kill him, Kerns."

"The dickens you did, Reverend!" Kerns returned, grinning. "The coroner—"

Daunt smiled.

"The coroner was not with me, that night. When I tried a key in the lock of the General's room, his own key fell with a clatter to the floor. I think it wakened him; and I think the shock finished what the excitement of my mere presence was almost enough to have brought about. For when I found him he was still warm!"

The Problem of the Uncomfortable Buddha

Mr. Suter tells us that his wife has been insisting that Stubbs, Daunt's efficient but strong-armed servant, be given a more prominent part in the stories about our clergyman-detective; and, also, that his secretary has suggested that a pretty girl or two be included in one of the tales. The following McGregor Daunt story complies with both demands, and it is dedicated with brotherly sympathy to all married men and all employers of secretaries.

1

———

TO WHILE AWAY a week he was spending in the city, in connection with his congregation's annual meeting, the Reverend McGregor Daunt was researching into Chinese ideographs. Lack of books on the subject hampered him at the start—clerks in local book-stores merely stared and shook their heads when he proffered his wants; but three days had brought a change. There had been time for parcel post response to the telegrams he had sent to New York. That morning had seen ten shipments arrive, by virtue of which he sat at his table in the city study, late in the afternoon, so hedged about with volumes that little of him would have been apparent to a visitor except the rounded dome of his intellectual head.

Not that any visitor was expected or desired. Had the Reverend McGregor been allowed three wishes just then by his fairy godmother, all three, doubtless, would have had to do with books on ideographs. None would have prayed for a visitor. Even Stubbs, who could be as unobtrusive as the bookcases themselves, had to clear his throat a number of times and knock over a chair before he could gain his master's attention to a repeated summons.

The chair turned the trick. It was solid and heavy, and it fell with a hearty crash. The reverend gentleman peered over his erudite ramparts.

"What the devil are you trying to do, Stubbs?" he demanded, warmly.

"I wasn't aiming to sock it all the way, Reverend," Stubbs

apologized. "I thought maybe if I give the chair a shove like, you would snap out of it, sir. The lady said she'd wait, but what's the use, I tells her, for if you'll see her when she gets through waiting, you're just as like to see her now."

Daunt half stood, so that his rotund face, bearing an outraged and apoplectic expression, rose like the moon from behind the books.

"The lady?" he exploded.

Stubbs explained.

"It's the blonde one, I mean, Reverend. There's two of 'em, but the one with the hayrick hair and blue eyes done the talking to me."

The clergyman completed the remaining elevation to an erect posture, and found words.

"Are you trying to tell me that two women are waiting outside?" he prompted, sharply.

"You've got the idea complete, Reverend. They're waiting to see you, and, if you'll pardon the liberty. I think I'd let 'em see me, sir, to save time."

Daunt sat down again, with the air of one who, having satisfactorily completed an item of business, passes on to the next.

"Tell them I am busy," he directed, shortly.

"I told them that, Reverend," returned Stubbs.

But the words failed to reach his master, who was sinking rapidly into the ideographs. Perceiving the situation, his faithful servant advanced to the edge of the bookish rampart, and, gazing down at the top of the clerical head, said, very distinctly:

"They said they'd wait, Reverend; leastways, the blonde one said so, sir. And she said if you wasn't ready to see them today, the other one would go out and bring in a lunch and some bedding, sir, and they'd keep on waiting till you *was* ready. That was what she said when I threatened to throw her out, you not wanting to be disturbed. Reverend. 'Throw me out,' she says, 'and it'll be a fine story for the newspapers!'"

Daunt toiled on, oblivious to the fact that anyone was trying to make conversation with him; he toiled, that is, until the last word of Stubbs' harangue was reached. That word stung him into consciousness. Not only did it do so, but it proved a stimulant to his subliminal mind, or wherever it was that Stubbs' unheeded talk had been docketed. For newspaper publicity was one of the perils of his avocation which the eccentric clergyman genuinely dreaded. Its mere mention made him alert.

"Are they reporters, Stubbs?" he demanded, apprehensively.

Stubbs shook his closely cropped head.

"Reporters don't go round with a bud wrapped up in newspaper, Reverend."

"A bud?"

"That's what they said it was—the little blonde, I mean, Reverend. It's about the size of a—a rabbit, sir, but she says it's a bud. And she says there's a mystery about it, and that's why she wants to see you, sir."

Daunt wiped from his high forehead a film of perspiration which mention of the newspapers had brought forth upon it. He sighed.

"You may as well show them in, Stubbs. It will be the easiest way to get rid of them. I hope they are not young women?"

"Young and regular stunners, Reverend," grinned Stubbs. "The Prince of Wales would be glad to dance with either of them, sir."

With the last word, he was gone, leaving no opportunity for

The UNCOMFORTABLE BUDDHA

By J. PAUL SUTER

this information to change his master's mind. Daunt sat back in his chair. His face wore the bitterly resigned expression of a Puritan culprit awaiting his turn in the stocks.

But the suspense, though severe to the reverend gentleman, was brief. Stubbs had hardly left before he returned; and his returning was accompanied by the soft swish of skirts.

Daunt rose. This was worse than he had expected. The blonde one was of the petite, rosebud kind one views incredulously on magazine covers but never really meets. The brunette was beautiful—tall, lithe, and everything that is popularly supposed to go with those qualities. They were both self-possessed. Daunt could have wished them less so. But he had no opportunity to wish, for Stubbs was introducing them—the blonde one first:

"Miss Diggs, Reverend; and Miss Marsden."

Then the clergyman found voice, and some portion of his usual manner.

"I am exceedingly busy," he declared, with dignity.

The little blonde answered. She and the other were taking chairs which had not been offered.

"Yes, isn't it awful, Mr. Daunt? I'm so busy myself I scarcely have time to run down to Tony's at noon for a hot dog and a slice of rye. I'm an artist, you know—silly little landscapes and all that sort of foolishness, but they sell. I could get rid of twice as many if I painted with my toes, too. It's a shame—don't you think—that when one has two sides to one's brain, one side can't be trained to make the toes do something useful?"

The Reverend McGregor turned gently pink. The conversation had become embarrassing. Theoretically, the proprieties never bothered him, but there was nothing theoretical about his visitor.

"I have never considered the subject," he said, stiffly, as she paused.

"Of course you haven't! What ever started me on it? I didn't trot over here to talk about my toes. I came to show you this."

She exhibited the package mentioned by Stubbs as containing a bud. Daunt had noticed it, though only casually. His conscious mind had been too actively engaged with the lady herself to look closely at what she carried. She smiled as she unwrapped the package, and explained for his benefit:

"We started out without any paper on it, at all. There never is any paper in our house, you know. But we saw a rough-looking man on the street eyeing it, so I bought a newspaper to put around it. There! I'll set it here!"

Hesitating only a moment to decide upon a suitable location, she placed upon the most solid-appearing pile of books a small marble statue of the Enlightened One, the exponent of the Threefold Way, the great Buddha.

Daunt started with unexpected pleasure. His embarrassment vanished. He forgot the ladies utterly in the presence of something of genuine interest.

"Why, this is unique!" he exclaimed, warmly. "This is a most unusual specimen! I never before saw a Buddha with that expression."

"You like it, Mr. Daunt?" the blonde inquired, demurely.

He became aware of her once more, and turned, with the enthusiasm of the connoisseur.

"I find it intensely interesting. Though it lacks the characteristic expression, I should classify it as undoubtedly Oriental."

"It came from India."

Daunt fingered the delicate stone, appreciatively. He longed to ask a question, yet dreaded to do so, for fear of receiving an unwelcome reply; however, he brought himself to the point.

"Is it for sale?" he inquired, diffidently.

"No, Mr. Daunt."

"Ah!" He could not quite cover his disappointment.

The young lady continued, with a twinkle of her crisp blue eyes.

"It is not for sale, because we brought it as a gift. It is yours, Mr. Daunt."

The clergyman glared at her. "Glare" is the word, for he felt that she had forced him into an impossible situation. He desired exceedingly to possess the image. He longed to study it, to puzzle out the meaning of that peculiar expression. But he could hardly accept the thing as a gift.

"This Buddha is valuable," he began. "It is of exquisite marble—"

He stopped, with an abrupt sensation of outraged dignity. They were giggling! Both blonde and brunette were giggling at him! But they cut their giggles short with bewildering suddenness, and became deeply penitent.

"Oh, *please* excuse us!"—It was the blonde, whose blue eyes gazed up appealingly into his. "We're *so* sorry. We didn't mean to hurt your feelings, Mr. Daunt, really. You looked so funny telling us mamma's Buddha is valuable that we had to laugh. We know how much it's worth. Of course we know. Do you think we'd give something cheap to *you?* Oh, Mr. Daunt!"

The clergyman was seldom barren of words; but that was exactly his predicament now. They had risen to go, and he had found no rejoinder. Nor was that the worst of it. For while he was still speechless, the little blonde, who had already pushed her companion into the courtyard, blew him a kiss with her tiny pink hand, and exclaimed:

"It's yours, Mr. Daunt! Yours to keep! Keep it if you can!"

He rushed to the door, but they were scurrying across the courtyard and rounding the corner of the church. They looked back at him, standing aghast in the doorway, and they both giggled.

And then he realized that he had forgotten their names, and that he had not the remotest idea who they were or where they lived.

2

HE RETURNED TO the study feeling decidedly discomposed and unsettled. The thing was outrageous. A transaction which could easily have been handled so as to observe all the business proprieties had been made impossible. He would have purchased the Buddha. A high price would have been no deterrent. But to accept it as a gift… from two young women entirely unknown to him… The only reaction to the situation he could think of was to ring for Stubbs.

"Stubbs," he began, when that efficient servant appeared. "Those women—what did they say their names were?"

Stubbs opened his mouth, and closed it. An embarrassed grin spread itself over his red face. He coughed, confusedly.

"Ain't that the perkiest thing now, Reverend? They told me their names, and I told *you* their names. And they didn't leave no cards. You wouldn't think a thing would slip off your mind that way, would you, sir? Now, if you hadn't of asked me—"

"Do you know where they live?" his master interrupted.

"No more than I know where the Pope's brother lives, Reverend."

"Have you ever seen them before?" Stubbs scratched his head, earnestly. "Maybe I have, and maybe I ain't. When you put it up to me that way, Reverend, I'm hard set to tell you. If they was in a crowd, now…."

The clergyman cut him off, sharply.

"Do you *remember* having seen them before?"

"Not any more than I remember cutting my first tooth, Reverend."

"You may go, Stubbs."

But before the serving-man had reached the door, Daunt recalled him.

"Is the dark one dumb, Stubbs?"

"Dumb, Reverend?" Stubbs looked his bewilderment.

"Can she talk? I seem to recall that she said nothing while here in the study."

Stubbs grinned.

"Like as not the little one with the robin's egg eyes and the fuzzy hair didn't give her a chance, Reverend. She can talk, all right. She was at it in the hall like a can of gasoline meeting up with a lighted match, sir. Did you ever see a female that couldn't talk, Reverend? Ain't all the deef and dummies you ever see men?"

Daunt became thoughtful. The suggestion was novel to him, and it required consideration. He dismissed Stubbs without replying.

Left alone in the study, he turned with a sort of hopeless determination to the ideographs; but fate overtook him speedily. For within a quarter of an hour, he had pushed aside a dry and fat volume on the Tree Radical to give himself up to the little marble image.

It was the expression which intrigued him. He could have ignored an ordinary Buddha, covering up the mysteries of eternity with its conventional smirk. The sweetish, ironical smile of Buddhas in Indian temples, all monotonously alike, all benignly tolerant and contemptuous of their worshipers, had never appealed to him as a subject for study. One could not get behind such a smile, to lay hold of its meaning. But the little Buddha on the pile of books did not smile so.

He lifted the image down from its printed pedestal, and set it before him on the table, where he could scrutinize the little face. At once, he found its study much more interesting than the ideographs. The countenance was fashioned like that of the conventional Buddhas. Its lips curved upward, as if to smile. The eyes were slightly crinkled in mirth. Yet, under careful scrutiny, there was no suggestion of levity. The unknown hand which had chiseled the features had been driven by the urge of genius. Handicapping its creation with the mechanics of mirth—the eyes, the curling mouth—it yet had succeeded in portraying a face of portentous evil.

On impulse, the clergyman rang again for Stubbs; and, as usual, his call was promptly answered.

"Stubbs, look at this image," his master directed. "It is an Indian idol. What effect does it produce on you?"

The manservant looked. His gaze was long and earnest. He shivered.

"It makes me uncomfortable, Reverend," he reported.

"That will do, Stubbs. I wished to know whether your mind reacted to it as mine does. It makes me uncomfortable, too."

When Stubbs was gone, Daunt rummaged in the table drawer for a magnifying glass, and meticulously went over the surface of the image. He found nothing to explain its expression; but just at the point where the squat neck merged into the base was some tiny and almost indistinguishable lettering. Under the glass, it read:

"Suraj-ud-Daula. Calcutta. 1756."

The clergyman breathed rapidly as beneath this he noted a shorter legend, in still smaller lettering. It was so infinitesimal that, though he used his best magnifying glass and manipulated the image in various lights, he could not arrive at the purport of the words. With a sigh, he postponed the task until he could procure a more powerful microscope, and turned instead to the article on Calcutta in his encyclopedia.

What he read there interested him, so that he rang for Stubbs and gave him an urgent mission to the optician's.

But the smaller legend, when finally deciphered, proved commonplace. It merely read, "E. Reilly."

The book on the radical maintained itself insistently on his table, and Daunt returned to it, at length; but his interest was not there. The Buddha's uncomfortable half-smile continued to intrude. So did the date on its base. That was one of the sinister dates of history. What had the marble image to do, the clergyman wondered, with the Black Hole of Calcutta?

He wondered throughout the afternoon and evening, mingling his surmises with what little solid work he did on the ideographs; and when finally he snapped out his study light, and walked amid the moonlight through the stone-flagged courtyard which connected study and manse, his thoughts were still with the Buddha.

The little Indian image even invaded his dreams. His sleep seemed concerned with baffled attempts to solve the mystery of that marble expression. He was undergoing a peculiarly harrowing experience as one of the doomed band in the Black Hole, when a slight sound aroused him from uneasy slumber, and he turned over to find Stubbs bringing in his breakfast.

"Slept well, Reverend?" the manservant inquired, amiably.

"No!" his master snapped.

Stubbs nodded his sympathy.

"It's been a bad night all around," he observed; "I slept well myself—I generally do; but may I ask, Reverend, did you do anything with that heathen idol—that marble bud, or whatever you call it?"

Daunt became fully awake, and propped himself up on one elbow.

"The Buddha?" he inquired. "I left it on my table in the study."

Stubbs clucked, significantly.

"I was thinking you did," he said. "Or why should anyone open your study window, Reverend—you not leaving it open yourself, I'll go bail, on a chilly evening like last night? You may have put that Chinese thing on the table, Reverend, but it ain't no more there now than the crown of England's on my head, sir. It's been took!"

3

WHEN THE REVEREND McGregor reached his study, after breakfasting rather heartily on muffins and tea, he found the window which overlooked his courtyard wide open, and the wind making free with such of his papers as had not been weighted down. Even less to his taste was a sparse vanguard of thin October snow, settled impartially on the table and on the volumes of ideographs. He grumbled a little, but made no changes until he had completed the investigation for which Stubbs had thoughtfully left the window open. The manservant had been with his master long enough to know that the first duty of him who discovers a crime is to leave things as they are.

Daunt's examination of the window told him nothing, except that he seemed to have left it unlocked—which was more than likely. There were no telltale traces in the study. The ground outside the window was too hard to show footprints. By whatever means the Buddha had disappeared, its abductor was not to be followed through any clue he had left behind.

Daunt shut the window and rang for Stubbs to dust off the snow. Then, with a little shiver—for the struggling fire in the grate, even though helped by a strictly modern radiator, could not at once overcome its handicap—he set to work on the ideographs.

He was not to occupy himself with them for long. He had barely found his place in a bulky volume and begun the labor of note-taking, when Stubbs re-entered.

"She's alone, this time, Reverend. It's the blonde one," the manservant announced, when he had caught his master's eye.

Daunt started; which was sufficient encouragement for Stubbs to essay another item of information.

"She's got something in paper under her arm that she carries like she didn't want to drop it, Reverend. It looks to me like another one of them heathen buds, sir."

The clergyman considered. Curiosity overcame his natural dislike for entertaining female visitors. He nodded to Stubbs.

The blonde young lady seemed to have a way of acting quickly and of inspiring speed in others. Daunt wondered how she could have put it into the slow-moving Stubbs. For that worthy reappeared almost immediately, redfaced and blowing, and she was behind him.

She was not at all the volcanic personality of the day before. Her blue eyes appealed, rather than flashed. She smiled brightly, but a sort of wistful hope tinged the brightness, and she bit her lip diffidently.

"I know just what you think of me, Mr. Daunt."—She had the first word. She was herself to that extent, at least.—"You think I'm forward and bold, and—and—an impudent little hussy. You needn't deny it!"

"I do not deny it," the clergyman retorted, stiffly.

She started; and suddenly the appeal vanished from her eyes, and she laughed. There was nothing forced about the laugh. It was musical, and not at all unladylike—even Daunt admitted that to himself; but it tinkled on as irresistibly as a brook.

"Now I shall have to beg your pardon twice," she gasped. "For kissing my hand to you yesterday, and for laughing at you today! I'm truly sorry, Mr. Daunt, I am, indeed! But you're so funny!"

She laughed again; and the reverend gentleman felt that he should be mightily offended. Yet, somehow, he was not.

"You're funny because you're brilliant, and there's so much power in you, and you know so much more than other people; and you're not bad-looking, either—for a clergyman—" She gave him an appraising glance, which was manifestly impersonal. "And yet you're afraid of women!"

"Did you come here to discuss me?" Daunt demanded.

She shook her head soberly, though a wicked tremble still played about her mouth.

"I came to apologize, Mr. Daunt— though I suppose that's no use, now. I never mean to be rude, you know. It's the artistic temperament, or something. And I came to return this."

She indicated the package, which she had laid on the table. The clergyman glanced toward it, inquiringly.

"It's the same Buddha," she confirmed.

"You broke in last night and took it back?" he demanded, incredulously.

"I did not, Mr. Daunt. I haven't the least idea how it was returned to us. Shall I sit down and tell you all I know about it? I came for that purpose, too."

The reverend gentleman's mind was quick enough in most directions, but she had been moving too fast for him along unfamiliar paths. He awakened now to the fact that they were both standing, and made haste to remedy the oversight.

"Is there something queer about the Buddha?" she suggested, breathlessly, as soon as they were seated. "Have you noticed it? Something that the mere chiseling of the features can't account for?"

Daunt hesitated a moment, then answered her. This young

person's own utter frankness demanded the same quality in him.

"I have noticed something of the sort," he admitted.

"You don't think it's just—just in the marble?" she persisted.

"I am not prepared to hazard an opinion."

She sighed.

"Oh, well! I thought maybe you would get to the bottom of it—you being a clergyman and a detective, too. Helen and I never could. You see, Mr. Daunt, we are half-sisters, and it comes down to us through our mother from our great-great-grandfather. We don't know much about history, or about anything but our specialties. We seldom even read the newspapers. Art is my line, music Helen's, you see. But we know great-grandpa had something to do with the Black Hole of Calcutta."

"Did he die in the Black Hole?" the clergyman asked, gently. He felt, suddenly, an obligation to be gentle with her; not for her own sake—her behavior deserved no consideration from him—but for the sake of her ancestry. This vivid, unstable child (she was really quite young, he was sure) seemed weighted with an inheritance of deep tragedy. Could some of the essence of that tragedy, he wondered, be lurking in the enigmatic marble which had come down to her?

She shook her head, in response to his question.

"He wasn't in the Black Hole, Mr. Daunt. He had some connection with it, and after the massacre was over, he chiseled this Buddha. He had been a promising young sculptor—very great promise, mother said—in England, but something happened, and he had to skip to India. That's really all sister and I know about the Buddha. His wife—our great-great-grandmother—brought it back to America, after his death."

"His name was Reilly?"

She nodded.

"I don't know what the other name on the Buddha—the Indian name—is. Mother never talked about that. I suppose we could have found out, but that isn't our line, you see."

The clergyman regarded her with some amazement. To his speculative mind, interested in the whole curious drama of life as it passed before him, it seemed inconceivable that anyone could ignore such a mystery as this, providentially placed in one's own household. But there were such people. He had met them. And artists and musicians were quite likely to be among the number.

"If you have had this image for years, I cannot understand your sudden increase of interest in it," he observed. "Why did you bring it to me?"

She laughed again; the same tinkling ripple of merriment which could not offend, though he felt it to be directed at his denseness.

"Of course, you are wondering about that! And here I am telling you everything about the Buddha except the one thing you really want to know! We haven't had it for years, Mr. Daunt. Dear mother died only a year ago. She left it to us with a very queer condition—that if the time came when we no longer wanted it, we should not sell it: we should give it away, throw it away, or destroy it. The time *has* come!"

"We have had it a year—and the time has come." She accompanied the repetition with a curious little twist of the mouth, and shrugged her shoulders. "I'm glad you've felt the queer atmosphere about that thing, Mr. Daunt. But for that, you wouldn't understand me, at all. Suppose you had lived with it for a full year—what would it have done to *you*, I wonder? It has driven me nearly crazy! And Helen is ill in bed at this minute because of the way it came back last night."

"How did it come back?" the clergyman interrupted, with interest.

"In a minute, Mr. Daunt. Don't ask me that yet. I must tell you everything—and there's something to tell before we come to last night. And yet...."

She stopped, and her vivacious face became drawn and tragic. "The really important part of the story is a little beyond me. I can't tell it. You will simply have to take my word that there's something devilish about the Buddha. Sister and I have studied the face for hours, trying to make out what it is. I've been especially interested, of course. Any artist would be. But the most I can say is that there is a fiendish cruelty in the expression—an almost human cruelty—which grows on you if you have to live with the thing, until it seems a personality by itself, that stalks about the house at night. Why, Mr. Daunt...." She laughed, nervously. "I've come into our sitting room in the dark, when I couldn't see the image at all, and I've felt that expression. Do you understand me?"

He nodded, gravely.

"Such an experience is psychological—possibly psychical. It is rare, but not unknown."

She brightened, and a little of her natural self flitted across the mobile face.

"I'm glad you said that. I don't feel nearly so foolish now in owning up that Helen and I finally determined to get rid of the Buddha. We argued about it for quite a while. Of course, we never even considered selling it. But whom should we give it to? Not a single one of our friends wanted the thing—not one! I suggested to Helen that we throw it into the river, but she thought that would be sinful—because it really is valuable, you know. Do you know what we did, at last?" She giggled at the recollection. "We took it to the city dump, there among all the old tin cans and things, and rolled it down the hill. We picked out a nice, clean place. When it landed in a little pile of soft, brown dirt, I kissed my hand to it, and we trotted over to De Klynn's to celebrate. We thought we were rid of it. Just think—we thought we were rid of it!"

This time, his medical instincts rose against her laugh. It sounded hysterical. He raised a hand in warning, but she pulled herself together at once, and continued, slowly:

"We went to bed as usual that night, and locked the doors. I am sure they were locked, because after we had retired, Helen called from her room to ask about them, and I got up again to make certain. The doors were locked, and the Buddha was on the dump; yet in the morning, there was the Buddha in its usual place on the mantel. It was rather dirty, but quite all right, otherwise. Helen woke first, and saw it there. Her screams roused me. You're not laughing at me?" she demanded, abruptly.

"On the contrary, I am deeply interested," the clergyman assured her.

"I shouldn't blame you if you did laugh. It seems so ridiculous, doesn't it? But the whole thing was quite awful. Helen went into hysterics, and we both swore to have that Buddha out before the day was over. I suggested another plan. It seemed splendid to me!"

She sighed; but a mischievous smile came to wipe away her gloom.

"What we did, Mr. Daunt, was to take the Buddha to a second-hand dealer. And when we offered it to him, he thought we'd stolen it! The more we pleaded, the surer he was. We actually had to give him the telephone number of the conservatory where Helen teaches, so he could call up and inquire about us. In the end, he put it on his shelf, but he handled it like a hot potato, and I believe he was no more astonished than we were at what happened afterward."

The clergyman looked his inquiry, and she nodded.

"Yes, Mr. Daunt. Locked doors and windows again—we're both careful about such things, and we were especially so that night. The junk dealer did say his upstairs windows were unlocked, but no one could have climbed to them from the street. Yet there was the Buddha in the morning, on our mantel!"

"Which morning was this?"

"Yesterday morning."

"You decided then to come to me?"

"It was my idea again. By that time Helen simply had cold feet. I think she is even more anxious than I to see the last of the Buddha, but she seems afraid to do anything about it. She agreed to come here with me, on the condition that I shouldn't expect her to say a word to you. And she *didn't* say a word. You may have noticed that. I thought it would be a better test just to give you the image and say nothing about its history. Then when we were here, and you were so embarrassed, I couldn't help having a little fun at your expense. I didn't mean any disrespect, really."

Daunt hastened to divert her conversation into a less painful channel.

"You found the Buddha on your mantel, this morning?"

She nodded.

"This time it was a little too much for Helen. It put her to bed. The doors and windows were locked, as usual."

"Was your sister the first to see it, as on the previous morning?"

"I was the first, Mr. Daunt. I saw it there on the mantel, and I must have screamed, for Helen came running in. She fainted. The doctor told me to keep her in bed today, but I knew she wouldn't be comfortable with that awful thing in the house. Neither of us would. So I brought it back to you."

"Do you intend to return directly home from here?" he asked.

"Oh, yes, Mr. Daunt. I have been gone too long now."

"Stubbs and I will accompany you."

He rang for that able functionary; and the response was swift. The door opened and Stubbs entered, accompanied by Chief of Detectives Kerns.

Daunt usually was glad to welcome the tall and smiling police officer. Some of the clergyman's most diverting problems had come to him through Kerns. Though a little startled by the unexpected intrusion, he rose with outstretched hand. Kerns grasped the hand, apologetically.

"Didn't look for me, eh, Reverend? I might at least have had Stubbs announce me. Fact is, I thought you wouldn't be very long, so I just waited in the hall; but when you rang, I came along with Stubbs. I'm in a hurry, but I couldn't pass without telling you the latest. It strikes rather near home. What do you say to a dead man in your own yard?"

Stubbs' departing shoulders, and the angle at which he himself had entered had prevented the detective from seeing Daunt's visitor. But now she rose excitedly, with rounded eyes and a sharp intake of breath which he could not fail to hear.

He turned, and bowed.

"I beg your pardon! I supposed the lady had gone out through the yard."

"It's quite all right, really." She smiled, with forced nonchalance. "Won't you please go on, Mr. Kerns?—if you don't mind me? They'll tell about the murdered man in tonight's paper, I suppose, but it's so much more thrilling to hear of it at first hand!"

"Murdered? I did not say 'murdered!'"

The detective regarded her with sudden sharp interest; but she shrugged her shoulders and pouted up into his face.

"Didn't you? I must have taken that for granted, since you came in to tell Mr. Daunt. Oh, well! I suppose it's too much to expect that I should be in at a murder mystery!"

Daunt now recollected the amenities, and made a move to introduce the detective; but fortunately—since the lady's name still escaped him—that proved unnecessary.

"I know Detective Kerns, Mr. Daunt. He was very lovely to me when I made some police studies a year ago for a magazine. Do go on, Mr. Kerns, and tell about the murdered—I mean the dead man."

"He may have been murdered," Kerns observed, gravely. "That is rather probable, in fact. He was lying with his head crushed, at the street end of the walk."

"The narrow walk at the side of the church?" Daunt inquired, with an anxious note.

Kerns nodded, carelessly.

"Don't attach too much importance to the thing, Reverend. It was Red Brannigan, the yegg—not a month out of the pen. Very likely, one of his pals knocked him off, and it's a safe bet he had it coming. But for the fact that it happened where it did, I wouldn't even have mentioned it to you."

"Now that you *have* mentioned it, what do you wish of me?" the clergyman demanded.

"Not a thing—unless you happen to have some information."

"I have not."

"Then that's that, and I'll be off—if you will excuse my hurry. It was probably just a fight between yeggs. If anything interesting should happen to turn up on it, I'll let you know. Goodbye, Reverend. Goodbye, Miss Diggs."

The little blonde had been standing with strained face, listening. As soon as the door had closed behind Kerns, she sank into her chair, and, to Daunt's annoyance, began to cry. He stared at her with some indignation; but in a moment the weeping fit was over, and she smiled up at him.

"I'm ever so sorry," she apologized. "You can't imagine how I hate myself for breaking down! You see, it was a shock, Mr. Daunt. Oh, yes, it was a shock, all right!"

She broke into a thin, falsetto laugh, which instantly aroused his apprehensions.

"Stop it!" he commanded, sharply.

"I will. I'm not going into hysterics." Her bosom rose and fell, and her hands clenched spasmodically, but she was silent. When she looked up at him, it was with an enigmatic smile.

"Unwrap the Buddha, please, Mr. Daunt. It is just as it was when I took it from the mantel. You will find the bottom of it covered with blood!"

4

FOLK OF NORMAL dispositions and habits have been known to live in New York for years without ever meeting their next-door neighbors; and possibly the same situation occurs in other large cities. The Reverend McGregor Daunt discovered that his clients, the blonde Miss Diggs and the brunette Miss Marsden, had carried on the offices of life for more than a twelvemonth within two short blocks of his manse; and he had known far less of them than of certain Chinese emperors prominent in connection with the ideographs.

The house to which the lady visitor conducted him was really a suite in a terrace, but it extended down a side street, as a projection from the main structure, with which its only link was a sort of Siamese twin bond in the extreme rear of the suite. Daunt had brought Stubbs along for a purpose in addition to the important one of chaperonage. Stubbs' career as a burglar of note in his younger days peculiarly fitted him for such investigations as the present, where the problem of locked doors and windows was under discussion. Others might theorize on that subject; he could speak with authority.

"You would like to talk with Helen, I suppose?" Daunt's fair client suggested, at the front door of the suite; but the clergyman shook his head.

"Not for the present. I merely wish to see the mantel, and to have Stubbs examine the doors and windows. We can take the windows in your sister's room for granted. You assure me they were locked in the same manner as the others?"

"They were, Mr. Daunt."

The mantel—of the over-elaborate apartment house variety—was quickly examined. The Buddha had been its only ornament. With that gone, it stretched baldly for its inadequate length, with no mark of distinction save a sinister ring of red, where the image had been. Daunt inspected this imprint under a pocket microscope, but its nature was apparent without that. Before he had finished, Stubbs returned.

"Well, Stubbs?" his master prompted.

"I seen 'em all, Reverend, upstairs and down. The blonde one fixed it so I could go into the other one's room, and look them windows over, too. They're as tight as a Scotchman's pocketbook. It's the kind of lock you can't jimmy from the outside, either."

"The doors?"

"Two doors, Reverend—front, and one at the side of the kitchen. Did the blonde one tell you they were locked, sir?"

Daunt nodded.

"Well, she didn't tell you half. There's bolts on the inside, as well as the locks, and she says they always shoot the bolts. She never thought of mentioning that to you, sir. Kind of took it for granted, I guess."

"In your judgment, Stubbs, has anyone broken into this house lately?" the clergyman demanded.

"No more than they've broke into the Bank of England, Reverend. Santa Claus hisself couldn't have slithered down the chimney. It's too narrow."

Miss Diggs had remained considerately in the dining-room, but by raising his voice slightly Daunt was able to reach her.

"I will keep the Buddha at the study for further investigation," he announced. "And I will talk with your sister tomorrow.

You might hand Stubbs the address of the second-hand shop. Though the main features of this problem are entirely clear, I should like to devote some time to the details."

His manner precluded the questions which evidently bubbled to her lips. Nor was he more communicative with Stubbs. He remained in the rear seat of his sedan until the second-hand store was reached, and then slowly got out.

He did not enter the place, but gazed thoughtfully at it from the front, walking past on the opposite side of the street. Crossing the street at length, he darted into a narrow passageway between the dingy frame building and its nearest neighbor, and emerged into the backyard of the store. He stopped beneath a fire-escape, and, jumping tentatively for its lowest rung, fell short by about a foot; which seemed to satisfy him, for he returned to the street and re-entered the sedan.

As they moved off, Stubbs divorced one hand from the steering wheel long enough to turn and wave solemnly toward the second-hand store. His master observed the action.

"Why was that, Stubbs?" he demanded.

The manservant permitted himself a cheerful wink.

"Elderly party, Reverend," he explained. "Consumed with curiosity, as you might say. Old Charles the First wasn't any more interested when the hangman came a-twirling the axe than the old party was in you, sir. Followed you around, he did, inside the store. Front windows, side windows, and, I'll lay my head, rear ones, too—though I didn't go back there. When you toddled out to the car, he came to the front door, and give his eyes a real treat. So I waved to him, friendly like, sir."

The clergyman nodded, absently. His mind was back with the ideographs.

With them—in particular with what a learned Chinese emperor had said about them in the fourth century, B.C.—he remained throughout what was left of the day, and through the evening, after dinner. As he worked, the Buddha eyed him, with its uncomfortable smile. He stopped occasionally, to return its stare. There were intervals when he was fairly obliged to lay the ideographs aside, and yield to the image's disquieting influence. But he did not cover the thing from view, nor did he even trouble to examine the bloodstains under a microscope. He was merely marking time until conditions were propitious.

At about eleven in the evening, he shut smartly a broad, sheepskin volume which had been occupying him, and laid his notes precisely in the table drawer. The Buddha was somewhat secluded, in a little niche between two tall piles of books. He chose another location for it—a spot to the left of the taller pile, where it would be visible from the courtyard window. With the electric light out, however, much of this visibility would be gone. So he heaped coal upon the grate fire until the responding flames promised adequate light from that source— their own robust glare, and a burning glow from the ruddy coals when that should have vanished. He ended by unlocking the courtyard window, and ringing for Stubbs.

"I expect to spend at least part of the night in the study, Stubbs," he informed that worthy. "You may retire."

"Shall I put on the light in the yard, Reverend?" the manservant inquired, diffidently. "If you're looking for a caller, it may save him banging his toes agin the corner of the church. A church is a cold, hard place when you run on it in the dark, sir."

The suggestion, thus thoughtfully proffered, was not accepted.

"The visitor whom I expect would find light of no assistance," Daunt returned.

Stubbs made for the door, but halted with a start and turned aside to the window.

"This thing's unlocked again, Reverend," he observed.

"I unlocked it. If my visitor comes, that window will be the means of entrance."

Stubbs whistled.

"Is it someone to steal the heathen bud again?" he asked.

At his master's nod, his face assumed a dogged expression.

"I don't like it, Reverend! Climb into bed, and I'll nab your party for you. When it comes to the watching game, I'm smooth as butter, sir. I could give correspondence lessons to a cat at a mouse hole. Let me do it, Reverend, and your man won't know he's caught till the police sergeant signs him up on the blotter."

"I prefer to handle the matter myself, Stubbs," the clergyman returned, coldly. "You will go to bed."

"Very good, Reverend."

When his man had gone, Daunt donned hat and overcoat, switched off the electric light, and left his study by the courtyard door, locking it rather noisily. He walked briskly through the yard to the rear of the manse, and let himself in with his pass key. But he remained within only long enough to go through the house to the front door. Closing that softly behind him, he stood on the porch and looked about.

The manse was on a side street—a rather quiet and dark backwater to be so near the important thoroughfare on which the church faced. The long stone wall of the greater edifice, with its little door leading to the choir room and the church parlors, also was on this street. Having satisfied himself that the shadows were as innocent as they seemed, and that no one was likely to observe him, Daunt left the porch and walked swiftly to the little door.

In a trice, he was within the hallway leading to the church parlors, with the door locked again behind him. The soft, warm darkness of the place enveloped his mind pleasantly, tempered as it was with the feeling of ample space contributed by the great auditorium above. He was sensitive to such impressions. Even his most acid moods had been known to yield to them. He remained for a few minutes luxuriating in the large serenity of the place, and it was with a glow of unwonted benevolence that he felt his way at length into the thickly carpeted parlors.

The glow remained when he had passed through them to the little room at the farther side. From this room opened the door leading into his study.

Still benevolently inclined, he unlocked the door—very quietly. He was enjoying the experience. The visitor he expected—the thief of the Buddha—was not likely to be especially sinister. The adventure of watching afforded a welcome thrill, with no accompanying apprehension of danger.

He peered into the study. The fire was burning cheerfully. Its warm yellow painted the back of the Buddha, and exaggerated the shadows on the face; so that the inscrutable features, more sardonic and cruel than they appeared in the daylight, were just perceptible. The clergyman stood still, watching, with a kind of artistic fascination, that demoniac play of light and dark. It was all illusion, but it held him. For a space he forgot the adventure on which he was there. The space might have been longer, had he not been reminded abruptly by a pressure on the back of his head. The pressure was cold, hard, and unmistakable.

"Hold the position, please," directed a suave voice behind him. "Should you move, even slightly, my finger might slip on the trigger. That would be unfortunate, would it not, Mr. Daunt?"

5

THE CLERGYMAN DID not move, but he essayed to speak; and his throat must have produced some sort of gurgle, for the voice went on, softly:

"My finger is very sensitive. Any loud noise—such as a cry for help—will have a disastrous effect upon it."

Daunt recovered his voice.

"I have no intention of crying for help," he returned, with dignity.

"That is wise. I was sure you would see it in the proper light. I am removing the pressure from your head, but allow me to remind you that the weapon which produced it is still in readiness. May I trouble you to place your hands behind you?"

The clergyman complied in silence. His hands were seized promptly, and one crossed over the other. A few twists of cord were bound about his wrists. But suddenly his captor hesitated.

"This should be unnecessary between gentlemen," he observed. "Suppose you engage not to attack me or in any way interfere while I am in your study; and you might give me ten minutes start before sending for Stubbs or otherwise raising an alarm. Have I your word?"

"You have," Daunt replied, shortly.

His hands were unbound, and he was pushed gently toward a chair in a corner of the study.

"You will oblige me by turning the chair around and sitting with your face to the wall," his visitor suggested.

The clergyman did so. Argument on the subject seemed

unwise. But, in the act of turning the chair, he contrived, as the electric light was snapped on by his visitor, to observe that the latter was a tall, slender man, who wore a full-length domino, adjusted to hide his face completely.

"I am taking the Buddha," the tall man remarked, pleasantly. "Your pocketbook, too—will you oblige me? I will remove the currency from it, and return it to you. Your watch, also; and was I mistaken, or did I observe a ring upon your finger? I shall take pleasure in forwarding you the pawn tickets for the watch and ring, by mail."

Despite the affability of his companion, who seemed to be appraising the study as a whole lest he overlook anything valuable, Daunt was careful to obey directions. Though smooth on the surface, the voice possessed hard undertones. But questions had not been forbidden.

"Do you intend to sell the Buddha?" the clergyman asked.

The man stopped moving about.

"I do," he responded. "It could not be pawned very easily."

"You have a purchaser?"

"Not as yet."

Deliberately, the clergyman turned. It was safe, he felt, to do so. And indeed, his tall visitor, who stood regarding him thoughtfully through the slitted eyeholes of the mask, offered no objection. Daunt returned the look quizzically. Though the situation had been unpleasant, it was beginning to have distinctive features.

"Would you consider me as a purchaser?" he continued.

The man laughed.

"You are true to your reputation for originality, Mr. Daunt. This is the first burglary I ever conducted in which the victim offered to serve as a 'fence.' Am I to understand that you make me an offer?"

Daunt shook his head.

"I am not sufficiently informed as to values. If you will set a price, we may arrange the matter at once."

The man in the domino sat down in a convenient chair. He did so quite as a matter of course, as any visitor might have done. He appeared to be thinking. Suddenly, he slapped his knee.

"I'll tell you what I will do," he said, explosively. "We are playing a game, you and I. I have you checkmated. You have resigned the game. Now you wish to buy back your king. I do not know the value of this statue; neither do you. Suppose I leave it, and make some inquiries tomorrow as to values? I shall return in the daytime, and set you a price. If we agree as to that, you pay me; otherwise, I take the statue, at that time. You engage not to prosecute?"

Daunt began to incline his head, but he left the nod only half completed. His gaze passed over the expectant man in the domino, and he smiled.

"I agree to nothing," he replied. "Will you please remove your mask?"

The man started, and reached toward his hip pocket; but the clergyman went on, evenly:

"I am curious to see your face. If you care to glance toward the door which leads to the church, you will perceive that what you mistook for checkmate was merely a temporary check."

"And the Reverend is a-going to fill in the amount of that there check," Stubbs observed, stepping into the study from the church.

"You'll pardon the intrusion, Reverend," he continued. "I did go to bed, like you told me. But I couldn't rest easy. I kept a-turning and a-twisting, like a man with a flea down his back. So I thought it wouldn't do no harm, seeing I couldn't sleep, to slip through the church and make sure everything was nice and peaceful with yourself." He turned to the man in the domino. "How are you, Slippery? You're still slinging the language as pretty as ever, I notice. I seen by the paper your time and Red Branigan's was up a month ago. You ought to be able to get back now, so as not to miss the Thanksgiving feed."

With unabashed dignity, Daunt's visitor removed his mask, disclosing a smooth and sallow face, the whole effect of which was length: upper lip and chin both deeper than ordinary; the small, squeezed mouth overhung by a pendulous nose; dark, humorous eyes peeping out under the high, narrow forehead.

The man smiled and shrugged his shoulders.

"You will find my gun on my right hip, Stubbs," he directed, easily. "How long have you had me covered?"

"Since about the time you began to make yourself at home in the chair," Stubbs returned, relieving him of the revolver. "You'll excuse me for horning in this way, Reverend? I watched through the slit in the door till I thought he was starting to bother you some. I used to know Slippery Emory in the old days, when I could crack a crib with the best of 'em. He's got the smooth chatter, has Slippery, but he wouldn't hurt a fly— not if the fly had him tied hand and foot and covered with a gat."

The tall man grinned, appreciatively. The inversion of circumstances by which he had become the captive instead of the captor seemed to affect him but little. He was still at his ease.

"You will pardon my lighting up, Mr. Daunt?" He extracted a box of a popular brand from his vest pocket. "I am, I regret to confess, something of a cigarette fiend. You do not care to join me? Nor you, Stubbs?" He made a gesture of regret, and blew his first smoke ring coolly into the air. "One's opportunities for harmless enjoyment of this sort, in the government institution with which I have been connected these last few years, are not what they might be. Oh, to be sure!" He smiled, and removed the watch he was wearing. "This timepiece is yours, Mr. Daunt. A Swiss, is it not? And your ring! I put it on my finger, for safe keeping."

He leaned forward, gracefully, to return the jewelry to his clerical host. To do so, he was obliged to reach in front of Stubbs, who still had him covered. He apologized, with a little bow in Stubbs' direction, for this slight breach of etiquette; and, at that moment, he dropped the watch.

Stubbs lunged for it—just too late. The tall man lunged, also, and his fist came into sudden contact with the manservant's eye. Possibly the contact was intentional. For, in the same instant, Daunt's guest leapfrogged high in the air, and, with a dextrous kick from his descending foot, catapulted Stubbs so violently against his master as to upset them both. Immediately, he was gone, and there was a sound of rapid footsteps in the church parlors.

"Stop him, Reverend, stop him!" Stubbs exclaimed, incoherently, unconsciously stepping on his master in the haste with which he rallied to his feet.

The clergyman, breathing heavily, did not reply, but painfully struggled to an upright position on his own account. His head felt light, and rather tender where the corner of the table had prevented it from reaching the floor. His left ankle, too, seemed lame. That was the one Stubbs had stepped on.

The manservant had lumbered through the doorway into the church, in keen pursuit of the fleeing Emory. Daunt followed, more slowly. From the medley of sounds within the staid precincts of the church parlors, it seemed evident that the fugitive had lost his way, and that, with Stubbs not far behind, he was running about in search of a street door.

Stubbs' voice rose, hoarsely. His master was visible to him, framed in the lighted doorway of the study.

"He's gone into the Sunday School room, Reverend.... He's out again.... There he goes up the stairs to the church! I'd pot him, but I'm afraid of breaking the stained windows."

Daunt essayed a rejoinder, but changed his mind. By the dim light which filtered in from a street lamp, he saw Stubbs bounding up the stairs, with the agility of an elderly bear.

Without undue haste, but with an interest in the chase which was momentarily growing keener, the clergyman also mounted to the pulpit door, and pushed through it into the church audi-torium. There he had an idea; an obvious idea, which seemed to have escaped Stubbs in his lively effort to head their visitor from the street door. He stepped back into the hallway, and turned on the church lights.

The sound of pursuit abruptly ceased. As Daunt peered through the doorway to learn the cause, he perceived Stubbs in the farther aisle, alertly holding his revolver.

"Behind a pew, Reverend," the manservant explained.

From an invisible location at the front of the church, the voice of the tall man rose in comment.

"He puts the situation correctly, Mr. Daunt. May I call your attention to the fact that the game is now at stalemate? Neither of us can proceed without moving into peril. My good friend, Stubbs, has the passage to the door covered. I shall not attempt to chance his marksmanship. But, just before we left the study, I was able to secure your watch again as it fell to the floor. It is a beautiful watch. I should be indeed reluctant to damage it. And the large stained window behind me is artistic in the extreme—truly a masterpiece, is it not, Mr. Daunt? Need I describe to you how it would pain me, should Stubbs advance a step farther down the aisle, to toss your watch through that window? I see a hymn book or two within easy reach. I could contrive to keep under cover and toss them through, also."

The clergyman considered this turn of the game, moodily.

"Are you aware that Stubbs has it in his power to shoot you dead?" he demanded.

Their hidden guest laughed.

"In the church? Hardly, Mr. Daunt! Consider the proprieties! I am sure you would permit nothing of that sort."

Daunt bit his lip, and retired again into his thoughts. It was Stubbs who broke the awkward silence.

"Reverend, I steered you into this mess. I'm slowing up—that's what ails me. I ought to have had Slippery safer than a dead jail-bird. Let me handle him now—as a favor, Reverend!"

"You will not shoot in the church, Stubbs?"

"Never fear, Reverend. He's too cute to come out till he's made terms about that."

The voice rose suavely from behind the line of pews.

"My terms are complete immunity. You are not to prosecute, either now or later."

Stubbs glanced at his watch. He appeared to be thinking,

deeply. But his face by no means showed the emotion which his words conveyed.

"My ears ain't so good," he said, scornfully. "I heard you wrong, I thought you asked me to let you go and call all bets off."

"I will return Mr. Daunt's watch; also his ring, which I still have."

"Say, listen to me!" The manservant spoke firmly. "You might put that over on the Reverend—I'm the only crook he's used to dealing with. You'd return the things, all right—you will if you hope to go on living. And after you put 'em down, you can waltz to the door of the church—and shut it after you. Then the hunting season opens."

"Five minutes' start?" their visitor suggested.

"Not five seconds."

"I am sorry." There was plaintive regret in the tall man's voice. "I shall be under the necessity of remaining here until better terms are offered."

Stubbs consulted his watch again, and suddenly became magnanimous.

"I don't want to be too hard on you, Slippery," he remarked. "Here's what I'll do. It ain't very far to the street corner at the end of the church, is it? You'd no more cut around it than I could be after you with my gat. But it's all of an eighth of a mile to the north corner, where the cigar store is. I'll let you out, and I won't take after you till you've rounded that north corner. If you're on, beat it!"

There was an interval of silence, in which Stubbs once more looked at his watch—rather impatiently. Then the tall man quietly rose, behind the fourth pew from the rear. He bowed, ironically.

"I thank you for your courtesy, gentlemen. You will note that I have been playing, not the ancient game of chess, but the good, old poker trick of 'bluff.' I could not possibly have bombarded the window from where I was concealed…. Shall I present you with the watch and the ring, Stubbs?"

"Lay them on the seat and get out!" directed the manservant.

The tall man complied. As he opened the great door of the church, Stubbs was just behind him, with drawn revolver.

Some ten minutes later, the manservant returned to where his master, a trifle shaken with the evening's occurrences, was resting in one of the pews. Stubbs grinned, cheerfully.

"I heard it said once, Reverend, that if you want a really good laugh, you should take your giggle after everyone else is through having theirs," he observed. "I'm taking mine now. Maybe you saw me look at my watch a couple of times, sir?"

"I did observe that, Stubbs," the clergyman admitted.

"Old Pat Murphy is the patrolman on our beat, these nights. You could set the town clock by Pat. Right on the half-hour he comes, round the corner of Feinstein's cigar store, and on past the church. I started Slippery off prompt at half-past-twelve, Reverend. You know that bootblack stand, two doors the other side of Feinstein's?"

The clergyman nodded, interestedly.

"That was where him and Pat met up. He tried to dodge, did Slippery. Nothing doing! So he went off with Pat like a lamb. If you want to talk to him in the morning, Reverend, his address will be care of the hoosgow."

6

"I'M NOT WHAT you'd call superstitious, Reverend. I'll walk under a ladder as cheerful as any man, if there ain't some bird with a can of paint atop of it. But I've just paddled up to my trunk, sir, and dug up a rabbit foot that I salted away five years ago. He was a blind jack rabbit, Reverend, shot by the light of the moon. That rabbit foot's in my pocket this minute, sir."

The clergyman yawned, threw back the bed clothes, and by a significant glance toward his slippers indicated his intention of rising forthwith. This was an occasion when he preferred to eat his breakfast out of bed. A perpendicular position quickened his thoughts; and he needed to think.

"I suppose you are about to tell me, Stubbs, that the Buddha is gone again," he suggested.

Stubbs paused, the slippers in his hand.

"You knew it, Reverend?"

"I expected it."

"But Slippery went to jail. You don't think he's broke out, sir?"

Daunt paused in the act of adjusting one of the slippers to the position of utmost comfort. He was particular about his feet.

"I should like you to visit the police station, this morning, Stubbs. Talk with Emory. Learn from him all that he can tell you about this affair. You might inform him that you and I intend to avoid appearing against him, if that is possible."

"That last will open his mouth better than a dentist could, Reverend," Stubbs declared, heartily. "I'll go over as soon as

I've got you properly dressed."

Though usually careless about his toilet to the point where his man covertly accused him of disdaining a valet's services altogether, upon this morning the clergyman was almost finical. He rejected the blue tie laid out by Stubbs, in favor of a fashionable gray—the color which men inclined to be stout should not wear, but invariably do. He criticized the crease in his trousers. He even inspected both shoes, side by side, to insure that one was not more highly polished than the other.

"I have a delicate task before me," he explained to the astounded Stubbs, "one in which psychology will play an important part. There must be no flaw in my appearance to distract attention from the issue at hand."

Stubbs shook his head, perplexedly. He could not arrange the events of the last twelve hours in his mind. But he did not venture a question until his master was finishing the second cup of coffee.

"If it's not asking too much, Reverend—were you expecting *everything* that happened last night?"

Daunt put down the emptied cup.

"If I had foreseen everything, Stubbs, my head would be far less tender, this morning—and your eye not so black. What I did foresee, however, appears ultimately to have occurred."

His manner discouraged further queries. In a moment, he rose from the table, donned hat and overcoat, and made his way deliberately down the stairs, out of the rear door of the manse, and across the courtyard to his study.

The window was open, as on the previous morning.

He shut it, and examined table and books perfunctorily, in

case any clue worthy of note happened to have been left. There was nothing. Without having removed hat and coat, he quitted the study again, and started across the courtyard for the passage which led to the street.

Just at the corner of the church, he halted, considered a moment, then turned back. This time, he went on to the manse, and, letting himself in, called sharply for Stubbs.

The manservant appeared from his own quarters, also wearing his outer garments.

"I was just going to the policemen's hotel, Reverend, to see Slippery," he explained.

"I recall that you have a small valise, Stubbs," his master remarked; "one which you used to carry in your burglary days, and which has a number of tools in it."

Stubbs nodded.

"It's in my room, Reverend. It's still got my jimmy in it, and a chisel, and a little saw. And there's a peach of a hammer—one of them short, stocky sockers, not so big, but with a wallop like a billy goat's forehead. I used to knock the combinations off small safes with that hammer."

"I should like to borrow the valise, as it stands," the clergyman indicated; and, thus equipped, he left the manse, a few minutes later.

He proceeded directly to the terrace of the two young ladies—a short distance, and the morning, bright and with a pleasant snap in the air, was ideal for walking. At the door of the suite, he hesitated a moment, before ringing the bell. Perhaps Stubbs' chaperonage would have been wise—a wealthy bachelor is obliged to be careful. But a private interview seemed desirable, too. He pushed the button.

"You beat me to it, Mr. Daunt!"— It was the little blonde, in street clothing, and the door was open. "Another five minutes, and I'd have been on my way to see you. Helen wished to come, too, but she really is not able."

As she ushered him in, he glanced at the mantel. The Buddha was there. Sinister, inscrutable, it stared back unwinkingly. Its expression seemed that of sneering proprietorship, as if it knew its rights, and declined to be ejected.

"Since Mr. Daunt is here, Millie, don't you think I should be the one to talk with him?"

"By all means!" the little blonde acquiesced.

The clergyman turned, with a curious feeling that this contralto voice, deep and limpid, was exactly what he had expected of his silent brunette visitor. She stood in the doorway of the inner room. Her face was a little tense and drawn in the harsh glare from the front window, but the soft, natural flush of youth showed beneath its transparent olive, and her eyes, in the worst possible light, were still darkly beautiful. She stood a moment, looking at him breathlessly—almost shrinking from him; then said, impulsively:

"Oh, Mr. Daunt, I think you know!"

"Yes, I know," he returned, gravely.

She came slowly into the room.

"Millie has gone upstairs. She said if I could talk to you alone, that would be best." She stopped. The clergyman waited in silence. He was not quite sure how to handle the situation. Suddenly, to his consternation, she dropped to her knees and grasped his hand.

"I can't save myself, Mr. Daunt!" she sobbed. "You can save me! Oh, I know you can!"

"Possibly I can," he answered, in a matter-of-fact voice. "Have you a pastry board?"

She stared at him incredulously, and he seized the opportunity to urge her to her feet.

"A board for mixing pastry, kneading bread, and such tasks," he elucidated. "I believe there is one in most kitchens."

His unemotional manner was having its effect. Her sobbing ceased.

"We have one," she said, haltingly.

"Get it. Also, I should like a newspaper." He checked himself. "I understand newspapers are hard to find in this house. Suppose we say a towel, instead? There is a cellar to this apartment?"

She nodded.

"You and your sister will take these articles into the cellar. I will follow."

He allowed a reasonable interval and when, from the sound of wondering voices, he judged that the latter part of his instructions was being carried out, stepped to the mantel. The Buddha eyed him sardonically. An imaginative man might have read defiance in its cold aloofness. Though Daunt was highly imaginative, he nevertheless seized the image, tucked it carefully under one arm, and took Stubbs' grip in his other hand. Thus prepared, he was ready to follow the sisters.

He found them at the foot of the cellar steps—two nervous and pretty pictures of perplexity; but nothing in his manner toward them indicated that such pictures registered even faintly in his mind. In fact, he accorded them only a passing glance—enough to note that the brunette had procured, not a newspaper, but a towel, according to his second suggestion.

His gaze roamed appraisingly over the cement floor of the cellar, and stopped with approval before the front window, high in the tile wall.

"This place will be satisfactory," he observed. "The other day, you offered me the Buddha as a gift. Is that offer still open?"

"It is, indeed, Mr. Daunt," the little blonde assured him. He turned to her sister, standing almost apprehensively at the foot of the stairs. She nodded.

"I accept the gift. Miss Marsden, you will place the board upon the floor, just beneath the window, and lay the towel upon it. The light there is good.

He set the image upon the towel, and turned to his audience.

"Stand where you can see the Buddha distinctly. I should like to solve this problem in some other way, but I fear there is no other way."

As they came forward, he opened Stubbs' valise, and, rummaging in it, brought out the chisel and the heavy hammer.

"Bear in mind that this is my property," he reminded them.

Before they could reply, he had directed the point of the chisel downward upon the sinister head, and struck the tool a heavy blow. The marble was stubborn. He was obliged to strike repeatedly before a large piece split from the image. Behind him, the sisters gasped. Miss Marsden was sobbing. He ignored them, and continued to strike with calm determination, choosing his points of attack so that the sardonic face split away first, and the remainder of the image slowly disintegrated. Suddenly, he stopped. The chisel had struck something metallic. He turned the base of the image upside down, and scrutinized it.

"A cemented cavity," was his verdict. "Done so well that I

missed it entirely in my first examination. The bottom is countersunk, and the sunken portion is all of cement, which exactly matches the marble. The maker was a clever mechanic, as well as an artist."

He was really talking to himself. Without attending to the excited comments of the girls, he chiseled downward, carefully. The metallic object proved to be a long, plain box. After disengaging it from the cement, he pried at the lid, with his chisel. There was no lock. When the stiffened hinges were forced to yield, he drew forth a single sheet of paper, closely written in faded ink.

The brunette spoke.

"Mr. Daunt, I think we should read that first."

But the clergyman eyed her coldly.

"I am the present owner of this image and its contents," he remarked; and, turning his back upon her, he held the manuscript to the light.

He read rapidly, but with close attention. His hostesses exchanged indignant glances, but said nothing further. At length, he folded the paper, and once more recognized their presence, but did not speak. He was gazing at them thoughtfully, as if not quite certain what to do.

The little blonde smiled diffidently at him.

"May we have it now?" she requested.

The question seemed to clear his lingering doubts. He returned her smile, in a really warm and human manner, for him. But he shook his head.

"I must run the risk of being misunderstood," he said, gravely. "The reading of this manuscript would be of no benefit to you, and would cause you both great unhappiness. Sometimes truth is less to be desired than mystery. This is such a situation. You may take my word for it or not, as you please. My mind is made up. I am acting now as a clergyman—your spiritual counsellor—to whom you have come for advice."

He pocketed the manuscript, and, gathering together the corners of the towel, carefully emptied into his valise all of the fragments and dust of the Buddha which it contained. Some of the pieces were scattered about the floor. These, too, he secured, while the sisters looked on in silence.

"I wished you both to witness this, so that you may know, beyond doubt, that the image is destroyed. I shall have Stubbs complete the task by pulverizing all these fragments and scattering them to the winds. We have nothing more to do here, I believe."

When they were back in the living room—Daunt in an armchair, the two sisters side by side on the sofa—he turned suddenly upon the tall brunette, who was staring at him in wide-eyed fascination.

"Miss Marsden, I wish to know everything that you remember of the night before last."

She trembled, but her eyes did not drop.

"Do you wish me to be under oath?" she inquired, faintly.

"Your word is enough."

She drew herself up with a kind of pride—the pride of inbred courage, it seemed, triumphing over temporary weakness.

"You have not asked me about the other nights—of what must have happened before this terrible thing—but I should like you to know that I remember nothing of them, at all. I must not have awakened. It must have been just as it was when I used to have this affliction before, as a little girl. Then I would do quite remarkable things in my sleep—dangerous things—and know nothing about them afterward."

"She would often dress herself, then undress again after it was over and go back to bed," supplemented the blonde. "We watched her, a number of times. We never wakened her, though."

The clergyman nodded without speaking, and Helen Marsden continued, speaking firmly but hardly above a whisper.

"Night before last, I did awaken, Mr. Daunt. I was just putting the Buddha back on the mantel. I was fully dressed, and my hands seemed wet. When I realized where I was, and turned on the light, I saw why they were wet. It was blood!"

"You remember nothing before that?" He looked at her keenly.

"Nothing whatever. I undressed and went to my room. But I didn't sleep. And I did not tell Millie until this morning, when I found the Buddha back on the mantel once more. I must have gone for it again last night, without knowing. Oh, Mr. Daunt, what can I do? What can I do?" Her voice sank to a horror-stricken whisper. "And what have I done?"

Her sister's arm crept around her; but the clergyman's calm smile was even more steadying.

"One part of you was willing to give up the Buddha—your conscious part," he declared. "But your subconscious part—your dream mind—refused. Probably there was a mistaken conviction, deep within your brain, that the image should be kept, out of loyalty to your mother. Now you have seen it destroyed—utterly destroyed. You cannot possibly bring it back. I believe that will cure you."

"But the blood!"

The clergyman glanced at Millie Diggs. She shook her head, slowly. Fortunately for the occasion, he did not share the prejudice against lying held by most members of his cloth. Usually, the truth is desirable; but falsehood is a tool which has its offices, too.

"The blood need not trouble you," he prevaricated, easily. "Nothing has come to light which will explain it. Possibly a slight bleeding from the nose may have been the cause. I believe that often accompanies somnambulism."

He did not refer again to the sanguine evidence on the Buddha until, the examination over, Millie Diggs was bidding him farewell at the door. Then it was she who brought up the subject.

"Oh, Mr. Daunt, do you think that she—"

He understood her meaning, and replied:

"I think that, while she was walking in her sleep, with the Buddha in her arms, she was attacked by a ruffian. She had a fixed idea—to bring the image back. He interfered. To her dreaming mind, he was not a man, at all—merely an obstacle. She struck out with savage strength, using the heavy weapon already in her possession, then returned with no knowledge of what she had done. She has not seen the newspapers?"

"We seldom have a paper in the house, as you know; and I have been especially careful not to buy one lately."

"Then act as her censor for a while, until the thing blows over. She has not been guilty of a crime. She is really a public benefactor. There is no reason why the matter should trouble her."

7

"THEY'VE GIVE SLIPPERY the third degree already, Reverend," Stubbs informed his master, a little later, in the study. "They've been prodding him about that bird that was killed out there by the church. Nothing doing on that for Slippery. He's got a better alibi than Napoleon had on the robbery at the City National, after they'd cooped him up in Saint What-you-call-it. He's got all four of his wisdom teeth, has Slippery, and he's teetotally dry behind the ears."

"Why did he come for the Buddha?" demanded Daunt.

Stubbs grinned.

"Ask me something hard, Reverend. The answer to that is so simple it hurts my pride. Him and Red was pals, you know. They both were in the pen for the same job, and they got out together, a month ago. Red spotted two ladies that first morning. They started out with the heathen bud unwrapped, sir—didn't have no paper handy in the house, I guess. They bought a newspaper on the corner to wrap it up, and that was when he seen them. He figured it looked like a valuable statue, and when they come here, he was sure of it—you've got a reputation, Reverend. He spotted just where they put it—must have come into the yard. But when he called around at night to lift it, something happened to him. I don't know who crowned him, and Slippery don't know; and the police don't. But Slippery had heard enough from Red so that he took a chance on it the next night—he not having anything more important on hand, and figuring he had brains enough to pull it off even though

Red couldn't. He got in through the church, with a skeleton key; and what should he do but meet up with you! And there you have it, Reverend. I tipped him off not to mention the bud down at headquarters, and told him we wouldn't talk, neither."

The clergyman nodded thoughtfully in the direction of his manservant's valise, which had not yet been emptied of its contents.

"Stubbs, the remains of the Buddha are in that grip. I should like them completely pulverized and disposed of. You may consider them as evidence, to be put where they will do no harm. Can you do a good job?"

His man received the commission with apparent enthusiasm.

"Can I do a good job, Reverend? I'm old Mr. Alibi, himself. I've been putting evidence away since before I can remember. Why, when I was a infant in the cradle, sir, and my mother used to feed me milk in a bottle, I had a trick of emptying out what I didn't want, so she wouldn't spank me for not drinking it all, sir. You couldn't have come to a better stand. If they want to put that heathen bud together on the Judgment Day, they'll have to start ten years beforehand to gather it up."

He hesitated.

"And there's something else I'd like to tell you, Reverend."

His master being silently expectant, he went on:

"I want you to know that I figured out how this heathen bud came and went away again. After it was gone that last time, my brains woke up. I had a pal once that used to walk in his sleep. He paraded into a jewelry store one night, and the judge gave him a year's free board—he being that unlucky, Reverend, that he happened to have a jimmy along in his pocket when he went strolling. Was it the tall, dark one, sir?"

Daunt nodded.

"I figured it was. She looks the part more'n the blonde. It was the fire escape she climbed up at the second-hand store, wasn't it? It would take a good sleep-walker to do that without waking up, but then she must be a good one, and she's tall. And the night Slippery happened in—you were looking for her and not for Slippery, Reverend, and she came all right later, but you didn't care to wait around after Slippery got through with you. You were ready to hit the hay then, sir. Is that the dope?"

The clergyman smiled.

"You have covered the ground thoroughly, Stubbs."

"I couldn't miss it, Reverend. There was only one way the bud could get through the bolted door of that apartment, and that was in the paws of one of them females. And I didn't think either of them would do it awake. As for who it was crowned Red Brannigan, I'm not figuring on that, Reverend, and I'm not a-going to, sir."

He was about to retire with the valise when his master recalled him.

"I should like you to witness what I am about to do, Stubbs." He held up the yellowed manuscript which had been inside the Buddha. "This is an intimate personal document. I have read it, and I intend that no one else shall read it. But since you have worked upon the problem with which it is connected, I shall tell you this: that it was written by the man who made the Buddha. He was a genius. He put into the countenance of that image the very soul of the man he portrayed—so much so that the evil soul seemed to peep out from the marble, and make everyone who saw the Buddha shiver. You and I have felt the power of his craftsmanship. Those two girls were affected by it until they could endure the thing no longer. He was a genius, Stubbs, and yet a vile traitor to the white race. History says nothing of him, but it was his treachery which made possible the horror of the Black Hole of Calcutta. He confesses everything in his manuscript. It is in my power to spare the feelings of his descendants; to prevent an additional record of human frailty from reaching the pages of history. That is why I do this."

With an abrupt gesture, he flung the paper into the blazing fireplace. Stubbs watched with fascination until the last yellowed line of writing had perished, writhing, in the flames. Then he asked, hesitantly:

"Whose picture was the bud supposed to be, Reverend?"

Daunt stepped to the book-case and plucked out a volume of the encyclopedia.

"You will find him here, under 'Calcutta'," he said, handing the book to Stubbs. "I do not know why he is depicted as a Buddha; unless, it be, possibly, through an ironical twist in the sculptor's mind. Not a bad twist, either! Only a genius could have handicapped himself with the upturned lips of Buddha, and still have shown the black soul of Surajah Dowla, the Nawab of Bengal. You might put on a little more coal, Stubbs. It is rather chilly in here, and I have a quantity of work to catch up on the ideographs."

The King of the Earth

The old objection to mystery stories—that the Author is always so busy creating a plot with which to fool his readers that he has no time for character delineation—never holds when Mr. Suter is the Author. And we always have the Author so busy that creating a plot this good is a real mystery.

1

RHYMING SAM, THE Hobo, awoke from a pleas-
ant afternoon sleep in the August woods, to find himself
surrounded. He did not arouse of his own accord. He could
have slept with enjoyment until evening. What brought him to
consciousness was an imperative hand, twisted into the collar
of his threadbare coat. The hand yanked him, still dreaming,
to his feet. Even then, he might have gone on slumbering—he
had been profoundly asleep—had not the other hand of the
big, red-faced man who held and shook him slipped a rope
around his neck.

"Up with him, Luke!" urged someone in the crowd, grimly.

"Just a minute."

It was the red-faced man, who wore a butcher's apron. He
stepped back, ignoring the jostling crowd about him, and gazed
calculatingly at the lofty limbs of nearby trees. The next tree to
the one Sam had slept beneath won his approval.

"This'll do," he declared, with brisk avidity. "Bear back till I
throw the rope over that limb." He turned on a man who was
pressing too close. "Give me room, you! How can I throw it
over with you hanging on my arm?"

The snarling voices impacted on the prisoner's mind like
figments of a nightmare.

"Out of his way, there!... Get back, fellows, he wants to throw
the rope over!... I'm getting back, ain't I... Get back, yourself!"

A heavy voice, forceful but unexcited, cut in beneath the
others. Sam glanced bewildered toward the speaker, and

The KING of the EARTH

by
J. PAUL
SUTER

A PROBLEM OF THE REVEREND McGREGOR DAUNT

perceived him to be a tall, sinewy man in a leather apron—apparently the village blacksmith.

"There's a better tree over here, Luke. Notice that low branch on the one you picked. He might make out to stand on that and save himself for a while."

"So he might," the butcher acquiesced, readily. "Come on, hobo."

"Come on, you damned murderer!" echoed a shrill voice on the fringe of the crowd.

They bustled him along. Those near enough aimed blows at him. One—a sallow little man who had wormed his way up from among the stragglers—kicked him suddenly in the shin, and laughed.

It was the kick that fully awakened Sam. He had been in a waking dream. Now he planted his feet with an abruptness that brought his captors up short for a minute.

"Of what do you accuse me, gentlemen?" he demanded.

His voice was deep and pleasant. He seemed the least excited of the party. But his question unmasked a chorus of howls.

"D'ye get that? He wants to know what he done!... Hear

the professor, boys, the professor's going to make a speech!…
Come on, hang the damned murderer! First thing you know,
the sheriff… To hell with the sheriff—we'll hang him, too, if
he butts in!"

The tall man in the leather apron spoke. Excepting the prisoner, he was the calmest person there.

"Look here, hobo, you were in Trexford village this morning.
No use denying it. You were seen."

The crowd quieted, to hear their captive's denial; but they
were disappointed.

"I was there," he admitted, with queer dignity.

"He owns up to it!" howled someone. "Come on, get that
rope over the tree!"

"You were seen coming out of Mrs. Phelps' house."

"The large yellow house? The lady was kind to me. She gave
me two cups of coffee—two separate cups at the same time,
so as not to delay her washing while she went back to fill the
second one." The prisoner chose his words deliberately, like a
man making a speech.

"Come on, John Chandler! That's enough talk. Let's go!"

The blacksmith turned patiently to the sallow man, who had
spoken.

"In a minute, Plimpon. We don't want to make a
mistake." Then, before the crowd could drown him out—"You
had a club in your hand, hobo—a club with blood on it."

The captive smiled—a thin, elfish smile, which emphasized
his extreme frailty.

"That was the blood of a rabbit. I had killed it just an hour
before, for my breakfast. Usually, I wash my club, but this
morning I neglected to do so."

The crowd would listen no longer.

"Hear the professor!" derided a village wit. "Something else you want to know, John? Ask him. He'll tell you. He'll tell you anything...."

"Come on, get him kicking in the air!" a sterner voice interrupted.

The blacksmith stepped back from Rhyming Sam.

"I guess you did it all right, hobo," he said, rather sadly. "Come on with your rope, Luke. Make the thing short."

Sam's arms were seized from behind. Someone began to bind them to his sides. But once more, by sheer suddenness of movement, he broke free and won an opportunity to speak.

"What am I charged with? You have no right to hang me without telling me the charge!"

The crowd hooted him down; but John Chandler's powerful voice in turn over-ruled them.

"That's fair enough, hobo. We'll tell you the charge. You are charged with the murder of the Widow Phelps—Mrs. Mary Phelps—the lady who gave you the coffee."

The ragged wanderer's eyes widened. He seemed to forget his personal danger entirely in horror at this news.

"Why she—she is not dead!" he stammered.

"She *is* dead—murdered!" the blacksmith contradicted, sternly. "And you are her murderer!"

"I am not!"

Ignoring the contradiction, the blacksmith spoke softly to the man with the rope. His voice reached the hobo distinctly, in spite of the crowd's commotion.

"Throw the rope over, Luke. No use arguing—he's got it coming. Let's not drag it out any more'n we have to."

"I tell you I did not do it!" the prisoner cried, desperately.

The crowd took up his words, snarling and deriding. With a final accurate cast, closing one eye as he threw, the butcher succeeded with his rope. It cleared the limb and came snakily down the other side. He began jogging it, to bring the loose end within reach. It descended part way, but he could not persuade it further.

"Somebody'll have to shin up, I guess," he announced, with chagrin.

The crowd had been watching him expectantly as a circus audience watches the preliminaries for a diverting feat. They were quiet enough for the sallow man to make himself heard again. He came out with a new suggestion, in his weak tenor.

"Don't hang him here, fellows! Take him back. That's the place to hang him!"

Mobs are curious creatures. The idea, coming at what seemed the critical moment, caught the popular fancy. It opened an opportunity to play, cat-like, with the victim.

"Yeah, take him back!" agreed one or two of the others.

"Make him walk back!" supplemented the sallow man.

The blacksmith's heavy growl found a path once more beneath the lighter voices of the others.

"You bet he'll walk back—if he goes. What say, Luke? Ain't that the place to string him up—right there where he did it?"

The butcher scratched his head.

"I'm for anything the rest of 'em want," was his decision.

"Take him back!" concurred others of the crowd.

"Drag him back!" the sallow man added, with fresh inspiration.

Still maintaining his strange calmness, the hobo wondered,

as they hustled him through the woods, why they did not tie his hands now. They came out into the dusty road. Two big farm wagons stood there, a team of patient horses hitched to each. The off horse on each team turned his head, with an air of intelligent question, but both the farther animals continued their stolid stare up the monotonous road.

Suddenly, they remembered his hands. It was the sallow man who remembered. The captive observed him more closely now, as small and rather flashily dressed, in contrast to the farmer and tradesman clothes of the others.

"Tie him by his wrists to the back of the cart and drag him after it," was his new suggestion.

The blacksmith turned, his heavy hand on Sam's shoulder, and looked at the sallow man.

"I thought you wanted to hang him in the village, Plimpon," he said, coldly.

"Sure I do; but let him stand the gaff a little on the way back."

"He'll stand the gaff enough if he walks. From the looks of him, he mayn't be able to do that. I'm for hanging him and treating him rough, but murderer or no murderer, I'll be no party to torturing the man to death."

The little man had pushed his way importantly to the front, but he wilted under the other's dogged, rather contemptuous gaze.

"Oh, all right," he agreed, with the suggestion of a sneer.

The blacksmith seemed definitely to have taken charge. He secured one end of the rope, which was still loosely around the hobo's neck, to the back of the forward wagon.

"If you'll drive, Luke, I'll sit in the back and watch him," he suggested to the eclipsed butcher. "It's up to someone to be responsible, and I might as well be the one."

The butcher nodded—willing, it seemed, to resign the leadership; and at that moment Sam caught the blacksmith's eye, squarely.

"I am not guilty!" he declared.

He spoke in ringing tones, which all could hear. But the crowd merely laughed, grimly. From the tones of that laugh, Rhyming Sam, who had pondered much on human nature in his solitary wanderings, recognized that argument was useless. One and all, they were sure of his guilt.

The butcher cracked his whip.

"Pile in, boys!"

Another man had taken the reins of the second wagon. The members of the mob found places. Though the wagons were crowded, they all managed to scramble on. The blacksmith had produced a double-barreled shot gun from beneath where he was sitting, with his face to the rear.

He addressed Sam, curtly:

"Any time you want to be wounded in the leg before you hang, try running for it!"

2

THEY WERE ENTERING the confines of the village, by the same road Rhyming Sam had taken that morning. He saw the hospitable yellow dwelling where he had partaken of the coffee. He saw it, however, from a different viewpoint. He was not now the carefree wanderer. His eyes were rimmed with the yellow dust of the road. They smarted intolerably. Though the rope still hung loosely, it had chafed a raw place on his neck. Yet he was neither footsore nor exhausted. His open-air life and continual wandering had lent him an iron endurance which his seeming frailty disguised. Too fast a pace might have worn him down; but the blacksmith had been watchfully lenient, and had insisted that the team should not go beyond a rapid walk. Sam appreciated this consideration, but understood the reason for it. His captors did not wish him to collapse from exhaustion on the road, and so, possibly, rob them of a victim.

A little knot of people were collected in the yard of the yellow house. As the wagon came into sight around the last bend of the road, they were augmented by others, some of whom ran forward to meet the approaching procession. The two teams drew up before the house, and the blacksmith untied the ignominious rope from the wagon.

"Into the yard with you, hobo!" he commanded, briskly.

Half a dozen hands pushed Sam toward the gate. As it swung wide before him, he realized that the tree toward which he was stumbling was one against which he had leaned his club that morning, when he had applied at the back door of the house.

The butcher rose into prominence again. He seemed to be the recognized expert on ropes. As the prisoner was brought to a jarring stop beneath a high, horizontal limb, he came forward and tightened the noose around Sam's spare neck, then stepped back to gauge his throw over the limb. But he was interrupted, as on the first occasion. The blacksmith laid a detaining hand on his arm.

"I'm thinking, Luke, we should take him in and show him his work before he dies. That's usual. It'll make things more regular."

The sallow man protested.

"Hell, no! String the dirty murderer up! We've let him live too long now!"

"A few minutes more or less won't matter," the blacksmith declared, firmly. "He'll be a long time dead. Come on, hobo!"

The sallow man was disproportionately furious.

"I won't have it!" he shouted, in his weak tenor. "I've traveled all of fifteen miles to catch that damned murderer, and now I want to see him get what's coming to him. What d'ye say, men?" He turned to the crowd. "Ain't it right to hang him now, without any more palaver?"

But the speaker was not especially popular, after all, it seemed, and the blacksmith was. There was silence; then a heavy-set farm laborer growled:

"Let John Chandler have his way. If John says it's regular for him to look her over afore he swings, I'm for John."

Amid a grim chorus of approval, which again wilted the sallow man, the blacksmith slipped the noose from Rhyming Sam's neck, and taking the hobo by his shoulder, walked him to the front door of the house.

The door opened. It became evident that the parlor was filled with excited women, who had been watching the proceedings through the drawn shutters. Sam looked about, with a flicker of hope, for the cheery woman who had given him his coffee. He saw her, instantly. As if by mutual agreement, everyone else in the room drew back, so that he might see her.

She was lying on a sofa, against the inner wall. She was dead.

For one blinding instant, the wanderer stared, speechless. Then he broke away, impetuously, from the lightly-laid hand of the blacksmith, and a sudden white heat of fury swept over him. So fierce and accusatory was his attitude as he stood erect in his rags, confronting them, that even the blacksmith retreated a step.

"Who did this?" he demanded. "Where is the man who did it? She was a good woman. She gave me two cups of coffee."

At that, the blacksmith appeared to shake himself loose from a spell. He resumed his hold on the hobo's shoulder.

"Come on," he commanded, though rather uncertainly.

"John Chandler!" It was a slim little woman who suddenly spoke up. She elbowed herself out of the knot of frightened feminine onlookers. "You ain't agoing to hang him without proof? Don't tell me he killed Mary. He don't look like it."

"We've got the proof on him, Mrs. Gillespie," the tall man defended, half apologetically.

"What proof?" she demanded. The blacksmith answered, readily.

"He was seen to come out of here; and he was seen drinking coffee on Mary's back porch. We've got the club he did it with. It's all covered with blood."

"I don't care! He never did it. That man ain't no murderer!"

She placed herself, a diminutive but determined figure, between him and the front door—incidentally pushing out the butcher, who had looked in to learn the cause of the argument. The blacksmith scratched his head, thoughtfully. Combat with women was not his forte. But he was spared a decision by a new element which was injected into the discussion by way of that same front door.

The new element was of an essentially quiet character—a slow-moving, silent, tubby little man, with no marks of distinction save a pair of unusually bright eyes in his round face, and a large revolver in each of his plump hands.

He appeared suddenly in the doorway; calmly and wordlessly viewed the various occupants of the room, including the pathetic figure on the couch; and meanwhile kept a revolver pointed casually toward the front yard. Because of his precarious position, it seemed likely that a hostile move might catch him unware; but a glance at his face made the probability of such a move seem rather remote. Something in the droop of his mouth—from one corner of which a stubby, unlighted cigar projected like a spike; something ever more ominous in his bright eyes—discouraged opposition.

He singled out the blacksmith, still maintaining his grasp of Rhyming Sam.

"John Chandler, raise your right hand!"

The blacksmith returned his gaze with mingled defiance and respect.

"I don't know, Sheriff, as I—"

Curtly, the fat little man cut in:

"This appears to be a case of mob violence. The law empowers me in such emergencies to compel the assistance of responsible citizens. Raise your right hand!"

The blacksmith's fingers, resting lightly on Sam's shoulders, slowly relaxed. Even more slowly, with a suggestion of the stiffness of a mesmeric subject, his hand was raised, until it stopped, with the arm bent but undeniably held aloft.

"You do solemnly swear to do your whole duty as a deputy sheriff, under the laws of the State of Ohio, until released by the proper authority. Say, 'I do!'"

The blacksmith was silent. The sheriff stepped forward—one short, determined step.

"Say, 'I do!', John Chandler! You and I were kids together. Are you going to make me fight this mob alone?"

All his life, Blacksmith John Chandler had stood for law and order. He was one of the staunchest timbers of the village ship of state; one not to be blown about by every wind of doctrine. The murder of Mary Phelps, coming at his very door, with the slayer apparently identified beyond doubt, had swept him from the moorings of years, into mob violence. But the sheriff, knowing his man, had asked the one question that could steady him again.

The tall man looked his interrogator in his bright eyes, and slowly rumbled:

"I do!"

"Take this gun, Deputy Sheriff John Chandler, and stand guard while I remove the prisoner. Clear the house, and let nothing be disturbed. This man"—suddenly fixing the hobo with his eye—"may or may not be the murderer. That is for us to find out.—What is your name?" he demanded of the captive.

Rather brokenly, but not without pride came the answer:

"They call me 'Rhyming Sam.'"

"Come with me, 'Rhyming Sam.'"

The little man did not touch his prisoner. He even led the way, secure in the conviction that Sam would follow. Enough of the crowd had peered through the open doorway to catch the drift of things, at least sketchily. They had passed on their information to others. This was rendered definite when, just after the sheriff with Sam in his wake descended the steps, John Chandler appeared in the doorway, a revolver in his capable hand, and sheepish determination on his face. Before any of them had time to address him, he spoke, quietly, but in tones that carried.

"I've been sworn in as deputy sheriff, boys. I'm going to kill the first man that lifts a finger. If anybody here don't like me doing this, I'll go into the matter with him, fair fist or rough-and-tumble, just as soon as I'm a private citizen again."

Those were the last words of the controversy—if controversy there was—that reached Rhyming Sam's ears. He was invited curtly into a rig beside the tubby sheriff; and he had hardly settled himself on the worn blanket which softened the seat before the fast-stepping gray horse between the shafts had begun his trip to the county jail, five miles away.

They had but rounded the first corner, which shut the village from sight behind a clump of pines, when the sheriff, looking sidewise at his companion out of his bright eyes, demanded suddenly:

"Did you do it, hobo?"

The wanderer shook his head, silently; whereupon the sheriff nodded his.

"That's my judgment, too," he agreed. "I don't believe you did it. But who did?"

They were some ten minutes out of the village, jogging briskly, when the railway station came into sight. At the same time there appeared also, on the platform, a lanky blond young man, the station telegraph operator. He waved, and the sheriff waved back. It seemed, however, that there was serious purpose in the operator's waving. He sauntered out into the road, and waited for them.

"That your man, Sheriff?" he inquired, sizing Sam up with interest.

"That's the man I took away from a bunch that wanted to lynch him," the official answered.

"Well, let me tell you something." The operator spat, deliberately. He was an exceptionally deliberate young man. "I just got something on the wire from the junction. There's another crowd up there. Tough bunch!" He spat again. "They saw you going up, and they figure on taking this bird away from you if you've got him. I tell you what you'd better do—better hop on twenty-seven. She's about due. Trouble is, she ain't going your way. She's the Cleveland train."

The sheriff frowned silently for a minute on this disquieting information.

"Cleveland train, is she?" he echoed. He turned to his prisoner. "Say, Sam—if I should take you on a little trip, will you promise not to try getting away—at least, not till I bring you back?"

"I will promise," the wanderer answered.

"Then I'm going to do something I've wanted to do for a long time. And I'm going to double-cross that crowd so bad they'll have to hang one of their own bunch to keep their pride up. You're a good salesman, Henry—you've sold two tickets to Cleveland. Look after my horse till I get back. And if anyone asks you where we went, tell 'em we're gone to Timbuctoo or to hell—any place but Cleveland!"

3

THE REVEREND MCGREGOR Daunt had been sitting up late in the comfortable library of his hunting lodge—where he hunted thoughts, rather than beasts or birds. A research begun some months before into ancient Chinese ideographs—specimens of which, in a crude and modern form, may be secured from any Chinese laundry in exchange for a bundle of dirty collars—had held him into the early morning hours.

The ideographs appealed to him from several angles. Some curious Chinese laws are couched in them—and he had dabbled in law for a time. He had once gone into the study of medicine, too—which doubled the interest of certain ideographic prescriptions, written in the fifteenth century by a physician on the shores of the Yellow Sea. His theological leanings, of course, were intrigued at every turn; the greater part of the documents he studied were saturated with the teachings of Confucius. And lately his most recent interest, that of philosophic detective reasoning, had received an unexpected jog. For on a priceless manuscript, seared by the breath of twenty-two centuries, he had come upon a cleanly-cut thumb print, which he had reason to surmise might have been impressed by the august digit of Emperor Hsun Tzu himself, in the third century B.C.

The better to study his find, Daunt had purchased a book of finger prints. That new science, it seemed to him, had possibilities.

That night, he had been working assiduously on the Emperor

Hsun's thumb print. It showed interesting characteristics—whorls which were undoubtedly Mongolian, and some which, from their conformation, raised the piquant question of how much the fingers of humanity had been modified by twenty-two centuries. The reverend gentleman was reluctant to leave his cheerful library and ascend to a lonesome bedroom where, though the surroundings were equally cheerful, he lacked the companionship of the illustrious dead.

He did ascend, however, and, clad only in pajamas, dressing gown, and slippers, relaxed in an easy chair. Before retiring for the night, he purposed tracing a few more filaments of thought connected with the Emperor Hsun's whorls.

He had almost ceased to think and begun to drowse when the great brass knocker on his front door downstairs sprang into pulsating life. Its summons was definite and insistent. It thundered a continuous roar, which beat like a hammer on his ear drums. He was properly indignant; but since indignation was not likely to abate the nuisance, he seized an automatic, kept handily in the bedroom, and, still in dressing-gown and slippers, shuffled down the broad stairs to the door.

"I have you covered through the door," he announced, taking inhospitable advantage of a brief period when the knocker was at rest. "Who are you?"

The reply followed sharply, along with total cessation of the knocking:

"The Sheriff of Prall County, with a prisoner."

Daunt was indignant.

"This is not a jail," he declared, still through the door.

"It is tonight," came back at him, distinct and imperturbable.

The hunting lodge was strongly built. Its doors could hardly have been forced by anything less persuasive than a battering ram. The reverend gentleman's logical course would have been to return to bed, leaving the unwelcome applicants to sleep on his porch, if they so elected. But curiosity—*scientific* curiosity, he would have termed it—bulked large among Daunt's many excellent qualities. The sheriff's bold retort had aroused his interest. He snapped into place a heavy chain, so that the door would open only six inches, and opened it that far, at the same time switching on the porch light.

He saw before him a short and tubby man, of about his own build, with remarkably bright eyes; also another man, very slender and frail, in rags.

The short applicant was cool and business-like. He plunged at once into his justification.

"This man"—he indicated his companion—"has been accused of murder. I rescued him from a mob of lynchers. On my way to the county jail, I received warning that we were to be headed off. So I stopped at a railroad station, and we came here."

"Why here?" the clergyman demanded, in astonishment.

The Sheriff of Prall County smiled.

"Your reputation has reached us, Reverend Daunt. I am something of a detective, myself, and I have long wished to present you with a case worth your attention. This one *is* worth it."

Daunt abruptly loosed the chain.

"Come in," he invited them.

When they were seated in his library, he eyed his visitors keenly.

"You seem exhausted," he remarked.

"We are."

"I can furnish you with food and stimulant."

When he returned with a laden brass tray, the sheriff thanked him, warmly; but the slender man smiled, apologetically, and shook his head.

"I broke my fast this morning. It is not yet time for me to eat again. But I shall appreciate a draught of water."

He drank deeply of this, lingering so long with enjoyment over his beverage that he was hardly finished before his rapid-eating companion. The clergyman noted mentally that this was a unique type of murderer.

Suddenly the sheriff pushed away his tray, and exchanged his relaxed expression of gastronomic enjoyment for his usual brisk mien.

"I've been told you have a wonderful cook, Reverend Daunt," he observed. "Now I believe it. Did I introduce myself? I'm Bram Harvey, Sheriff of Prall County. This is 'Rhyming Sam,' the hobo. Doesn't answer to any last name, so far as I can learn. A party of my neighbors wanted to send him to heaven this afternoon at the end of a rope. Evidence seems against him, but I took him away from them. I'm glad I did. He told me his version on the way over. He even wrote it out for me, under oath. And, by George, I believe it!" He paused. "How about having him tell you, Reverend? It's your quickest way to get the facts."

The clergyman hesitated. There was still time to decline this case. His investigation of the Emperor Hsun's thumb print was but fairly begun, and he disliked to interrupt it. But the prisoner's oddity intrigued him. Also, he knew the Sheriff of Prall County by reputation, and rated him as one who would not lightly consider a case worth while.

"Tell me your story," he said abruptly, to Rhyming Sam.

The wanderer smiled—that elfish, unworldly smile of his.

"It is the story of a rabbit," he returned, meeting his host's sharp gaze with whimsical frankness. "He paid for my breakfast with his life. Now I seem in danger of paying for him in the same coin. Perhaps I owe him that. Have you ever killed a rabbit with a club?"

The clergyman intimated, rather curtly, that he never had.

"It is unusual; but I, too, am unusual." Again, the narrator smiled. He was at ease in his host's company; and his ease was not bravado. It was the poise of a cultured man. "I am unusual in that I am a king. You will admit that to be out of the ordinary. Kings do not, as a rule, travel about on foot and in rags."

The clergyman may have looked what he thought; the sheriff certainly looked it. But the prisoner continued, imperturbably, as one willing though not obliged to tell his story.

"I was at one time a professor in a small college. What were my subjects?" He paused, reminiscently. "Ah, yes—English Literature, and, in particular, Poetry. I was a bachelor, and, I fear, very dry, very dull." He sighed. "I might be there still, though it was many years ago. But fate came to my rescue. Fate decreed for me an incurable disease. You know these incurable diseases? Doctors term them so. But mine needed not doctors, but fresh air, the open country, the woods and fields. I was not rich. I could not buy my fresh air on the rear of an observation car. So I became a wanderer. I have wandered ever since, following the birds; north in the summer, and south again when the breeze becomes chill. And for some years past, I have been king!"

He paused once more. This time, his smile was one of genuine amusement at the transparency of his hearers' opinions of him.

"What is a king? One who has power, or is supposed to have. A king who had everything he wished would be very great, would he not? He might be called the King of the Earth. I have everything I wish—everything—the north in the summer and the south in the winter. I can recite poetry—immortal poetry—to the birds and the woods, where I will. Therefore, I am a king—without a crown or a throne."

"You were going to tell the Reverend of your experience in Trexford," the sheriff interrupted, with something of the tone one would take with a child.

"There is little to that," the wanderer declared. "I have already told the important part of my story. I am expert with the club— one becomes so, from practice. I killed the rabbit with it, from a distance. He was my breakfast, I neglected to wash the club, having a poem in mind, and wandered on to the yellow house. There, the mistress of the house—" He stopped, and his voice trembled. "The very kind woman who is dead—gave me two cups of coffee. She was washing. She had come up from the laundry to answer my knock. She gave me the two cups at once, so as to be rid of me without further interruption to her work. I wished only the coffee, though she offered me food. I had already eaten, and one meal is enough in a day." He spread his hands, with an eloquent, smiling gesture. "That is all of my story. I came away then, and wandered far. I slept, at last, beneath a tree, in the late afternoon. And I awakened to find a rope about my neck, and to be called a murderer."

His face became painfully reminiscent, and he was silent. The clergyman had been listening absorbedly; but when the recital was finished, he did not speak. Instead, he turned expectantly to the sheriff.

"I haven't much to add," that official volunteered, in response to his glance. "I was so busy getting this chap away from the mob that I had to swear in a deputy and leave him in charge till I could come back. He must be pretty tired by now. I haven't *been* back."

"What was the nature of the injury that caused death?" Daunt inquired.

"I talked to one or two outside the house while I was getting my bearings. And I saw for myself when I looked into the room where the victim lay. She was terribly crushed about the head by some blunt instrument. They accused Rhyming Sam of doing it with his club."

The clergyman shot a sudden, searching glance at his ragged guest, and put to him the same question the sheriff had asked that afternoon.

"Did you do it?"

The hobo shook his head.

"She was my benefactor," he said. "She gave me kind words, which are priceless, and two cups of coffee."

"You walked through the woods here?" Daunt inquired of Harvey.

The tubby sheriff smiled.

"Wondering how we found our way? No trick, at all! Rhyming Sam knows these woods—and most other woods, too, I'll bet! Not finding you at your city study, we grabbed a taxi to come here, and Sam told me just where we should take to our feet and hoof it. He's got the instinct of a carrier pigeon. I'd hate to have him on my trail if I was wanted for something."

Daunt rose.

"My man Stubbs, who brings me supplies from the city, is due at five," he said. "I will go with you after he comes. Two bedrooms upstairs are at your disposal, or you can make shift with the couch in the library. I intend to retire."

The ragged man looked about him, mournfully.

"Must I sleep under a roof?" he asked; to which his companion made prompt reply:

"Sleep or not, under a roof you're going to stay. I'm not planning to spend the night out of doors. Though I don't think you'd try to run away, at that," he added. "I'll stay awake, thanks, Reverend. I'm on guard."

The clergyman nodded, and with a curt good-night, left the two of them to their own arrangements. He wished to sleep. And he was confident that the astute Stubbs, upon his arrival, would not shoot the interlopers as burglars, but would investigate their credentials, instead.

4

THE REPUTATION FOR originality which had already brought the Sheriff of Prall County to Daunt's attention was deserved; and his next move in the case of Rhyming Sam by no means diminished it. He had snatched Sam away from under the nose of a grimly determined mob, and had appointed the leader of the mob his deputy to have charge until his return; he had taken the suspect with him on his trip to find a detective— and a private detective, at that—to handle the case; and now he came driving back from the railway station to meet the mob, if they chanced to be still there, having with him not merely the reverend dilettante in crime he had secured, but also the very man he had spirited from the place not twelve hours before!

Sheriff Harvey was due for something of a jolt himself, as he pulled up before the fateful house; for the blacksmith was not to be seen. In his place, carelessly toying with the sheriff's gun as he sat on the front steps, appeared Luke Blevins, the butcher. A few curious villagers lingered in the road, but the yard was free of them. Luke's presence, it seemed, had something to do with this phenomenon.

As the rig stopped, the butcher glanced up, with amazement on his red face, and slowly ejaculated:

"Well, I'll be jiggered!"

"Where is my deputy?" the little sheriff demanded, sharply, at the very moment of alighting.

"John Chandler?" The butcher jerked a thumb backward over his shoulder. "He watched all night, John did, and along toward morning he got powerful sleepy. Nine o'clock's his regular bedtime, you know. So he swore me in as deputy's deputy, and he's pounding his ear in the kitchen. See that string across the gate?"

All three of the newcomers were now on the ground. The sheriff, having just reached the gate, examined the string with interest. It was stretched across from post to post, in such a manner that no one could walk in at the gate without displacing it.

"John tied that there before he went to sleep," the deputy's deputy explained. "If anybody breaks it, or comes under it, or jumps over it, I'm to plug him. Them's John's instructions. I sorta let it leak out, so as not to kill any of my neighbors that didn't understand, and I haven't had to do no shooting. If anybody came the back way, that counts same as breaking the string. Nobody's come, so far. There ain't been no trouble, at all. Of course, your crowd can come in, Sheriff," he hastened to add. "We're just keeping things till you're ready to take charge again."

Harvey broke the string, without comment, and walked into the yard, followed by Rhyming Sam and the Reverend McGregor Daunt. Coming to meet them, the butcher put in another word, in lowered tones.

"John and me are pretty much ashamed of ourselves, Bram," he said, humbly. "We ain't naturally given to lynching. I guess we lost our heads, and there was a lot of others in the same boat. You're perfectly safe bringing the hobo back. Since yesterday, we've been thinking things over, and we ain't so sure he done it."

It was Daunt who caught at his words.

"Why are you not so sure?" he demanded, sharply.

The butcher glanced doubtfully at Harvey, then seemed to yield to the clergyman's air of stern authority.

"We found a brick, sir, with blood on it," he explained.

"So you've been searching the house?" the Sheriff accused him.

"Just looking it over. We didn't touch a thing. No one has so much as laid a finger on that brick. It's lying down in the laundry, just as it was when we first saw it."

"Was the dead woman found in the laundry?" the clergyman asked.

"That's the queer part of it, sir. She was lying in the kitchen. Hank, my delivery boy, found her there when he went in to deliver the meat, and he come running back to tell me. Then I got John Chandler, and Mr. Plimpon, the notary, and we carried her into the parlor where she is now."

"How about a doctor?" demanded the sheriff.

"We called young Dr. Burman." The butcher lowered his voice, apologetically. "He's just set up in the village, you know, and everything that comes his way helps a little. We knew she was dead, all right, so he couldn't do no harm. I don't think he even touched her—just looked at her, and said he'd make out a certificate any time one was wanted."

Harvey nodded, with a half-smile.

"Very proper," he commented. "Mr. Daunt, I understand that you hold a medical diploma, along with your qualifications as a clergyman. Do you care to examine the remains?"

"I shall follow Dr. Burman's example," the clergyman answered. "The autopsy belongs to the coroner. Merely a view of the body will be sufficient, I believe."

"You are in charge of the prisoner, Blevins, and are relieved of your other duties," Harvey instructed the butcher, crisply.

The deputy's deputy scratched his head, and with a sudden though rather irregular impulse, shook hands warmly with the prisoner.

"Set down here on the step, Sam," he invited, cordially. "I'm mighty glad we didn't hang you. You can make it up to a man for most mistakes, but not for hanging."

Daunt spent only a minute or two beside the pathetic figure on the couch.

"Whoever did this, it was hardly done with a club," he remarked, reverently turning away. "The wound is too broad and even. I should like to examine the brick your man mentioned."

They passed through the living-room, in which a copy of a weekly farm paper lay face downward upon the broad window seat; and through the dining-room, also.

"Table not cleared," the clergyman commented, as they passed it.

The sheriff laughed, shortly.

"That won't tell you a thing, Reverend. You don't know the ways of country folks. Lots of women never clear the table on wash days till they get their clothes on the line. My wife don't."

"It tells me this—that you can release the hobo with a clear conscience. His visit occurred in the morning. The mob was prepared to lynch him on the strength of such a morning visit. But the victim evidently was living to eat her mid-day meal."

"How do you figure that out, Reverend?" the sheriff asked.

"Look about you!" the clergyman recommended, curtly. "Country folk who keep chickens eat plentifully of eggs, but the same person does not eat them served in two ways at one meal."

The sheriff grinned.

"I get you—the plate with the soft-boiled eggs for lunch is stacked on top of the one with the bacon and eggs for breakfast. That it, Reverend?"

But his companion had already progressed to the kitchen, where blacksmith John Chandler, on a chair perilously propped back in an angle of the outside wall, was enjoying profound and noisy slumber. Daunt merely glanced at him, but examined with interest the open door of the clothes chute, about half way up the wall and a little to the right of the stove. He peered into the chute, first upward, then downward.

"Come here, Sheriff," he commanded, abruptly. "What is this on the side of the chute?"

The plump official obeyed, and started violently at what he saw.

"Blood, by heck!" he exclaimed. "Right here on the side of the chute." He stepped back, to allow the light from the kitchen window, most of which he had been effectually blocking, to enter the small doorway. "Here's some below the door and a drop or two above. How could it splash like that?"

"Where was she lying?" the clergyman demanded.

In answer, Harvey went to the outside door, and opened it.

"Blevins! Come here a minute. Sam won't run away. I don't care if he does!"

"Blevins, you fellows shouldn't have moved her," he reproved the butcher, importantly, as the latter appeared around the corner of the house. "I don't suppose you can tell me within a yard of where she was lying when you found her."

The butcher smiled, broadly.

"Maybe we ain't such fools as you take us for, Sheriff," he

retorted, with satisfaction. "We moved her, sure enough. It didn't strike us as seemly to leave her there on the floor. And I'm not saying John and me mightn't have done it without giving the detective stuff a thought. But not that fellow Plimpon. He's a cute one! 'We'd better mark on the floor just where she lays,' he says. John here had a nail in the pocket of his apron, and he kneeled down before we even touched her and scratched a line right around her on the floor. She was laying on her face. Her head was towards the wall, where that blood stain is on the floor. And her feet, they was partly under the table."

Daunt had been scrutinizing the rudely scratched line, looking up occasionally to compare its direction with the position of the opening in the chute.

"There seems to be a little blood under the table, too," he observed.

The butcher glanced at it, and shrugged his shoulders.

"I don't know why. So far as I could see, she wasn't hurt, except about the head."

"Down cellar, I suppose, Reverend?" the sheriff suggested, as Daunt paused and appeared to be looking about him carelessly; but the clergyman had not finished questioning Blevins.

"Did anyone move the broom?" he inquired.

The butcher gaped vacantly, but suddenly brightened.

"Right there, hanging behind the door, Reverend," he replied, heartily. "I'll get it for you."

"I do not care for it," Daunt returned, sharply. "Answer my question, please."

"Did any of you fellows move it, Luke?" supplemented the sheriff, coming to the rescue of his bewildered neighbor.

"Why, no, it's been hanging there right along, so far as I

know. I didn't see no one touch it. What would we want with it?"

But Daunt, satisfied with the answer, already had turned in another direction.

"I shall take the cellar last," he informed Harvey. "The door to the second floor opens from the dining-room. If you prefer remaining here, I shall be gone only a minute."

The sheriff followed, however, with an air of tolerant perplexity. His clerical companion, climbing the stairs deliberately, had no interest in the various bedrooms which opened from the small upper hallway. He proceeded at once to the open door of the clothes chute, and began to fish in his pockets.

"Something I can help you to, Reverend?" prompted the sheriff.

"A match."

Harvey produced half-a-dozen. Daunt held their tiny flames, one after the other, within the open maw of the chute, then turned and started back down the stairs.

"I am done with this," he stated. "I merely wished to examine the walls of the chute. And I have seen what I expected to see—which is nothing."

He led the way to the cellar so swiftly that the rotund sheriff broke into a trot to keep pace with him. The chute ended some two feet above the cement floor of the laundry. A few white clothes, on one of which a smear of blood was visible, had fallen beneath it. At their edge the brick—a yellow enameled brick—lay on its side in the laundry. The sheriff squinted at it, professionally.

"What's it doing down here?" he demanded.

Daunt was making as careful an examination of the brick as

could be done without touching it.

"I've got more matches, Reverend," his interested companion volunteered.

The clergyman reached for them in silence, and—rather reluctantly—dropped to his knees on the laundry floor to make the most effective use of them. Something that he saw broke through his usual impassivity. He smiled grimly, as he rose and dusted his knees.

The sheriff noted these symptoms with excitement.

"Find something, Reverend?" he inquired eagerly.

"I should like a camera—a good camera, preferably of the roll film type; also a ball of twine," Daunt returned.

"A camera! By George, that's something of an order!"

A voice came from the stairs—the voice of the butcher, who had been watching with open mouth.

"Plimpon, the notary's, got a camera. I'll go get it. He'll be glad enough to lend it—he was mighty sweet on the widow. I'll get the twine, too."

With a curt nod, the clergyman accepted this help from above, and at once became interested in the white clothing left in the chute. He removed the garments, one by one, standing back with head to one side after each, like an artist laying the last pigments on his picture. Suddenly, he turned to the sheriff.

"Look at them," he directed, shortly.

Harvey handled them gingerly, wrinkling his brows with an appearance of intense thought.

"Blood on just one of them," he observed. "Top one, of course."

"I noticed that," Daunt returned.

"There ain't much more to notice, is there? Being a married

man, I could give a name to each one of them, which may be more than you could, Reverend, but I can't see that that counts."

Daunt was gazing expectantly toward the cellar stairs, beyond which the sound of approaching voices was audible.

"It does not," he agreed. "I should say, however, that the unfortunate woman worked in an unusual way. One does not ordinarily find cleanly washed linen at the bottom of a clothes chute."

The sheriff started violently, but any remark he had in mind was forestalled by the appearance of both the butcher and the blacksmith—the latter yawning broadly, and followed by a third man.

"I brought Plimpon along himself with the camera, in case you might want some directions about it," the butcher explained. "I've got the roll of film, too, and the twine. Charged 'em to the sheriff at the general store."

With one embarrassingly keen glance, which left nothing of Plimpon's too spruce attire unnoticed, Daunt took the film and the twine.

"Shall I load the camera for you, Mr. Daunt?" the notary suggested, but the clergyman shook his head, with brief thanks.

"I am familiar with this style of camera," he explained.

He did not at once load the instrument. He examined it carefully first, snapping the shutter the while he peered through the lens at the light from the cellar window.

"An anastigmat?" he inquired.

"Wollensak Velostigmat, F. 4.5," the owner answered, technically. "I brought along my portrait attachment, too, and the tripod."

"Let me have the portrait attachment," the clergyman requested.

He examined that, also, and fitted it to the lens; after which, having subjected the fastening of the film, too, to a meticulous scrutiny, he deftly loaded the camera.

"You've done that sort of thing before," the notary declared, with a laugh which revealed a rather massive jaw and teeth for so slight a man.

Daunt laid the camera gingerly on the cement floor.

"It is one of my occasional hobbies," he replied.

"Mine, too. I spend a good part of my time roaming the woods for pictures. Sometimes I go rather far afield. I have an excellent snap of your lodge, even—taken from the northwest corner. Rather an unusual view, I flatter myself."

But the clergyman declined to be drawn into conversation. He was painstakingly slipping two pieces of twine beneath the brick, in such a manner that, with the double ends knotted together, they formed a suspension-by which the pieces of evidence could be carried without the bearer's touching its enameled surface. He glanced up at the sheriff.

"Carry it up the stairs, with great care," he directed. "One of the others can bring a stool from the kitchen. I wish the brick set on the stool, just out of the sunlight, on the shady side of the house."

He himself brought the camera. When the stool with its burden had been placed to his satisfaction, he reached for the japanned metal tripod, which Plimpon had begun to polish idly with his handkerchief, and screwed the camera to it. When he next produced a jointed rule from his pocket and measured off the distance with it, the notary's sallow face wrinkled sardonically.

"It takes an expert to measure off with a portrait lens and get it right," he volunteered.

"I *am* an expert," the clergyman replied, simply.

He worked with a rapidity and sureness of touch which seemed to bear him out. Having first dusted various portions with a black powder—carried loose in his pocket—which proceeding seemed to satisfy the onlookers, he quickly snapped all six sides of the brick—including the side encrusted with blood.

"Put these things back now," he instructed the sheriff. "Be careful not to touch the brick."

He had returned the camera to its owner and was folding the japanned tripod for the same purpose, when he paused.

"This is an exceptionally fine camera," he observed.

The notary grinned, vainly.

"Nothing like it in the village, Mr. Daunt. I do some professional work with it, along with my amateur stuff. I'm quite a jack-of-all-trades. Would you care to drop in and see some of my pictures?"

The clergyman smiled.

"My train schedule will hardly permit that. But I should like very much to borrow this camera for a day. It is finer than any of mine. There are one or two views about the lodge which have baffled me so far. This instrument might get them. I expect to return here in two days, and to bring it back, if you care to oblige me."

The notary's assurances were profuse. He seemed rather astonished to learn that Daunt desired to borrow the tripod, also; but all other emotions promptly gave way to satisfaction at the undoubted envy with which he was regarded by the butcher, the blacksmith, and certain others of his acquaintance, who had gathered about.

Daunt glanced at his watch and addressed the sheriff.

"I have just comfortable time to catch my train. If you will drive me to the station, you may look for me back day after tomorrow. I shall develop this film tomorrow evening in my dark room at the lodge. Tonight, I mean to retire early."

"Have you got any suspicions?" Harvey inquired, in a confidential whisper.

The clergyman considered a moment in silence. When he replied, it was in his natural voice. He seemed to have nothing to conceal.

"Occasionally, unusual and bizarre circumstances bring about the appearance of crime where really there is none. Suppose, in the present instance, that some clothes had stuck in the chute, between the first and the second floors. The unfortunate woman might, conceivably, have tried to force them out by dropping a brick from the upper opening. If, because the clothes still remained stuck, with the brick atop of them, halfway between floors, she had poked her head into the kitchen opening in an effort to free them, she might have met with just such a terrible injury, when she succeeded and the brick fell. And the brick, released when she staggered back into the kitchen, would have fallen to the basement."

The audience were mute until Harvey found breath to exclaim:

"By George!"

But it was the blacksmith who added the ultimate thrill to their emotions.

"Where's the hobo?" he demanded explosively.

And a boy with curly red hair, who had wriggled his way into the front rank, answered at once:

"I saw him go up the street about an hour ago. I thought Mr. Harvey let him go. *Didn't* you, Mr. Harvey?"

5

THERE WERE TIMES when the Reverend McGregor Daunt, like most men of independent habits of thought, was guilty of apparent inconsistency. In the matter of the camera with the Wollensak lens, for instance—he had borrowed it from Plimpon and had promised to return it promptly. The day after his trip with the sheriff would have been excellent for photography. Yet he hardly emerged into the sunlit grounds of the lodge. He occupied himself throughout the daytime hours, with a research along new lines into the complexities of the Emperor Hsun Tzu's thumb print.

Not until long after his solitary dinner, when the summer night had fallen, did he descend to his dark room to develop the films he had taken on the previous day. Once there, he spent some hours at the task—hours as much given to reflection as to photographic work. When at last it occurred to him that thinking could be done more pleasantly in his library or on the broad front porch rather than below stairs, the grandfather clock in the hallway was striking midnight.

He chose the porch. On so clear a night, following the perfect summer day, it offered advantages over any chamber indoors. He subsided into a roomy willow arm chair, sheltered by vines from even the prying eyes of woodland birds and beasts, and began to plan his next move in the strange problem of the kindly woman's death.

A crackling footstep brought him to sudden attention—a

moment too late. A man with a leveled revolver in his hand was climbing the steps.

"Not a move, please!" the visitor directed, sharply. "I'm going to search you for weapons, but remember you'll be covered all the time!"

The voice was familiar. Daunt was mentally struggling to place it when a ray of light from the library window fell across his assailant's face, which had been in shadow.

"Good evening, Mr. Plimpon!" he remarked, calmly.

The sallow man desisted a moment from his task of carefully patting the reverend gentleman's clothing, in a search for suspicious protuberances. He laughed, without embarrassment.

"Didn't expect me to be doing this to you the next time we met, did you, Reverend?" he asked, chuckling. "I hardly did, myself. When you photographed the brick, I began to be alarmed, but when you borrowed the tripod, that cinched it. Clever work! Most men wouldn't have thought to ask for the camera, too, as a blind. I lay awake last night thinking things over, and it seemed to me I'd better pay you a nice, late visit."

"The fingerprints on the tripod were too much blurred to be of use," Daunt volunteered, still without excitement.

Plimpon continued his search, finding nothing, and dropped into a chair where he could watch the clergyman closely.

"Yes?" he returned easily. "I tried to fix 'em that way. But you found some prints on the brick, I take it?"

"Some very distinct prints. A little smear of blood on the smooth face of the brick retained them perfectly."

"Then you could have traced them to me soon enough. Odd, isn't it? I did a fairly good bit of planning on that job, yet I never thought of the finger prints till too late. Have a smoke?"

Daunt silently declined.

"Excuse me if I light up."

"Why did you kill her?" the clergyman demanded, suddenly.

He had not moved from his position of ease in the arm chair. As far as his attitude and the evenness of his voice; were concerned, he might have been quite unaware of the revolver pointed at his portly stomach.

His visitor answered, without hesitation.

"Love, Reverend Daunt—the good, old emotion. I loved Mary for herself, and even more—to be frank with you—for the very nice little property she had. The old boy left her well fixed when he died. I asked her several times to marry me, and she turned me down so hard that I saw red. I went over there, day before yesterday, to give her a final chance. I told her if she said 'No,' it would be close to the last thing she ever said. She said it anyway—and I kept my word."

Daunt startled his visitor somewhat by yawning.

"I suppose you are aware that what you say to me will be used against you?" he warned.

"Will it?" Plimpon laughed, unpleasantly. "I hardly think so, Reverend. If you're interested in just how I did it, I'm here to tell you."

"I *am* interested," the clergyman admitted.

"I planned to choke her to death. That would hurt some, and it's a curious kink in me that I like to hurt people—or animals. But after I got there, I saw the brick—she had used it for a door stopper in the kitchen—and I remembered suddenly that my fingers would leave marks on her neck. Queer, isn't it, that I should think of that and never consider the prints on the brick? I talked with her awhile, and toyed with the brick, till I was sure she meant 'No,' then I let her have it, before she could make a sound."

He blew a ring of smoke across the ray of light from the library window, and glanced down idly at his revolver.

"I did a nice little piece of work there. It *would* have been nice, that is, if I hadn't forgotten the finger prints. I threw some clothes down the chute and tossed the brick after them. That was something for the detectives to work on. A clever man, I figured, would be apt to reason that she had poked her head into the chute and been struck by the brick, coming from the second floor. Just as you *did* reason. But I don't think you really held that theory, did you?"

"I might have held it," the clergyman returned. "But a number of points told against it. For instance, there was a drop of blood inside the chute and above the entrance to it in the kitchen. Also, you used freshly washed clothing. That was a serious oversight. And there was still another weakness," he went on, thoughtfully. "You will grant, I think, that she would have tried to poke the clothes down the chute with some instrument, after the brick failed. Possibly not, of course; but that would have been her natural course. I found nothing she could have used for that except a broom; and it hung behind the kitchen door. She could not have placed it there after having been hit by the brick."

The notary laughed, with what seemed genuine merriment.

"And I thought I was clever! But I don't see yet how all this made you suspect me. You borrowed my tripod to study any finger-prints there might be on it. But why *my* tripod? Why did you pick on me?"

For answer, the clergyman gravely and deliberately pointed

to his own head.

"The light here is poor," he said. "You cannot see my ear very clearly. It differs from yours—for mine is a normal ear, set symmetrically on my head. When you have opportunity, I recommend two studies to you. First—books. You will find the works of the great Italian criminologist, Cesare Lombroso, and a later volume by his follower, August Drahms, especially informative. Secondly, I recommend a good mirror. In the mirror you will note several points; the shape of your ears; their asymmetrical placing on your head; your heavy, prognathic jaw. I could hardly fail to suspect you, since you were the only man associated with the neighborhood of the crime whose face was distinctly that of a murderer. Moreover, you yourself strengthened my suspicions when you wiped the tripod with your handkerchief before handing it to me. You thought to obliterate all finger prints. You were partly successful."

Plimpon laughed again—a laugh with a touch of chagrin in it.

"It looks like the one really clever thing I did was to come here tonight. My work with the tramp was better though."

"I have not quite followed your reasoning there."

"A little deep, even for you, Reverend?" He swelled a trifle, at this small sop to his vanity. It was visible, despite the shadows of the porch. "I didn't start the mob after the tramp, you know. Someone else who had seen him hanging around the village did that. But I joined it, for the fun of the thing, and where I did my real thinking was when they wanted to hang him in the woods. If I opposed that, of course, it would divert suspicion. No one would expect me to commit a murder, and then try to keep another man from being hanged in my place.

But I wanted to see them string him up in the end—I've never watched a man being hanged, and it must be interesting. And I wanted them to make him stand the gaff a little on the way back. Same old kink, you see—I like to watch 'em suffer. But I wasn't anxious to have him taken to look at her." He shivered. "Why wasn't I?"

"Have you ever killed anyone else?" the clergyman asked— still without raising his voice above a conversational tone.

"No. But I've always wanted to. And now I've begun. You will make the second."

Daunt's start was hardly noticeable.

"That would be a mistake," he said, quietly. "My servants in the house would be sure to capture you before you could escape. There is one of them in the library now, just behind you."

But the sallow-faced man laughed.

"No, you don't, Reverend! You think I'll turn my head, and then you'll jump for me and try to knock the gun out of my hand! I've been watching in the shrubbery all evening. You're alone in this house."

He paused.

"I don't mind killing you, you know. There will be quite a thrill in it. I never realized the thrill of murdering someone till I killed Mary."

Daunt's mind had never worked more rapidly, and to less purpose. That his visitor was in earnest he could not doubt. Plimpon was evidently a homicidal maniac, of the type that sometimes live respectable lives for years before committing their first crime. He was sufficiently sane to take all reasonable precautions. Even the chair where he sat was far enough away from his victim so that he could easily fire once or twice before a spring could reach him. The clergyman tried argument.

"Suppose I promise you to drop this case and give you the plates?" he suggested.

Plimpon chuckled.

"A forced promise—you wouldn't keep it! Why should I take chances? I've already stolen the brick from the sheriff and done away with it. Now I'll do away with you."

"By shooting?" The clergyman's voice was quite impersonal.

"You've guessed it!" his visitor laughed.

"You will hardly have the pleasure of seeing me suffer. Shooting is a quick death."

"I've thought of that, too. You ought to suffer—you've done your best to make things unpleasant for me. I shall wound you in the stomach. That will be fatal, but you will live for a time. You'll live in pain. There'll be a number of ways at my command to make sure of that."

Daunt had a sudden, almost overwhelming desire to cover his stomach with his hands; but he resisted the impulse, and forced himself to speak calmly.

"Have you ever enjoyed medical training, Mr. Plimpon? If not, I might make the evening more interesting by acquainting you with the various organs of the abdomen. A bullet in one of them might have an entirely different effect from a bullet in another. The stomach, for instance...."

But the notary interrupted him, with a harsh laugh.

"Playing for time, eh? I get the point, all right. Time might do you some good; there's always a chance of someone coming along, even to this out-of-the-way place. I think we'll have to call the game. If I need any information about the stomach, I can learn it from a book—after you're in your grave."

He raised the revolver, slowly but steadily.

"Do you believe in prayer, Reverend? You couldn't find a better time to try it out! When I count three, you'll get it. In the stomach, remember! One!"

Daunt seemed to crumple suddenly in his chair. The lunatic laughed.

"No, you don't! You can't slide away from me that way! Two!"

The clergyman jumped—straight for the mocking face in front of him. He had not crumpled—he had been gathering himself for that desperate leap. But the revolver exploded, twice.

"HE IS ALIVE, Mr. Daunt. Do what you can for him."

Daunt picked himself up from the floor of the porch, where he had fallen. He looked about him, in a daze. It seemed incredible that he should be unhurt. Yet he felt no pain. He wondered who had spoken to him. Then his eyes cleared, and he saw.

Almost at his feet, Plimpon sprawled upon the porch. Bending over him was Rhyming Sam.

"I was listening," the hobo explained, between paroxysms of a choking cough. "I came to thank you—but found a man lurking in the bushes. I have been guarding your house since early in the evening. You will pardon me?"

6

THOUGH THE REVEREND McGregor Daunt's experience as a physician had been some years in the past, his medical instincts remained with him. He turned from his rescuer to the prone figure on the porch floor, and in that brief space Plimpon became for him, not a would-be assassin, but a patient. He ripped open the man's collar; and, realizing the necessity for better light than could be had on the porch, dragged him through the hallway to the bright illumination of one of the living room lamps.

There he speedily diagnosed the case. The man was badly wounded, but he would live. Daunt applied first aid, and made his patient comfortable on the couch, not forgetting, however, to tie his hands with some strong cord procured in the kitchen. Also, he bound his patient's ankles together, and secured the cord to one of the legs of the couch. Even a wounded man may be dangerous. Then it occurred to the clergyman to send for help.

The telephone was in the library. He crossed the hall, but stopped, with a start, at the library door.

Rhyming Sam sat at the table, writing.

The hobo seemed strangely different from before. His dark eyes, their brightness accentuated by the livid pallor of his face, shone feverishly. His lips were compressed to a thin line with the intensity of his effort. He was incredibly frail. Yet he wrote rapidly, his pen scarcely touching the paper as it glided. Daunt recognized both paper and pen as his own, which he kept on the table. He was seized with an impulse to demand an explanation. Something forbade, however; he felt reluctant to dissolve the spell of that delicate, speeding hand, even by tiptoeing forward to the telephone. And, while he still stood there, the ragged wanderer laid down the pen, raised his eyes until they met Daunt's squarely, and opened his lips to speak.

His speech was as strange as his manner; halting, uncertain of its tones, and not much louder than a whisper. At the first word the clergyman started forward, apprehensively; but his guest held up one thin hand with a commanding gesture.

"You can do nothing. It was the first shot. I am nearly gone now."

He began to cough again, chokingly, but stopped himself, seemingly by a powerful effort of will.

"I have written briefly what I heard him say on the porch. You may need that. My mind has not always been clear, but it is clear now. You will compare this statement with the one I wrote on the train for the sheriff. That will identify the handwriting." He stood, slowly.

"Quick! Help me go outside! Let me die on the warm ground."

He laughed—the old, elfish laugh; but, despite its weakness, there was complete sanity in it.

"I used to call myself the King of the Earth, you know! I can't—" He choked, but finished the sentence—"—die indoors!"

Daunt lifted the light figure in his arms. There was no need for the wanderer's whispered:

"Hurry!"

Just beyond the steps, and a little to one side, the grass was thick and soft. Daunt dared go no further with his burden. He was barely in time, as it was. But as he laid the head back gently upon the sod, he heard what sounded like the ghost of a whisper from the gasping lips. He bent close to catch what might be said.

Rhyming Sam was chuckling—a chuckle so near akin to silence that it might have bridged the last infinitesimal gap between time and eternity. With the chuckle came the faint sighing of words:

"I seem to have paid for my rabbit, after all!"

With that last scrap of philosophy, the King of the Earth had abdicated his throne.

The clergyman turned slowly away, and went back into the lodge to telephone.

About the Author

DO MOST OF your writers plot their stories out in advance, so that they know just where they are going, from first word to last? I wish I could. My method is so unscientific that it becomes laughable. The murder mystery comes to me first. I get to wondering about it—what a heck of a thing for someone to do!—why should anybody pull off a killing like that?—who did it, and why, in the name of common sense? I wonder, without arriving at any conclusion; and then, some fateful evening, I sit down to the typewriter, throw Humberton onto the job, and let him do his stuff. As the story progresses, I begin to sense who the murderer is. Sometimes I am right; but more often, I find toward the end of the story that someone I did not suspect is the real criminal, and then, of course, I have to go back and do a lot of rewriting.

That, it seems to me, is about the hardest way to write a detective story. I know a lot of easier ways, but with me they don't seem to click. If I can tell in advance who did the horrid deed, the story is more than likely to be a flop.

As for my personal tastes, if they are of interest to anyone, I play volley ball and pitch horse shoes (doing neither very well), I believe in ghosts and am profoundly interested in all sorts of psychic phenomena. I like to read all manner of books, with a slant toward ancient Egypt. I don't drink or smoke, but I do over-eat—with the result that I have to diet, every once in a while, to keep the old waist line below my chest measurement. Also, I am inclined to "reach for a sweet," and you know what that does.

Married; five children, and about three thousand books. Wife can write much better than I, but she doesn't know it. Consider myself pretty nifty at humorous writing, but the editors don't. Turn out a few ghost stories each year. Do most of my writing at night, all alone, in a downtown office building. Have had the family train the Graflex on me a time or two, so you are likely to see a picture of me shortly. If it doesn't seem good enough for publication, let me know, and I will send a snapshot of my brother-in-law. He has "it."

www.ingramcontent.com/pod-product-compliance
Lightning Source LLC
Chambersburg PA
CBHW051145030726
47504CB00004B/1050